BETRAYED

BETRAYED

AMY CLIPSTON

FIVE STAR

A part of Gale, Cengage Learning

GALE
CENGAGE Learning™

Detroit • New York • San Francisco • New Haven, Conn • Waterville, Maine • London

Set in 11 pt. Plantin.
Printed on permanent paper.

LIBRARY OF CONGRESS CATALOGING-IN-PUBLICATION DATA

Clipston, Amy.
    Betrayed / Amy Clipston. — 1st ed.
      p. cm.
    ISBN-13: 978-1-59414-793-7 (alk. paper)
    ISBN-10: 1-59414-793-0 (alk. paper)
    1. Automobile racing—Fiction. I. Title.
PS3603.L58B48 2009
813'.6—dc22   2009016286

First Edition. First Printing: September 2009.
Published in 2009 in conjunction with Tekno Books.

Printed in the United States of America
1 2 3 4 5 6 7 13 12 11 10 09

For my loving pit crew—Joe, Zac & Matt—
with all of my heart.

ACKNOWLEDGMENTS

I'm thankful to many friends and family members who encouraged me during this long journey to publication. First, I want to thank my cohorts in Chesapeake Romance Writers and Carolina Romance Writers. Your friendship and encouragement guided me. I can't even measure the knowledge you all have imparted to me over the years.

Several friends deserve special recognition. Judi McCoy has been my unofficial mentor; her knowledge and words of wisdom have steered me in my writing career. The feedback from Maggie Halpin, Jennifer Spencer, and Sue McKlveen made this story so much better. I owe the premise of the story to Nancy O'Berry, whose wonderful plot ideas have aided my muse in creating my racing romance books. Without Nancy, this book would never have been written. Thank you also to Pam McCarthy for always believing in me and picking up my spirits when I needed that little push. Thank you also to Vannetta Chapman for her encouragement and support. And I'm grateful to Andrea Christy-Glover for taking my lovely portrait.

I am grateful to my agent, Mary Sue Seymour, who supported me through the piles of rejections and continued to query publishers on my behalf. Thank you, Mary Sue, for making this dream a reality.

I'm ever thankful to my wonderful editor, Alice Duncan, for loving this book and making it ever better. You polished my words in ways I never imagined possible! I appreciate your patience with my endless questions, too.

To my beautiful sons, Zac and Matt—your sense of humor and love of cars have always inspired me. Thank you for forgiving the times when I seemed more interested in my laptop than what you had to say. You both are my life and my heart. I'm blessed and privileged to be your mom.

My husband, Joe, deserves a medal for his patience with my endless barrage of racing and mechanical questions. You're my rock and my hero. I love you.

Without a doubt, the most influential person during this process was, of course, Lola Goebelbecker, my mother. She's always been my biggest fan, avidly reading my books with fervor, even the stories that were positively dreadful. Thank you for believing that one day we'd see my name on a cover. You proved once again that you're always right. I love you.

ONE

"I never thought my dad would get married before me." Lacey Fowler held her champagne flute up to her lips and rolled her eyes while her father beamed, dipping his bride again in the middle of the dance floor.

"Now, now, now." Her best friend Krista Wilson wagged a finger at her. "Your dad's entitled to some happiness. He's been single for what? Fifteen years now?"

"Sixteen. Mom died when I was five." Lacey swallowed her envy with the last gulp of the champagne then scanned the throng of wedding guests for the cute waiter with the tray of flutes.

Closing her eyes, she sighed. She wanted more champagne. She needed a buzz to deal with the strange, hollow feeling that filled her belly the moment she saw her dad and new stepmother kiss before the makeshift altar at the other end of the reception hall.

"Sixteen years is a long time to be alone." Krista's voice brought her back to the present.

"I can't even get a first date, but Dad met Veronica and married her in less than a year. He's forty-seven, and I'm twenty-one. How's that fair?" Lacey spotted the guy in the tuxedo vest carrying just what she was looking for. She waved, and he approached.

"You'll find someone. Just wait. This is your year. You'll meet some hot guy and—" Krista suddenly gasped, but Lacey ignored her friend's dramatics, smiling at the server instead.

"Trade ya." Lacey winked, handing him her empty glass and taking a full one. "Thanks."

"No problem," he said.

Lacey shook her head, catching herself studying his rear while he weaved through the crowd. *I've had too much alcohol already.*

"He's here." Krista gripped Lacey's arm and shook it to catch her attention. Her voice sounded over the blaring dance music pounding through the D.J.'s mega speakers.

"Hey! Watch my drink!" Lacey warned, balancing the flute. She took another sip while her dad kissed his blushing bride yet again. Her eyes narrowed. *Love is sickening.*

"Will you look? It's Reese Mitchell." Krista gasped again. "He's more gorgeous in person than on *Racing Today.* I think I'm in love."

Lacey's eyes darted to the other side of the room, and her breath caught in her throat. She knew all too well what it felt like to be in love with Reese. She'd fallen for him when she was just a kid, and, to her heart's detriment, the feeling seemed to only intensify over the years.

Reese was a superstar. The driver of the number 89 Ford for Southern Racing, he was one of the most popular race car drivers in the prestigious American Racing Association (ARA). Lacey's grandfather had built Southern Racing, and her father inherited it. Reese's father became a partner in the team when Reese was a toddler. Being five years Reese's junior and the daughter of his father's business partner, she knew she didn't have a chance of ever winning his heart.

But that didn't stop her from fantasizing about him.

Reese's gaze met hers, and his smile widened. Her heart fluttered and she downed more champagne, trying to calm her quickening pulse. He was so stunning in his black, three-button tuxedo that she couldn't force herself to look away. He looked like he'd come straight from a photo shoot for a fashion magazine, with his deep brown hair gelled and his adorable cowlick falling into his powder blue eyes.

"He's coming toward us," Krista whispered in Lacey's ear like an excited schoolgirl.

Lacey gulped still more champagne and teetered on her high heels. Her ankles swaying like noodles, she reached for Krista.

"Whoa there." Reese took her hand in his, grinning down at her. At nearly six-foot-two, he towered over her by almost seven inches. "You drunk, squirt?"

Lacey pulled her hand back and pushed a stray curl away from her face. She had to at least appear mature and sober, even though he always made her feel twelve again with that stupid nickname. She'd give anything for him to see her as an attractive woman instead of his surrogate kid sister. "I'm just fine. Thanks, Reese."

"You look lovely this evening, squirt." His azure eyes glided over her.

Lacey smoothed her hands over the ridiculous periwinkle strapless taffeta dress Veronica insisted she don as bridesmaid. "Thank you."

She cleared her throat, trying to ignore the way his gaze bore into her and made her nerves prickle with a strange awareness. But the nickname countered his bold assessment of her. She wanted to tell him he looked nice too, *really nice,* but she was afraid the alcohol would cause her to say something stupid, like *Reese, you look so hot, I want to take you into the limo and show just how grown up I am now.*

"Hi, Reese," Krista sang, sidling up to him. "You did awesome last week at Dover. I was screaming so loud for you to win, I nearly lost my voice. But second was good, too."

"Thanks," he said. Lacey immediately recognized the phony, professional "good loser" smile he flashed at her best friend.

She sipped more champagne, and studied Reese over the top of her glass. He was scanning the crowd expectantly. She couldn't help but notice once again how striking his features were—high cheekbones, a strong jaw, and smooth, tanned skin. His shoulders filled out his black tuxedo jacket to perfection. She'd seen him once without his shirt at her father's pool, and the sight of his well formed abs and taut pectoral muscles had made her cheeks warm.

He leaned in close, his warm breath caressing her neck. "Have you seen my pop?"

She inhaled the spicy scent of his cologne, and her mouth went dry. She held onto his powerful arm, squeezing it for balance and just enough to enjoy feeling it ripple while she spoke in his ear. "He was out there dancing with some brunette before, but I haven't seen him in a while. Where were you earlier? You missed the ceremony."

"I had this sponsor thing in Charlotte. I talked to reporters and smiled pretty for the camera." The annoyance in his tone couldn't be missed.

Releasing his arm, Lacey mocked him with the flutter of her eyelashes. "It's *so* difficult being a superstar."

He grinned and hugged her shoulders. "You're adorable, squirt."

She swallowed a sigh, while he turned and said something to a member of his crew who'd walked past. She'd give anything just for one kiss from Reese. Just *one* to satisfy the curiosity she'd had for all of those years . . .

She mentally shook herself. Now she knew she must've had too much champagne because fantasizing about Reese was just plain hopeless. He practically had to beat models off with a stick shift. And Lacey didn't fit his ideal woman's image. She wasn't tall, wasn't blond, and wasn't a model. She was just a nerdy college senior, the daughter of his team owner, and a redhead to boot.

To make matters worse, Reese had made the list of "Sexiest Athletes Alive" in the *Gossip Weekly* magazine after winning the American Racing Association championship last year. Thanks to that article, he had his pick of super models. Lacey was nothing but his "squirt" and always would be.

"You okay?" Krista's question slammed Lacey back to the present like a car hitting the wall at Darlington Speedway.

"Yeah." Lacey cleared her throat and met Krista's stare.

"I think it's time for the bouquet toss." Krista took the champagne from Lacey's hand and placed it on a table beside them. "Let's go."

"No. I hate that cheesy stuff."

"Don't be such a dish rag."

Lacey ignored her. Looking over her shoulder, she spotted Reese moving through the crowd, his gaze targeting a gorgeous blond model-type wearing a short, black, spaghetti-strap dress. He whispered in her ear, and the woman laughed a little too loudly and clung to his arm. Assuming the bimbo must be his flavor of the month, Lacey's stomach roiled. Why did she torture herself?

"Now, I need all of the single ladies in the room to come out on the dance floor for the bouquet toss!" The D.J.'s voice blared through the speakers along with the Dixie Cups' "The Chapel of Love."

"Let's go!" Krista dragged Lacey to the middle of the dance floor where two dozen women lined up behind the bride.

Lacey couldn't help fixing her eyes across the room where Reese stood with his arm around the blonde while sipping a beer. She looked toward the bride and found Veronica smiling over her shoulder at her. The bride winked then turned back toward the D.J.

"Okay, ladies! Let's pick our next bride." The D.J.'s voice

bellowed over the microphone. "One . . . Two . . . Three!"

Veronica's arm swept up over her head, and Lacey watched in horror as the bouquet of pink roses and baby's breath sailed in a high arch toward her as if in slow motion and then landed directly in her hands. Lacey stared down in revulsion at the bouquet while a gaggle of women enveloped her in a huddle of cackles and hugs.

"Oh, you're so lucky!" one woman yelled.

"You'll be a beautiful bride!" another insisted.

"Can't you just see Lacey in a glittering white gown with a crown on that gorgeous red hair?"

Lacey felt nauseated. She wanted the dance floor to swallow her up. She pushed her way through the crowd and started for the bathroom.

"Wait!" Krista yanked her back. "Don't you want to see who catches the garter?"

"I really couldn't care less." Frustrated, Lacey searched the room. "Where's the hot waiter with the champagne?"

"Let's get those bachelors out here and find a groom for our future bride," the D.J. barked while a funeral march sang through the speakers. "Let's go, men!"

"I gotta get out of here." Lacey held out the bouquet. "Here. You have a better chance of finding a man than I do."

"Knock it off," Krista chided with a hand on her small hip. "You caught that bouquet fair and square."

Eligible bachelors lined up on the dance floor as if before a firing squad. The D.J. produced a chair and set it before the bride and groom. Her father kissed Veronica, and the crowd broke out into a chorus of "ooohs" and "ahhhs," causing Lacey's frown to deepen. *Why does everyone have to encourage them? Don't they realize the mistake my dad has made?*

Tacky burlesque music blared while the bride lowered herself into the chair with the groom kneeling before her. Aghast, Lacey cupped her hand to her mouth while her father fished through the sea of crinolines in search of the garter. A chorus of catcalls, whistles, and hoots cheered him on.

"I can't watch this." Lacey turned her back to the scene. Where was that guy with the champagne? No, she needed something stronger. She needed to get drunk and drown out the image of the new woman in her father's life. Shaking her head, she started for the bar.

"Lacey. Lacey!" Krista's voice was faint over the music.

Lacey leaned on the bar for support, while cheers indicated that her father must've found what he was searching for under his bride's dress.

The bartender raised his eyebrows in question.

She slapped the bouquet on the counter. "I'll have more champagne, please."

Daring to look over her shoulder, she spotted her father standing with his back to the crowd, holding a blue garter over his head like a slingshot. She turned away again. "On second thought, make it something stronger."

"Sex on the beach?" the bartender asked.

"Excuse me?" Lacey's eyes widened.

The man grinned while mixing the drink. "Trust me."

Standing beside her, Krista's voice was urgent. "He's throwing the garter. You have to go back out there."

"I'm not going out there." Lacey shook her head, facing the bartender. "I'm going to get drunk, then sit right here and wait for my ride home. Uncle Carl said he'd take me around midnight."

"But Lacey—"

"Save it." She nodded toward the flowers. "Go be my stand in."

"Lacey . . ."

"I'm not doin' it."

"Lacey."

"This whole thing's stupid. Why my father had to get married again, I'll never understand. He doesn't even really know Veronica. Why couldn't they just date for a few years? What's the hurry? It's not like she's pregnant or anything."

"Lacey!"

"Can you get pregnant at forty-five? I hope not. I'm not ready for siblings. I'm too old."

"Will you shut up for a second? Reese caught the garter!"

"She's probably only after his money—" Lacey stopped when Krista's words finally filtered through her tirade. "Did you say Reese caught the garter?"

Krista's face was solemn as she nodded.

"Holy—" Lacey's eyes rounded with shock.

"Lacey? Lacey Fowler?" The D.J.'s voice rang out over the tawdry music. "We need you to come meet your future groom."

Two

Lacey's cheeks started to burn with fire while she leaned against the bar. Catcalls and hoots roared around the reception hall.

Reese stood in the center of the dance floor with the blue lacy garter wrapped around his muscular bicep like a rubber band. Their gazes collided, and a smirk spread across his sexy lips. To keep consistent with tradition, the bachelor who caught the garter had to put it on the bachelorette who caught the bouquet.

Reese had to put the garter on *Lacey's thigh.*

"I can't do this," Lacey whispered, her legs rubbery.

"Girlfriend, you're the envy of every woman here. Go!" Krista shoved Lacey, who stumbled toward Reese.

Reese held out his hand, and Lacey took it. The warmth of his grasp sent electric pulses roaring through her veins. He led her to the chair, and the cheers of the crowd surrounding them seemed to disappear. Lacey wondered if it was the effect of the alcohol that made it seem as if she and Reese were the only two people in the room.

She lowered herself into the chair and Reese yanked the garter from his sleeve. He peeled off his black tuxedo jacket and draped it across the back of the chair. Her heart turned over in her chest while he unbuttoned his sleeves and rolled them up. The anticipation was almost too much for her already frayed nerves.

Someone whistled, wrenching Lacey back to the ballroom.

Her eyes darted to the throng gathered around her and found every set of eyes focused on her and Reese. She thought her cheeks might spontaneously combust if they heated any more from abashment.

Lacey leaned forward as he knelt before her, almost bumping heads with him. "Reese . . ." she whispered. "Please don't do this. Let's just forget it, okay?"

His right eyebrow lifted in question. "Are you kidding? This is tradition, squirt." His smile faded. "I won't embarrass you, Lacey. I promise."

"Reese . . ." Her heart hammered in her chest while he lifted her foot, removing her satin periwinkle heel and gently massaging her foot.

He smiled up at her and her breath paused. She gripped the trembling bouquet as he placed the garter around her ankle. Heat surged from her veins into the pit of her belly when he pushed the garter up her leg, past her calf to her knee.

"Please, Reese," she whispered. "Don't."

His fingertips moved up to her knee and brushed her inner thigh, leaving the garter halfway up her thigh, between her knee and eternity. She gasped at the feel of his hands, and the bouquet shook harder in hers.

His hands traveled down her leg then he slipped her shoe back on her foot before taking her hand and lifting her to her feet. Her flesh prickled where his fingers had been.

"Here's our next bride and groom," the D.J. announced while the crowd cheered. "Now, let's dance."

Peter Gabriel's "In Your Eyes" filled the air and Reese pulled her close. "You're a good sport," he whispered in her ear, his hands resting on her hips.

Lacey swallowed and closed her eyes. Having him hold her was surreal. The air around them felt electrified.

"You seem preoccupied." His voice was husky in her ear.

"It's been a rough day." Lacey looked up into his Caribbean blue eyes. "I feel like I'm losing my dad, as immature and silly as it sounds."

He shook his head. "That's not immature. It's been just you and your dad for a long time, so I can understand why this is tough for you." His fingertip traced her cheek. "But you're a beautiful young lady. You'll have your own wedding soon."

Lacey blinked. Reese said she was beautiful and, for once, didn't call her squirt. Did he finally see her as an adult, as an equal?

"I bet you already have a boyfriend back at school who's crazy about you," he continued.

She shook her head.

His eyes widened with astonishment. "You're kidding."

Sighing, she rested her head on his chest. She had to enjoy every second of Reese's embrace. Soon he'd be distracted by his flavor of the month, and Lacey would be demoted to his squirt again.

"I find that difficult to believe." His fingers moved up and down her spine, sending shivers through her.

"Well, it's the truth. I haven't had a boyfriend in over a year." Lacey wrapped her arms around his neck. Why did being with him feel so right when it was obviously so wrong?

A hand on her back startled her. Looking over her shoulder, she found her stepmother grinning. Lacey grimaced. Veronica had a lousy sense of timing.

"I couldn't have staged it better myself," her stepmother said. "You two look adorable."

Lacey forced a smile. "Thanks." Veronica needed to learn when to disappear.

Reese shook her father's hand. "Congratulations, sir. Sorry I was late, but I had that sponsor appearance."

"That's okay, son," her father said. "We're happy you made it."

Her father hugged Reese, then tugged Lacey into the embrace. Reese's arm fell around her waist, and she thought her knees might turn to gelatin.

"You two mean the world to me." Her father stepped back, his eyes filling with tears. "Take good care of each other. I love you both."

"I love you, Daddy." Lacey's voice trembled. Although she never doubted her father's love for her, hearing him say the words always tugged at her heart strings. "I'm very happy for you." She gave Veronica a weak smile.

"Thank you, honey." He kissed her cheek then turned to his bride. "Let's dance one more before we slip out." Gathering her into his arms, they swayed to the slow love song.

Lacey's eyes met Reese. "The man has lost his mind."

"Love will do that to you." Letting her waist go, he took her hand in his. "Want to get a drink?"

"Sure." Still holding his warm hand, she followed him to the bar. "I had a drink waiting for me before I was dragged out onto the dance floor for the garter. Where's your date?"

His face showed no sign of emotion while he shrugged. "I don't know."

She watched his eyes for any sign of his thoughts and wondered what that shrug meant. Was the blonde just a one-night stand? Was she one of many? Why did Lacey even care? She was just his friend. Just his kid sister. Nothing but his squirt.

The bartender flashed a grin. "Your sex on the beach, Miss Fowler." He pushed her glass toward her.

Her cheeks flamed again. Lacey avoided eye contact and grabbed the glass. She was thankful Reese didn't comment as he snatched another bottle of beer.

He took her hand again and led her out to the balcony

overlooking the lake. The warm June air kissed her skin, and a slight breeze moved the skirt of her long dress.

He leaned on the railing and sipped the bottle. "Pretty night."

"It is." She stared out over the lake and sighed. "I love it here. Wish I didn't have to go back north."

"When are you heading back?"

"Tomorrow." She sipped the drink, wishing she'd only ordered a soda. Being alone with Reese was enough of a buzz.

"Why aren't you taking the summer off?"

She shrugged. "I got an internship, so I have to stay out there." She drank more, silently admiring how his azure eyes reflected the lights from inside the hall.

"How come you don't call me anymore?"

Lacey nearly choked while studying him. "What?"

"You used to call me and tell me how things were going. Are you avoiding me?"

She shook her head. "No, not at all." *Actually, I wish I could spend more time with you.* She pushed the thought aside. She'd really had too much to drink.

"So, why don't you call me?" He lifted his beer. "I thought we were buddies."

Buddies. She bit back a groan. "I've just been busy with school and you're super busy. I don't see how you could even fit in a call from me now."

He grimaced. "Please. I always have time for family."

"There you are!" An impatient female voice said behind Lacey. "I've been looking all over for you."

Lacey didn't have to turn around to know to whom the voice belonged. It was the flavor of the month.

"Sabrina, this is Lacey. Lacey." Reese touched her shoulder, and Lacey faced the gorgeous blonde.

Plastering a phony smile on her face, Lacey held out a hand to the woman. "Nice to meet you."

"You too." Sabrina studied Reese, ignoring the offer of Lacey's handshake. "Honey, can we please go?" she whined. "I'm bored."

Lacey shook her head. The woman was all charm.

"In a little bit, baby," he said. "I just got here."

Baby? Lacey's stomach twisted while envy slammed through her. She gulped her drink and leaned back on the railing. She did need the alcohol after all.

"Pleease, Reese?" Standing between his long legs, the blonde flashed puppy dog eyes. "I'll make it worth your while." Her smile was wicked.

"Okay!" Lacey stood up. "I'll give y'all some privacy." She smiled at the blonde. "Nice meeting you." She turned to Reese. "Nice to see you, as always."

Reese looked pained. "Lacey . . ."

Lacey started toward the door. "Have a great night and use protection." Lacey blinked her eyes in question at her quip. *Where'd that come from? Must be the alcohol talking.*

"Lacey. Lacey!" Reese yelled after her. "Call me."

"Yeah." She snorted with sarcasm and waved his comment off without facing him. "Whatever."

Lacey picked up speed when she hit the threshold and entered the ballroom. Her stomach soured at the thought of that bimbo snuggling up to Reese. She had to get out of there. The night had turned into a disaster. She marched over to Krista, who was talking to a member of Reese's pit crew.

Krista's eyes met Lacey's. Krista knitted her brow in confusion. "What's wrong?"

"Take me home."

Her best friend's eyes glittered with concern. "Why?"

Lacey jammed her hand on her hip. "I want to go home, and I'm too buzzed to drive. If you won't take me, I'll find someone who will."

Her expression softening, Krista tried to grab Lacey's hand. "Just calm down. Let's go talk—"

"Forget it." Lacey spun on her heel and stomped through the crowd while oldies beach music echoed in her head. She searched the sea of faces for her father's best friend and business partner. Where was Carl? He said he'd take her home. She maneuvered through the cluster of crewmembers and relatives.

Heading toward the back of the room, she spotted her father and Carl talking in the corner. Carl was nearly thirty years Reese's senior, but the Mitchell family males shared their powder blue eyes and rugged good looks.

The older men's glares came into view, and Lacey slowed her pace. They were angry. Her father shook his fist inches from Carl's face, and her stomach clenched. She'd never in her life seen such an angry exchange between the men.

What on earth was wrong? Why was Carl arguing with her father on his wedding day? Carl was like a brother to him.

Lacey bit her bottom lip and contemplated what to do. Interrupting them was probably not a good idea. Should she find someone else to drive her home? Her eyes darted back to the doors leading to the balcony and she groaned. Her head pounded at the thought of watching Reese frolic with his current bimbo for the rest of the evening. She had to go home or she was going to drink herself stupid and really embarrass herself and her father.

"Lacey." A hand pulled her back. "I'll take you home."

She met Krista's smile and blew out a sigh of relief. Krista had come to her rescue. "Let's go."

Reese gently pushed Sabrina back. "Knock it off." Her blue eyes widened with shock, and guilt gnawed at him. "This isn't the appropriate place." He pushed a lock of her long, golden hair back from her small shoulder.

"But you promised we'd have some quality time tonight." She gave a playful smile while she traced his chest with her fingertip.

He sighed. She just didn't get it. All she wanted was sex. Sure, he enjoyed it, but sometimes he felt cheap. Sometimes he longed for a woman who wanted more than just his body. He wanted someone he could talk to. Someone who would listen to him—*really* listen. He craved someone who loved Reese, the man, and not just Reese, the ARA Champion.

Sabrina's lips brushed his earlobe. "Let's go home and try that bubble bath I picked up last week in Dover," she whispered in his ear.

He scowled. "Sometimes I feel like I'm talking to a brick wall." Taking her arm, he gently moved her aside. "Excuse me." He sauntered toward the door.

"Reese!" she called after him.

Standing in the doorway, his thoughts turned to Lacey and his stomach tightened. He searched the throng for her. Why had she run off? Was it something he'd said? She'd seemed so angry, but he couldn't imagine why.

Her voice echoed in his mind. *Have a great night and use protection.*

She'd never been so crass before. Come to think of it, he'd never seen her drink so much. What would bring that on? Was it depression about her father's wedding, or was it something else?

Reese blew out a sigh. Why was he so worried about her? Why couldn't he get the sight of her creamy white shoulders peeking over the top of that sexy strapless gown out of his mind? Why did the way her body quivered when his hands slid up those soft, shapely thighs make his trousers suddenly feel tight?

Reese chugged his beer and shook his head. What was happening to him? How could he lust after Lacey? He'd watched her grow up. He'd been a shoulder for her to cry on when she had her first crush in junior high. She wouldn't ever look at him that way, but he was sure checking her out tonight. She was beautiful, no radiant, with her gorgeous auburn hair in those curls and her green eyes sparkling in the light of the dance floor.

Covering his face with his hand, he groaned. Did he need counseling? Had the pressure of the competition and demanding schedule finally take a toll on him?

"Reese?" Sabrina appeared next to him, touching his arm. "You okay?"

"No." He took another drink. "I think I need to see a shrink."

She looked confused. "Huh?"

Reese blew out a ragged breath and stared at the crowd moving in time to the blaring dance music.

"Never mind," he muttered. Stepping into the ballroom, he shook his head. It had been a long day. He longed to go home—alone. He scanned the room for Lacey and then fished his car keys from his pocket.

"We're heading out?" Sabrina asked, a coy grin tugging at the corner of his mouth.

"Yup," he said. "I'm going home. I'd be happy to drop you off on the way."

"You're a killjoy, Reese Mitchell," Sabrina snipped.

"Yup," he deadpanned. "So I've been told."

Weaving through the crowd, Reese considered how long he should wait before he broke up with Sabrina.

THREE

Lacey hummed on her way to her campus mailbox. The February breeze rejuvenated her after a morning full of lectures. Only three months to go until graduation! She was so ready to get out into the "real world," she could taste it.

After wrenching the heavy glass door open, she smiled and nodded to acquaintances while making a beeline to her box. She dropped her heavy backpack on the floor with a thud, then twisted the combination lock. Pulling out a stack of letters, she sifted through junk mail and stopped at an envelope addressed to her in her stepmother's writing.

Ripping open the pastel pink envelope, she smiled. She'd come to love Veronica during the past eight months. Her stepmother had turned out to be a warm, sweet woman, and every phone call home was pleasant and encouraging. Veronica encouraged her to do her best at school and offered thoughtful words when Lacey was frustrated in a class. It was as if her stepmother knew just what to say to give her the confidence she needed to succeed in college.

Even better, her father seemed happier than he'd been in years. He always appeared upbeat on the phone and was more relaxed when they discussed race team business. The elements of the business that used to stress him seemed replaced with his newlywed bliss.

Yes, Lacey had to admit her father had made a wonderful choice when he picked Veronica. Now if Lacey could only find someone to make her happy . . .

Pushing thoughts of her non-existent love life aside, she pulled out a pretty pink Valentine addressed to "Our Wonderful Daughter." Inside was a poem highlighting how special daughters are. At the bottom, Veronica had written with a flourish:

Lacey,

We just wanted to tell you how proud we are of your perfect 4.0. We're looking forward to coming to your graduation and cheering as you cross that stage. Keep up the good work. We'll send presents from Daytona.

Much love, Veronica and Dad

Lacey hugged the card to her chest and smiled. Despite the chaos of preparing for the start of the racing season in Daytona, her stepmother had thought to send her a Valentine. Sometimes she wondered how her stepmother knew when Lacey needed encouragement. It seemed that whenever she was feeling lonely and cut off from her family in North Carolina, she'd receive a card or a phone call from home.

Shaking her head, she stared down at the card, and guilt nipped at her. She had misjudged Veronica when they first met. She was lucky to have such a thoughtful stepmother.

"Excuse me, are you Millicent Fowler?" A male voice startled her from her thoughts.

She turned to a police officer. "Yes. I go by Lacey. Can I help you?"

He knitted his brow. "Ma'am, I need to speak with you."

"Why?" Her stomach clenched with alarm.

His expression softened a bit. "I think you might want to come with me so we can speak in private."

"No." She shook her head and gripped the card with her clammy hands. "Just tell me here."

His expression became grim. "I'm sorry to have to say this, but there's been an accident."

"An accident?" Her heart raced and hands shook. "What do you mean?"

"Ma'am, your parents . . ." He touched her shoulder.

Her body shook. "My parents what?" Her voice rose. "What about my parents?" When he didn't answer, she nearly shouted. "Tell me!"

"Please calm down." He touched her trembling hand. "I'm sorry to have to say this, but your parents perished this morning in a car accident."

Lacey screamed, collapsing in sobs on the cold tile floor.

Later that afternoon, Reese took another lap around the track, drafting behind his teammate, Tommy Reynolds. Pride swelled in his chest while he grinned. The two cars were a force to be reckoned with once they hooked up on the high banks of the track. They passed competitors as if the other cars were standing still. They crossed the start/finish line, taking no prisoners. And they loved every second of it—at least, Reese did.

"Reese! Reese!" His crew chief's voice crackled over the radio in his helmet.

Reese pushed the button on the steering wheel, activating the microphone in his helmet. "Yeah, Brett."

"Bring 'er to the garage."

"Why?" Reese nosed his front bumper millimeters from his teammate's rear bumper. "I was just warming up. Me and Tommy got some business to take care of on this track. We've got some cars to pass."

He smiled, approaching his fiercest competitor, Dylan McCormick, the star of Sinclair Motorsports. Oh, how he'd love to wipe up the track with that guy on Sunday. He'd show those Chevys these Fords can lead the pack too!

"Rod wants all Southern Racing employees in the team trailer pronto. Emergency meeting." After a pause, Brett added, "*Now,* Mitchell."

"Coming, Mother," Reese mocked with a salute only he could see.

"I think it's serious, man." From his crew chief's tone, it sure sounded serious.

Reese's grin faded. "Ten-four."

Tommy held his hand up, signaling to the cars around him that he was going low and slowing to merge onto pit road, and Reese assumed his teammate had received the same order from his crew chief. Reese signaled the car behind him then followed his teammate onto pit road. He watched the tachometer drop to 5,000, slowing to the mandated pit road speed of fifty-five.

Reese maneuvered the car into the garage area and parked in his team's stall. Removing his helmet, earplugs, and safety belts, he shimmied through the window and jumped onto the pavement.

Brett Turner leaned on the fender and tapped a pencil on his clipboard while reading statistics written on it. "That was your fastest practice session by far."

"Awesome." Reese removed the heat shields from his shins and dropped them onto the driver seat. "So, what's goin' on?"

His crew chief shrugged, hugging his clipboard to his chest. "Not sure really. Rod called an urgent team meeting. He wants us in the hauler in five."

"Let's go!" a crewman bellowed over the roar of an engine in a neighboring stall. The young man waved, and the team filed out like children heading to recess.

Falling in line, Reese's mind whirled with thoughts of practice. His car felt damned near close to perfect, the best it'd been since the practice sessions began three days ago. He itched to get back in it and turn more laps.

Reese smiled to himself while the line of men in matching uniforms headed toward the team hauler. He had a good feeling about his team and about Tommy. Together, they would make Southern Racing better than ever and take it to a higher level. They'd make their mark in the ARA. Reese could almost taste it.

The men climbed into the hauler, their work boots clicking up the metal steps, then they lined up along the supply counters.

Team Manager Rod Smith stood at the far end of the hauler by the door leading to the lounge. The middle-aged man's grimace sent a chill skittering down Reese's spine. Something was wrong, very wrong, and Reese had a sneaking feeling it had nothing to do with the practice session.

Conversations whirled through the hauler while crew members discussed everything from engine setups, parts, competitors, pretty girls spotted in the garage, and even what brand of beer to bring to the social gathering in someone's hotel room later tonight.

Folding his arms, Reese leaned against the counter and bit his bottom lip. He hoped to get the meeting over with and get back on the track before the end of the session.

Rod tried a subdued plea for quiet. When his weathered face turned red, Reese braced himself for the yelling to come.

"Quiet!" Rod's voice boomed off the walls, and the chatter abruptly stopped. "Thank you. Now, I need you boys to hear me out." He shook his head and closed his eyes for a moment. "I have bad news. Real bad news."

Reese sucked in a breath. He'd never seen Rod act so serious, so . . . distraught. What on earth was wrong?

"I got a call a little bit ago from Carl." Rod's gaze met Reese's, and Reese's heart paused at the sound of his father's name.

Reese's stomach clenched in anticipation. What had his father told Rod? And if it was so bad, why hadn't Carl called Reese too?

"And . . . ?" a wise guy in the back prodded.

"And he said that Greg . . . Greg . . ." Rod's voice vibrated with anxiety. He covered his face with his hands. "I can't say it."

"Say what?" someone asked. "Just get it out, Rod. We've got a practice session to finish."

"Have some respect, you schmuck," another chided.

"You're telling me to have respect?" the first guy challenged. "When have you ever shown any respect?"

"Guys, guys, calm down." Reese held up his hands and stepped into the center of the throng. "Let's all give Rod a moment. Apparently this is something big." He sidled up to the older man. "You okay?"

Rod shook his head, wiping his cheek with his shaky hand. His eyes were puffy and distraught. "I don't know how to say it, Reese."

"It's okay, man. Just say it the best way you can." Despite the anxiety washing over him, Reese forced a smile. "We're all family here."

The blood drained from the older man's face. "He's dead." His voice cracked like a kid going through puberty.

Reese gasped. "What did you say?" Had he heard him right? Someone was dead? *Who's dead? It couldn't be . . .*

Visibly shaking, Rod cleared his throat. "Greg and Veronica were killed in a car accident at two this morning on Interstate 95 somewhere in Georgia."

Reese's body trembled and his mouth dried. "What did you say?" he whispered.

"According to the highway patrol," Rod began, "they were speeding to get home, and Greg lost control of the car on some black ice. He hit a guard rail and the car rolled."

"What?" Reese repeated. His blood ran cold while he

stumbled backward, shaking his head. "Greg's dead?" he whispered. "Dead?"

The words echoed in his mind but didn't make sense. Greg Fowler was dead? The man Reese had called "Uncle Greg" when he was a child was dead? The man who'd taught him how to maneuver his race car through traffic at Bristol and who insisted his father let him move up to the ARA was gone?

Greg was dead.

Dead.

His eyes widened and Reese gasped. *Lacey.*

He moved toward Rod, weaving through the knot of coworkers gathering around him and shooting questions with the speed of a machine gun.

"Does Lacey know?" Reese asked, raising his voice over the barrage of voices. His pulse raced like a marathon runner while he paused for an answer and then repeated the question. "Rod, did someone call Lacey?" He grabbed the front of the team manager's shirt. "Do you know?"

"I don't know." Rod shrugged.

Taking deep breaths to calm his racing heart, Reese let Rod go and stalked through the door at the back of the supply area to the lobby. He dug his backpack out of his locker, fished his cellular phone from the pocket, and dialed her number.

Pacing back and forth, he silently urged her to answer. *Come on, Lacey. Answer the stupid phone!*

He needed to hear her voice. He had to know how she was coping. Did she need him? Was she alone?

Her voicemail picked up immediately. "Hi, this is Lacey," her sweet voice said. "I'm not here, so leave me a message. I'll call back when I can. Thanks!" Then a beep sounded.

"Lacey, it's Reese. Call me." His voice quavered, and he cleared his throat. He redialed, but her voicemail picked up again.

"No!" His hands shook, tears filling his eyes while he stared down at his phone. He felt as if the rug had been pulled out from under him. He had to get his emotions under control. He cleared his throat again, dialing his father's cell phone.

His father answered after one ring. "Reese."

A lump swelled in his throat at the sound of his father's voice. "Pop. Greg and Veronica . . ." his voice trailed off.

"I know, son," his father whispered. "I know."

"What about Lacey?" He dropped onto the overstuffed sofa and wiped a stray tear trickling down his hot cheek. He had to stop his emotions. Crying wouldn't bring Greg and Veronica back. He had to be strong even though he felt as if he'd just lost his second father.

"She's on her way home. Should be landing in about an hour." His father's voice was hoarse, and Reese wondered if he'd been crying too.

"Who told her?" He stared down at the toes of his racing shoes and tried not to imagine Lacey sobbing in some stranger's arms. She needed him. He needed to be with her. He had to see her.

"A police officer from—"

"A police officer?" Reese stood and paced again, his voice booming with ire. "A stranger told her? Why didn't you tell her? Or why didn't you have me tell her? Pop, what were you thinking?"

"Reese, just calm down." His father's voice was more confident, almost harsh. "Son, this was out of my control, understand? A highway patrolman told me, and he'd already contacted the Baltimore police. I had no say in this."

Reese pondered his father's tone. Why was his dad so defensive? Or was he agitated?

Letting the notion go, Reese changed the subject. "Who's picking her up from the airport?"

"She only wanted Krista. I guess she's turned off her cell phone because I haven't been able to reach her. Poor kid . . ."

"Yeah." Reese's throat constricted again with thoughts of Lacey losing the only family she had left. He had to help her through this. He needed to be her rock. "I'm coming home."

"Now, Reese, wait a minute," his father said. "You have obligations there. You come home in a few days after things are settled here. I'm going to help her through this. It's my job. Greg and I always said we'd look after each other's—"

"No, Pop." He shook his head. "She needs me. She needs us both, really. We're her only family. Someone else can practice my car. This is way more important."

His father sighed with defeat. "All right. You do what you have to do."

Reese nodded, glad his father finally realized he was right. "I'll call you after I arrange a flight."

"Okay, son. Be safe."

Snapping his phone shut, Reese headed out of the lounge to tell his team he was leaving.

FOUR

Lacey sank further into the first class seat on the jet and clutched the crumpled Valentine in her hand. She'd cried so much earlier that she felt devoid of tears. Her mind sped out of control with the confusion of the day. She felt cold, hollow, and so, so alone.

Her father was dead.

Her stepmother was dead.

Lacey was all *alone*.

None of it made sense. The police officer said they'd been the victims of a single-car accident. Her father was rushing back to Mooresville at two in the morning. He hit black ice, then the car hit the guardrail at an excess of seventy miles per hour, flipping at least five times.

Images flooded her mind and Lacey shuddered, hugging her arms across her chest.

They were dead.

Dead.

It was so clinical. So logical.

So utterly surreal.

The events of the day replayed in her mind. Carl had called her minutes after she'd spoken to the police and told her he'd arranged a flight from Baltimore to Charlotte. He had said he'd pick her up at the airport, but Lacey wanted Krista. For some reason, a warm hug from her best friend since junior high seemed more comforting. Sure, she loved Carl, but she could cry more easily with Krista.

Lacey opened the Valentine and ran her fingertip over her stepmother's handwriting again, the words smudged from her tears. She thought back to her call to Krista. Saying the words, "My dad and Veronica are dead" felt foreign. Sobbing, Krista had promised to be at the airport by four.

After that call, Lacey had turned off her phone and stuck it in her coat pocket. She wanted to close out the world and be alone. She knew the news would spread like wildfire through the racing community, and her phone would ring off the hook soon enough.

She bit her lip and shut the greeting card. Right now, she needed solitude to digest everything and figure out how the heck she was going to make it through the week. How would she plan a funeral for the two most important people in her life?

Closing her eyes, Lacey took a long, ragged breath. She hugged the Valentine to her chest and let the thoughts race through her head. She needed a dress, a nice black dress. Did she have any comfortable black pumps?

Her thoughts spun like a car blowing a tire and losing control at Talladega Super Speedway. Had Reese heard the news? Would he come back from Daytona?

Her eyes flew open. *Reese.* She hadn't spoken to him since the wedding. She'd spent a lot of energy trying to put him out of her mind but found herself thinking about him even more. Despite her best efforts, his gorgeous face, sexy smile, and memories of his gentle, tantalizing fingers on her thighs invaded her dreams.

He'd even called her a few times. However, she'd let her voicemail answer, and he'd left her messages asking her to call him. But she didn't. She couldn't. Her stomach still soured at the thought of that cheap floozy pawing him at the wedding.

Lacey shook her head. Was it jealousy? Was it anger? She

knew it was a mixture of both. In her heart, she knew she'd always carry a torch for that man, and she hated it. He'd never see her as more than just a kid.

Lacey pulled out her phone and stared down at it. She considered calling Reese, then jammed the phone back into her pocket. Hearing his voice would wrench memories of standing on pit road between her father and Carl, watching Reese practice his cars. Then the tears would start again.

Lacey closed her eyes, pushing Reese's handsome image from her mind. She needed her strength to get through today.

Tomorrow would be difficult enough.

FIVE

"Veronica's sister would like their service to be together," Carl said while he sat across from Lacey in her father's formal dining room later that evening. "She said Greg was Veronica's life and she'd want it that way."

"That sounds fine." Lacey's voice came in a hoarse whisper.

She stared into the mug of hot tea Krista had set before her. She felt as if she were moving through a horrible nightmare. Never in her wildest dreams would she have dreamt of planning her father and stepmother's funeral less than a year after they were married. How could this be happening?

"You and Veronica's sister will meet with their pastor in the morning. You'll have to see the lawyer on Friday."

Lacey nodded, contemplating the bright yellow happy face on her mug and swallowing a sarcastic snort. At the saddest moment in her life, she found herself staring at a happy face. Life was just plain ironic.

"We thought maybe Thursday would be a good day for the service. By then the news will be out, and people can come . . ." his voice trailed off.

"Mm-hmm. Thursday. Yes." Inhaling the scent of the English Morning Breakfast tea steaming in her yellow mug, she remembered cold winter nights when she'd sat by the fireplace with her father, watching the evening race report and enjoying the crackling flames. Back then, it was just her and her dad. No one else.

Now those days were gone—wiped away by a patch of black ice. This just wasn't fair. She'd give anything to have her father back.

"Lacey?" Carl's voice jarred her back to the present.

Her eyes darted to his blue orbs, finding them brimming with concern and compassion.

"Honey, are you okay?" he asked.

She considered the silly question. Was she okay? Of course she wasn't. Her father was dead. Her stepmother was dead. Her life was left in shambles. She had no idea how she was going to get through the week or how she was going to pay the mortgage.

The thought jostled more questions in her mind. Did the house even have a mortgage? Was the house hers? Was her college tuition paid in full? What would happen to the race team her grandfather had built?

No, she wasn't okay, and she didn't know when she would be.

"I'm fine." Lacey folded her hands on the table before her.

Carl raised an eyebrow with suspicion. "You sure?"

Lacey nodded with emphasis. "I'm just exhausted, and I'd like to go to bed." She stood. "Thank you for everything."

Krista marched from the kitchen, her blond waves bouncing. "Hold on there. You haven't eaten, young lady. I made you vegetable soup and a turkey sandwich." She gave Lacey a stern expression, resembling a mother chastising her child. "You're not going anywhere until you eat."

Lacey plastered a smile on her face. "Thank you, but I'm not hungry."

"Lacey . . ." Her best friend shook a spoon at her. "You need to eat. You need your strength."

Lacey shook her head. "I'm sorry, but I can't."

"Reese will be home tomorrow morning," Carl said. "He got a red-eye flight leaving at six. The airport wouldn't clear the team plane to take off tonight. Something about fog."

Lacey spun at the sound of his name. "Reese?"

"I talked to him earlier. He said he's been trying to call you."

"Why is he coming home?"

"For you, honey."

Glowering, Lacey shook her head again. "Tell him not to come. I'm fine. I'll see him . . . sometime." She couldn't face Reese. Not now. Too many emotions were already spinning like a tornado within her, and seeing him on the arm of some blond bimbo might push her over the edge.

"Sweetie." Carl approached, putting his hands on her forearms. "He was going to come back for the funeral anyway. The whole team is. But he wanted to be back in town early to give you some support."

"I have all of the support I need right here. Tell him I'm fine, and I'll see him Thursday." She pulled her arms back and padded out of the dining room.

She made her way up the sweeping open staircase to her room and then gathered up her favorite pajamas and slipped into the hall bathroom.

After stripping, she climbed into the stall, and took a long, hot shower, letting grief drown her while her tears flowed. She didn't want to meet with the pastor in the morning to discuss her father's funeral. She didn't want to talk to the lawyer about his assets.

She certainly didn't want to see Reese. Well, she'd love to stare at him and admire his gorgeous body, but she didn't want him to see her like this—vulnerable, hurt, lost, and lonely.

Stepping from the stall, Lacey wrapped herself in a big, fluffy purple towel. As she dried herself, she tried to put everything out of her mind. She was physically and mentally drained. It was all too much. She needed to sleep. She'd face it all in the morning. Somehow.

While pulling on her pajama top, a soft knock sounded on the door.

"Lacey?" Krista called. "Reese is on the phone."

Lacey groaned. Why was he calling her already? Couldn't he give her some time? She couldn't stand the thought of hearing his voice. She just wasn't ready to face Reese or the memories his voice would dislodge.

She cracked the door open to find Krista grimacing and holding her hand over the mouthpiece of the cordless phone.

"Tell him I'm not up to talking," Lacey said.

Krista adjusted her hand over the receiver. "The man's dying to talk to you. He sounds really upset."

"Well, so am I. Tell him I'm not here. I went back to Maryland."

Krista looked ready to challenge her then her shoulders drooped with defeat. Turning away from Lacey, she held the phone to her ear. "Hey, Reese? . . . Yeah, she doesn't want to take any calls . . . I know . . . I know . . ." She sighed, lowering her voice. "I told her that . . ."

Lacey retreated into the bathroom, closing the door behind her. She didn't want to hear the conversation. She didn't want to know Reese cared. It didn't matter. Hearing his voice would hurt too much, and she'd had enough hurt for one day. Heck, she'd had enough to last her five years.

She stared at her reflection while running a brush through her long, wavy strawberry blond locks. Her complexion seemed more pale than usual, and her green eyes were dull with exhaustion. All she wanted to do was go to bed.

The door burst open, and Lacey jumped.

Krista stomped into the bathroom, swinging her arms. "What's your problem?"

"Excuse me?" Lacey glared at her. "Can I have a little privacy here? I'm in the bathroom!"

Krista slammed the phone onto the counter. "Why won't you talk to Reese? He's worried sick about you!"

"Are you kidding me? *What's my problem?*" Rage trembled in her voice. "I just lost my parents! What do you think is my problem?"

Krista sighed and reached for Lacey's arm. "I'm sorry. I didn't mean that the way it came out."

Offended by her words, Lacey pulled back. "Whatever. Good night." She started past her friend.

"No. Wait!" Krista gathered her into a warm hug. "Don't go. I'm sorry. This is all too much for me too."

"Don't worry about it. Good night." Pulling back, Lacey blew out a sigh of defeat. She was emotionally spent. She just wanted to go to bed and forget the whole day.

Krista tilted her head in question. "I just don't understand why you're shutting Reese out. He's always been like your family. Don't you want to talk to him?"

"It's complicated." Lacey folded her arms. She wished Krista would just drop it. She was too tired to go into the intricacies of her jumbled emotions.

"Try me."

"Look, Krista, when I talk to Reese, I'm going to lose it, and I've cried enough today. I need to save some energy for the rest of this week. Talking to Reese will dig up some memories I'm trying to suppress right now." Her throat tightened and she hugged her arms to her chest as if guarding her heart.

"He says he's coming over tomorrow, and he's going to see you."

Lacey shook her head. "Tell him no. I don't want to see him."

Krista gave her a palms up. "Why?"

Lacey blew out a frustrated sigh. Why wouldn't she drop it? She didn't want to say *because I don't trust myself around him.* "I'm not ready for company yet. I just don't want to see anyone." *Especially him.*

Krista shrugged with defeat. "Fine, but he won't be happy."

Relief surged through Lacey. *Good. She dropped it.* "You can take him out and entertain him. You always liked him."

Krista snorted with sarcasm. "Yeah, like I'm in his league."

Lacey nodded. *Boy, do I know the feeling.* "Well, good night. Thank you for everything." She dragged her slippers across the carpet to her room, curled up in her bed, and cried herself to sleep.

Six

"Damn it!" Reese slammed the cellular phone onto the counter of his luxury motor coach parked in a secured section at Daytona International Speedway. Frustration mixed with ire boiled in his gut.

Cursing under his breath, he grabbed a bottle of beer from the refrigerator and dropped onto the leather sofa. He'd been trying to reach Lacey all day. He wanted to hear her voice and know she was okay. But she wouldn't answer her phone. He must've left six messages, all of them asking, no begging, her to call him.

Why hadn't she called back?

After twisting off the bottle top, he took a long drink, then grabbed the remote and turned on the large, flat screen television. The alcohol only dulled his irritation. The hurt still surged through his veins and tugged at his heart.

Flipping channels, he shook his head. He'd heard Lacey tell Krista to say she wasn't taking calls. Why the heck couldn't she say that herself?

She could've just said, "Reese, I'm not up to talking, but thanks for calling." Then he would've at least heard her voice and known for himself that she was okay. It wasn't enough to have her message delivered through her friend. Wasn't he worth the energy it took to speak for herself? She'd known him her whole life, for goodness sake!

He downed another drink, wishing the hurt in his soul would

subside. What was going on with Lacey? He could understand her avoiding other calls, but why his? They'd always talked when she was younger. But something had changed. What was it?

Reese flipped more channels. Settling on Sports Channel, he wracked his brain, pondering Lacey Fowler. Was she avoiding everyone or was she only avoiding him? He thought for a moment about the last time he'd spoken to her. It was at her father's wedding. He conjured the night in his mind's eye.

Things were going okay when he first saw her, and they'd talked. She caught the bouquet, and he got the garter. His mouth dried while he remembered putting the garter on her. He recalled the smell of her shampoo, the feel of her soft skin, and that long, gorgeous leg. He absently wondered if he should turn on the air conditioner in his bus. Had it suddenly gotten hot?

Reese's thoughts moved back to the night of the wedding. After their dance together, she'd changed. She'd left in a huff, and he hadn't spoken to her since. However, their silence wasn't his doing. In fact, he'd tried to call her a few times, but he kept getting her stupid voicemail.

What on earth was going on with her? Was it something he'd said? Something he'd done?

Why is it bugging me so much?

On the screen, the commentator sitting behind a large desk and wearing a suit drew Reese's attention. When a photo of Greg Fowler flashed up on the screen, Reese groaned. The news was out, and he could only imagine how painful it would be for Lacey to see the story of her father's death in the news.

"On a sad note today, the racing community is mourning the loss of one of its own," the commentator said. "Team owner Greg Fowler and his wife Veronica died in a car accident early this morning."

"Oh, man," Reese whispered, shaking his head. A flood of

grief drowned him as if he were hearing the words from Rod all over again.

"The couple was heading back home to Mooresville, North Carolina, after attending pre-race events at the Daytona International Speedway," the reporter said. "Greg Fowler was the chief executive officer of Southern Racing, which owns the number 89 Ford driven by last year's American Racing Association champion Reese Mitchell, as well as the number 91 driven by Tommy Reynolds. Our thoughts and prayers are with the Fowler family and the Southern Racing organization. In other racing news . . ."

Reese turned off the television and tossed the remote onto the coffee table with a clatter. He could only imagine the newspapers, magazines, and websites that were featuring stories about the Fowlers' death. Lacey would soon be inundated by reporters and mourners. She needed Reese to support her through this difficult time. Why didn't she realize that?

He cursed the air traffic controllers for not clearing the team plane for an earlier flight. He cursed himself for not climbing into a rental car and heading home as soon as he'd heard the news.

He also cursed Greg for trying to drive home in the middle of the night. What was he thinking? Everyone knew temperatures were going to dip below freezing overnight. What could've been so important that he'd risk leaving that late at night?

Reese gripped his bottle and silently vowed to be Lacey's rock. Whether she thought she needed him or not, he was going to help her through this.

Lacey kicked off her shoes and gingerly placed her feet on the ottoman in front of the leather sofa in her father's den. The day had flashed by at lightning speed. She'd spent all morning in the office of Pastor Paul Tyson, listening to him and Veronica's younger sister, Brenda, plan the funeral.

Lacey had stayed silent as images of her mother's funeral sixteen years earlier flooded her memories. Details she'd never realized she'd filed away in her mind washed over her—the brilliant yellow of the gown in which her mother was buried, the scent of the gorgeous lilies that had filled the church, the sound of the choir singing "Amazing Grace" in perfect harmony . . .

It had been too much for her to relive the memories. Overcome by a smothering grief, twice she'd fled the pastor's office and sobbed in the bathroom. Brenda offered several times to take her home, but Lacey stayed and listened, wishing she could wake up from the awful nightmare and go back to her mundane life of classes, term papers, and study groups.

Life had been so simple a week ago. All she had to do was study and prepare to graduate in only three months. Now she had to bury her father and stepmother and figure out how to go on with her life.

She lifted her mug of hot tea to her lips, the aroma and warmth filling her senses but only dulling the hollow feeling gnawing at her. Sipping the tea, she reflected on the afternoon, which hadn't gone any better than the morning. She'd spent it with the funeral director, talking about the reception, food, caskets, gravestones, and cemetery plots. The finality. The *end*.

"I didn't hear you come in," Krista said, and Lacey jumped, nearly dropping her mug. "I didn't mean to scare you." Her best friend sank into the chair across from the sofa. "When did you get back?"

"About twenty minutes ago." Lacey grabbed the remote and flipped on the television. She could feel her best friend watching her, but she kept her gaze glued to the screen. She didn't feel like talking.

"I must've been upstairs."

Lacey stopped on Sports Channel, where a commentator

droned on about practice sessions at Daytona. ARA cars thundered around the track, and her heart thumped when she spotted Reese's 89 Ford stockcar. She'd wondered how Reese was doing, but she still couldn't face him—not yet. Her heart ached enough without seeing the man she'd loved from afar for most of her life. She dropped the remote on the end table and sipped her tea.

"So, how'd today go?" Krista asked.

Despite the awareness of Krista's eyes boring into her, Lacey shrugged and didn't speak. She didn't want to relive the stress of the day by recounting it to Krista.

"Are things set for Thursday?" her best friend asked.

"Brenda wanted to postpone it for another week, but I wanted to stay with Thursday," Lacey said, staring at the television and absently wondering how her father's team was coping with the news. "I need closure. The burial will be Saturday with just the family."

"How are you? How are you *really?*"

Keeping her eyes on the screen, she shrugged again. "I'm fine."

"The phone never stopped ringing today. I checked the machine, and there were messages from reporters, fans, and racing officials. Most of them wanted to express their sympathy. A few asked for calls back. You can listen to them whenever you feel up to it."

Lacey ignored the sorrow surging within her from Krista's description of the outpouring of condolences. Knowing many other people were missing her father and thinking of her caused tears to well in her eyes.

"Reese called about six times," Krista continued. "He said on one message that he stopped by too."

"He did?" Lacey met her gaze, her heart hammering in her chest at the mention of Reese's name.

Krista gave a knowing look as if reading Lacey's thoughts. "You should call him."

Before she could respond, the television wrenched her attention away from Krista's comment. A photo of her father flashed in the upper corner of the screen. She gasped and cupped her mouth with her hand. Seeing her father's face sent tears spilling down her cheeks and a renewed grief soaking through her soul.

"American Racing Association team owner Greg Fowler and his new bride, Veronica, died in a car accident early yesterday while traveling from Daytona to their home in Mooresville, North Carolina. Greg was the second generation owner of Southern Racing, which houses the 89 Ford driven by series champion Reese Mitchell and the 91 driven by Tommy Reynolds."

Lacey sniffed, swiping away tears with the back of her hand.

"A memorial service will be held Thursday in Mooresville, and a private burial is planned for Saturday. In lieu of flowers, the family requests donations be made to Racing Charities," the reporter said.

"News travels fast in this town," Lacey whispered, swallowing more tears.

"American Racing Association superstar Reese Mitchell left Daytona early this morning to go home to Mooresville to be with the Fowler family. In his absence, rookie Chandler Quinn will practice and qualify his car. In other racing news . . ."

Lacey hit the mute button and cleared her throat. "I saw the paper this morning. It's all over the news about my dad and Veronica, huh?" She bit her lower lip.

Krista nodded and folded her hands.

"Thanks for staying here with me. I don't know what I'd do without you."

"What are best friends for?" Her best friend's lips formed a sad smile.

Lacey's mind clicked off a laundry list of things to do in preparation for the service for her father and stepmother. "Can you take tomorrow off and go shopping with me? I need a new dress. And some shoes. I need to get my mind off this stuff somehow. Shopping's a good distraction."

"You know I love to shop." Krista's smile deepened, but sadness glittered in her eyes.

"Thanks."

The phone rang, and her friend stood. "Hold that thought." She crossed the room and snatched the cordless receiver from the cradle.

"I'm not here," Lacey said, folding her arms and settling back in the chair.

"Hello . . . Oh, hi Reese. How are you?" Krista's blue eyes darted to Lacey, who shook her head to indicate she didn't want to talk. "No, she's not here . . . Oh, okay . . . Hang on one minute." Her friend held the phone to her chest. "He says if you don't talk to him, he's going to come over and sit here until you do."

Lacey sighed with defeat. She knew she was stuck. She didn't want him to come over. She wasn't up to facing her feelings for him in the flesh, especially after spending the day planning her parents' funeral.

"Gimme the phone." She held out her hand.

Krista smiled as she brought Lacey the phone. "He even sounds hot over the phone," she whispered.

Lacey took a deep breath and prayed her heartbeat would slow. She grasped the phone and held it to her ear. "Reese?"

"Hey, squirt . . ." his voice quavered, wrenching more sorrow from deep in her soul.

Memories crashed over her like a tidal wave. Images invaded her mind's eye—Christmas dinners with her father, Reese, and Carl. Hanging out in the shop with her father, Carl, Reese, and the crew. Watching their drivers practice at the racetrack.

When the tears started, she couldn't stop them. She jumped up, tossed Krista the phone, and retreated to her room, where she curled up in the fetal position on her bed and sobbed into a pillow.

"Lacey? Lacey?" Reese shook his head. Where'd she go? He'd heard her voice and then the line went dead.

"Reese?" Krista's voice called through the phone.

"Krista? Where's Lacey? I thought . . ." He dropped into his favorite wing chair in the den of his Mooresville home.

"She lost it." Krista sighed. "I guess hearing your voice was too much for her."

"Crap." Reese leaned back in the chair, looking up toward the ceiling, guilt pouring through him. "I never meant to upset her."

"I know. I think the stress of the day took a toll on her. She had to plan the memorial service, and she just saw a news story about her dad on Sports Channel. I think it all got to her."

Defeated, Reese blew out a ragged breath. "I'm sorry. I guess I was being insensitive insisting she talk to me."

"It's not you. She's just hyper-sensitive." Krista paused. "Look, you might want to just give her space until the service on Thursday. She wants me to go shopping with her tomorrow to get a new dress and shoes. I'm going to keep her as distracted as I can."

"All right," he said. "I'll keep my distance." *As much as it's going to kill me.*

"Good night, Reese."

"Good night." He disconnected and scanned the room until his eyes fell on a photograph. Taken last season, it featured his team, along with Greg, Veronica, Lacey, and him grinning in Victory Lane at Richmond.

Staring at her smile, his heart ached for Lacey. He wanted to talk to her and tell her that he was going to help her through this. He hated to back off, but he knew Krista was right. He had to just bide his time and give her the space she needed.

But come Thursday, he was going to get her alone and take her into his arms. Then he'd let her cry for as long as she needed.

Whether she wanted to or not.

SEVEN

Standing room only.

Lacey shook her head as she surveyed the crowd packed into the large hall at the funeral home late Thursday morning. There had to be at least five hundred people, if not more, and they all had come to pay respects to her father and Veronica.

Standing at the front of the hall, she scanned the sea of faces, recognizing Southern Racing employees, ARA officials, reporters, sports commentators, friends, and relatives. Then there were the strangers—too many of them to count. She marveled at the crowd, and her heart swelled with a mixture of admiration and grief. All of these mourners somehow held a common bond of having known her father and stepmother.

"There's Reese," Krista whispered.

Lacey's stomach clenched when she spotted him walking through the doorway with a tall, thin, leggy blonde holding onto his arm.

That jerk.

"He's such a ladies' man," Lacey seethed. How dare he show up to her father's funeral with a date! Some things never changed. She shook her head, gritting her teeth in disgust.

"Don't you know it?" Krista sounded as disappointed as Lacey felt.

Lacey pursed her lips. The nerve of Reese to sound so concerned on the phone the other night. It was all a crock! He didn't care about her. All he cared about was looking good.

Even Sports Channel reported that ARA Champion Reese Mitchell had rushed home to be with the Fowler family. He'd only rushed home as a publicity stunt.

Lacey studied him. He shook hands with members of his crew. He frowned as if he were truly upset. It nearly killed her that he looked so good in that dark Italian suit. He was clean-shaven, and his hair was styled to perfection. His blue eyes glittered across the large hall. He was so handsome. No, he was drop-dead gorgeous, and she resented him for it. She also resented that model-perfect blonde by his side.

Krista placed a hand on Lacey's arm. "Let's have a seat. The service should be starting soon."

Lacey lowered herself into a seat in the front row with Veronica's family to her right. She nodded to them, and they returned the gesture with sad expressions that mirrored her mood.

The pastor began the service, and she breathed a sigh of relief. She wanted to get the day over with. The anticipation had kept her awake and her stomach in knots all night long.

Lacey was grateful the closed caskets sat at the other end of the podium so she didn't have to stare at them. While the pastor went through the motions of the service, her mind wandered. She pondered what would happen next in her life. Although she only had a couple of months left in school, she longed to stay home in North Carolina. She assumed her father had left her some money to live on, so she could transfer to a local college to finish up her degree. Then she could work for her father's company full-time.

She was lost in her thoughts when the pastor offered the microphone to members of the crowd to pay their respects in an open forum. A few of Veronica's friends and relatives took turns remembering her, and Lacey wiped her eyes during their stories of her loyal friendship and great sense of humor. When some of the Southern Racing employees spoke of her father,

Lacey fought tears and blotted the ones that escaped with tissues Krista had handed her. She missed her father so much that their words made her heart ache.

When the pastor returned to the microphone, she sucked in a breath. Next she knew she'd have to face the long line of guests expressing their condolences and she dreaded it. Their stories and love of her father and stepmother would send renewed grief rushing over her. She longed to put her feet up in front of the fireplace and close her eyes, erasing the images of the caskets and the mourners.

"If no one else would like to speak, then we'll close the floor now," Pastor Tyson said.

"Wait," a voice from the back announced. "Please, I'd like a chance."

Lacey's heart thumped, and her stomach plummeted. She knew that voice. Could it be . . . ?

When Reese stepped up to the podium, she gasped. No, he couldn't possibly want to speak. Hearing his voice and his sentiments for her father would send her sobbing. She didn't want to lose her cool in public. It was just too much for her. She started to stand to leave, but Krista's strong hand yanked her back.

"Listen to what he has to say before you run off and hide," Krista whispered.

Lacey shook her head, nonplussed. How did Krista know her so well? She sank back down in the seat and snatched a handful of tissues from the box beside her.

Reese cleared his throat. "Thank you for the opportunity to share my feelings. My name is Reese Mitchell, and I've known Greg Fowler my whole life."

Lacey's throat constricted and fresh tears flooded her eyes. Her hands trembled while she absently ripped the tissues.

"My pop and Greg have been best friends since they were

teenagers. Pop always said Greg taught him everything he knows about race cars. I know it's true because Greg also taught me." His eyes scanned the crowd. He smiled, indicating he found the face he'd sought. "Right, Pop?"

"Greg loved life." His smile faded and his blue eyes sparkled with sadness. "He loved to laugh, and he loved his race team. He always believed in me, and I'll be eternally thankful for that. He gave me a chance by convincing my dad to let me race, and I don't think it turned out too bad for me or the team."

The lump in Lacey's throat swelled and tears stung her eyes again. Hearing Reese talk about her dad was tearing her apart inside. She had to get out of the hall before she dissolved into sobs in front of the crowd.

"Greg's family meant more than anything to him, especially his beautiful daughter Lacey." When Reese's gaze met hers, she heard herself whimper.

Then her tears started. She covered her mouth with her hand, trying in vain to quiet her weeping.

"After his wife died suddenly sixteen years ago, Lacey was his life," Reese said. "She was his pride . . . and his joy."

Fighting back tears, she stared down at the toes of her new black pumps. She couldn't bear to gaze into those crystal blue orbs that were pulling her in like a magnet.

"Greg's family grew less than a year ago when he wed Veronica, a wonderful, warm, caring woman. He once told my dad that she completed him." His voice wavered, and he paused to clear his throat again. "It's truly a tragedy that Greg and Veronica were taken from us. We'll never forget them. All of us at Southern Racing will miss our friends. And I will miss a part of my family."

Applause spread through the crowd like wildfire, indicating Reese was finished. Sobs wracked Lacey's body and her soul. She popped up and hurried toward the door, slamming into

Reese on her way.

"Lacey?" he asked, his deep blue eyes full of concern. "Wait."

Ignoring his pleas to stop, she pushed past him and kept going. She needed to be alone to gather her thoughts and suppress the grief bubbling through her like a river. Wrenching the door to the hallway open, she hurried down toward the parlor, where she had dressed before the service.

"Lacey!" Reese yelled after her. "Lacey, wait!"

Reaching the parlor, she pushed the door open and stood before the mirror. She lowered herself onto the bench, and wept as Reese's speech echoed in her mind.

"Lacey," Reese said.

Looking up, she found him in the doorway, a confused expression clouding his handsome face.

She stood and pointed toward the door. "Get out of here!"

He held his hands up in surrender. "Lacey, wait a minute."

"Get out! Just leave me alone." She gestured toward the door behind him.

"What's going on with you? Why are you shutting me out?" He stepped toward her.

"I want to be alone. Why can't you understand that? I just lost my dad and my step-mom, and I need time to grieve." Her voice trembled with a mixture of sorrow, frustration, and anger.

His azure eyes pleaded with her while hurt spread across his face. "Why are you treating me like the enemy? I only want to help you, but you've been pushing me away."

She took a deep breath and glared at him. He had a heck of a way of showing he wanted to help her. "How dare you bring a date to my father's funeral?"

He tilted his head in question. "What date?"

"That blond bimbo on your arm when you came in." She gestured toward the lobby. "You can't go anywhere without your flavor of the month, can you?"

A smile twitched the corners of his mouth. "My flavor of the month?"

"Yes!" She grabbed a tissue from the counter behind her and dabbed her eyes, absently wondering if her eyeliner had run. "You have an endless stream of trollops. It's like you thrive on the attention. You're so freakin' gorgeous and popular that you can't help but bring your entourage with you everywhere you go—even to a funeral!"

"You think I'm gorgeous?" He folded his arms across his wide chest.

She was running out of patience. "Are you even listening to me?"

"Yes." He nodded. "Intently."

"Well?" She gestured for emphasis. "What do you have to say for yourself, Reese Mitchell?"

"First of all, Gina's not my date. She's my new PR rep. Your dad hired her a few weeks ago."

Her cheeks burned with embarrassment. "Oh. Where's Sabrina?"

"Sabrina?" He raised an eyebrow in question.

"The tramp that hung all over you at my dad's wedding."

He shrugged. "We broke up six months ago."

She dabbed her eyes again. "You did?"

"Yes." He stepped toward her.

"Where's your current flame? I'm sure you have one."

"Actually, I don't right now."

She cleared her throat in an effort to hide her surprise. "I find that difficult to believe."

"So. You think I'm gorgeous?" He stood before her, and she inhaled his cologne, a popular spicy male fragrance that he endorsed as one of his sponsors. The scent made her crazy.

"I never said that." Vulnerability spread through her gut, overpowering the anger from a few moments ago. Her cheeks continued to burn, and she wished he'd just leave.

"Actually, you did. I heard it myself just a few minutes ago." He flashed a sexy grin, causing her pulse to leap to hyper speed.

"Well, I didn't mean it." She folded her arms.

His grin faded. "Why are you pushing me away?"

"Because I can't handle the fact that he's gone, and I'm all alone." Her answer came in a hoarse whisper, her body shaking with grief.

"You're not alone." Reese opened his arms, beckoning her to him.

She let him embrace her as if an invisible tractor beam yanked her to him. Burying her face in his chest, she cried while he rubbed her back and whispered his sweet words of condolence and sympathy in her ear. His body heat and warm voice comforted her, and for the first time since she'd gotten the news of her father's death, Lacey felt safe.

EIGHT

Reese stood near the end of the hallway while the seemingly endless line of guests streamed through to shake hands with Veronica's family and Lacey. He leaned against the wall and studied Lacey. She looked tired—no exhausted. Her creamy white complexion was paler than usual with dark circles shining beneath her emerald eyes, despite her efforts to disguise them with make-up.

But she still was beautiful, more beautiful than he remembered at the wedding. Her red hair hung in waves past her slight shoulders and halfway down her back. She wore a simple black dress that hugged her curves and stopped at her knees. Tan-colored stockings encased her shapely legs, and when he remembered the feel of her thighs his cheeks warmed.

Reese cleared his throat and looked away for a moment. What was his problem? He'd never before thought of Lacey as sexy. But there she was all grown up and looking like a woman, not the kid he'd taught to drive a stick-shift in his restored 1969 Camaro in the back lot at the race shop when she was sixteen.

His eyes found her again. She shook hands and nodded to the mourners with grace that seemed almost robotic, giving each person the same expression. She wasn't the Lacey he knew. She was cold, distant, and troubled. And it was killing him, filling him with an insatiable urge to comfort her.

His mind wandered back to their conversation in the parlor. What had she meant when she commented about his flavor of the month? Did she mean to imply he was some sort of playboy? Why did that comment bug him so much?

A smile tugged at the corner of his mouth. Why had she said he was gorgeous? Was she admiring him as much as he found himself admiring her? When they'd hugged, she'd held onto him for dear life. Holding her felt so natural.

Reese shook his head. Lacey was only twenty-one, and she'd been like a sister to him. He had to get his head on straight and concentrate on being her rock. He had to let this strange attraction go before it drove him to the brink of distraction.

"Reese Mitchell." A voice beside him slammed him back to the present. "How on earth have you been?"

He turned to find his ex-girlfriend Sandy Webb staring at him. "Sandy? How long has it been?"

His gaze raked over her. Still the same Sandy—long golden hair, slender legs, and curves in all the right places. They'd had a whirlwind love affair filled with late nights in his bus at the track. Then she'd abruptly left for some big-time marketing job on the West Coast.

"Four years, right? How are you?" She opened her arms.

He gave her a quick hug. "I'm all right. How are you?"

"Fine. I just came back from California." She flipped her hair behind her shoulder.

"Really? What brought you back here?" He leaned back against the wall.

She shrugged. "Things just didn't work out. I was going to see if I could get a job with the team again. I was really surprised to hear . . ." her voice trailed off.

He folded his arms. "Yeah, it was a shock."

Sandy stepped toward him and lowered her voice. "How's Lacey?"

He shook his head. "She puts up this solid front, but I can tell she's barely hanging on." He glanced over to where Lacey hugged one of his crewmembers.

"She was always a tough kid, but this is a low blow."

"Yeah." He met Sandy's gaze again. "So, have you found a place and everything?"

"I'm back in Mooresville. I've got an apartment for now, but I'm looking at condos. I made some money on my place in California." Her eyes darted toward his hands and back up again. "No lucky girl has snatched you up yet, huh?"

"Who, me?" He chuckled. "Nope. Still single."

She raised her eyebrows and a coy grin spread on her ruby red lips. "We'll have to get together for old time's sake." She whipped a pen and paper from her purse, wrote down a number and handed it to him. "Give me a call."

"Sure." He shoved the paper in his pocket.

"Good seeing you." She winked then gave him another quick hug. "Call me." Her voice was husky in his ear.

Watching her swagger off, he pursed his lips together. Although the invitation sounded good, he couldn't see himself falling back into a relationship with her. Their expectations never seemed to mesh. All she ever wanted was a good time. However, while the sex was good, he longed for something more, more of a personal connection.

Reese's gaze collided with Lacey's, and her eyes narrowed before they turned to the next person in line. His stomach clenched, and he wondered if that glare was meant for him.

After nearly two hours, the line finally dissipated to only a few folks left to express their condolences. Reese had spent the time talking to other visitors while keeping an eye on Lacey. Her complexion seemed dull, and her eyes looked heavy. He was getting more and more concerned about her as the afternoon progressed.

When she held a hand to her temple, he rushed to her and put his arm around her waist to hold her steady in case she stumbled. "Are you okay?"

She waved him off. "Let go. I'm just tired."

She was more than tired. She looked almost sickly. He worried that the stress of the day and lack of food had gotten to her.

He glanced around the room and spotted Krista near the back talking to his teammate Tommy. She would know if Lacey had eaten at all during the day.

"Krista!" he called.

The blonde caught his eye and rushed over with Tommy close behind her. "Is everything okay?" she asked, her blue eyes twinkling with concern.

"When was the last time Lacey ate? I mean really ate, not just snacked?" He held Lacey close to his chest, feeling her body heat mix with his.

Krista shook her head and scowled. "She had a half of a sandwich at lunch yesterday, and that's about it."

"I had a bagel this morning." Lacey started to sway, grabbing Reese's arm for balance.

"Tell the truth, Lace," Krista chided. "You didn't even finish half."

Lacey's countenance paled to a light greenish color. "I don't feel so great." She hugged her stomach.

Alarm bells sounded in Reese's head. She needed food and needed it now. "Let's go," he said. "You're going to eat something." He kept a firm hold of her waist for support and started down the hallway.

"Let's just eat here." Lacey motioned toward the reception hall.

"The food's gone. Let's go out." Krista handed Lacey her purse while moving toward the parking lot.

"We'll all go out to eat. My treat," Reese said, walking out the door.

"I can eat at home. I don't feel like going out," Lacey said as they approached his deep metallic blue sports car.

"Well, you're going to." She wasn't going to push him away. Right now she needed food, and he was bound and determined to make sure she ate. He yanked out his keys, hitting the unlock button.

Lacey jammed her hand on her small hip. "You can't tell me what to do."

"I just did. Get in the car." He opened the door for her. Spotting Krista's gaping mouth, he suppressed a smile. He had a sneaking suspicion that no one ordered Lacey around.

"Reese Mitchell, you're not my keeper." Lacey wagged a finger at him. "I can do whatever I want."

"Just get in the car. I don't want to embarrass you in front of Tommy and Krista." When her face flashed from anger to shock with her green eyes wide, he bit his lip to stop his laughter.

Her cheeks flamed as she faced Krista. "Take me home. I'm not having dinner with this jerk."

Krista shrugged. "Well, Tommy and I are. You'll have to find another ride home." Her best friend padded toward her sedan. "Come on Tommy. I'll drive."

"Krista!" Lacey bellowed. "I thought you were my friend."

"I am," Krista replied over her shoulder. "You need to eat, and Reese can afford to buy you a nice meal."

Lacey's green eyes glistened with anger while focusing on Reese. "You're a pain in the rear."

"Thank you." He opened the passenger door wider and smirked. "Get in."

"I will, but I want you to know this is against my will."

"Point taken. Get in."

She huffed and climbed into the passenger seat. Heat roared through his veins as her dress slipped up to her mid-thigh. He noticed her cheeks flush while she smoothed the skirt down. He gently closed the door and hurried around to the driver side.

After folding himself in the seat, he slammed the door, attached his safety belt, and jammed the key in the ignition.

"Why are you angry with me?" he asked as the engine rumbled to life.

"I'm not." With a sideways look, he found her arms folded and her gaze turned out the window.

"Your demeanor has changed since our discussion in the parlor." He pulled out of the parking space and motored through the parking lot. A quick glance in the mirror found Krista's sedan following him.

"I told you. I'm tired."

"You seem more hostile than tired, squirt."

"I'm not hostile, and my name isn't *squirt.*"

He raised an eyebrow, stealing a gaze at her. She was still staring out the window while he drove on the highway. She was adorable, and he enjoyed looking at her.

"You've always been my squirt," he said.

"I'm twenty-one. I'm not a kid anymore."

"Got it. No more squirt." He nodded. "So, what did I do?"

"I'm just tired. Will you drop it?" she snapped.

"Are we still friends?"

She groaned as if he annoyed the crap out of her. "Yes, Reese. We're friends. Drop it."

"All right. Just checking."

Lacey continued to stare out the window as they drove. Reese seemed to grasp for conversation, chattering on about how nice the service was and how touching it was that so many people came. She bit her lip, wondering how he could read her feelings so well. How did he know she was upset with him? Was she that transparent? She cut her eyes to him for a quick moment and wondered if his baby blue eyes could read the depth of her soul.

Glancing at his waistline, she wondered if that piece of paper was still in the pocket of his suit trousers. She clasped her hands together while anger and envy slithered through her veins. Yeah, he was right when he called her "hostile." In fact, she was more than hostile; she was enraged that he had the nerve to pick up a date at her father's memorial service. What was worse was that he'd picked up Sandy Webb!

Her stomach twisted as she remembered four years ago when the rumor mill at Southern Racing and at the track buzzed with Reese Mitchell and Sandy Webb, the new Marketing Manager. She'd heard stories about Reese and Sandy rendezvousing in the team hauler, in the supply closet at the shop, in the mechanics' bay after hours, and in his bus parked at the tracks. The stories made them sound like regular bunnies, and it made Lacey sick to think about that woman digging her claws into Reese.

Lacey did a mental head slap. What was her problem? Reese didn't belong to her, and she couldn't decide with whom he spent his time. But there it was—that green-eyed monster surging through her soul. And, darn it, she wanted to scream at him for disrespecting her father's and Veronica's memory by hooking up with another floozy at their memorial service!

"How does Tony's sound?" Reese's question broke through her mental tirade.

"I'm sorry?" She plastered a phony smile on her face.

"You were off in another world again, squirt. Oops, I meant Lacey." He slowed to a stop at a light and leaned over to her. "I asked if you wanted to eat at Tony's."

She blinked, bewildered for a moment. Darn him for offering her favorite restaurant on a night when she really needed it. How could he be such a slime-ball one minute and so wonderful the next?

"It sounds wonderful. Thank you." Her answer came in a hushed whisper.

"Good." He leaned over, and her breath caught.

Was he going to kiss her? Oh, no, not now. She was such an emotional mess that she feared she'd throw herself into his arms and beg him to take her virginity right there in the front seat of his sports car with Tommy and Krista watching in the next car.

She felt his breath on her face and closed her eyes in anticipation. His lips brushed her forehead with the softness of a summer breeze. When she opened her eyes, his gaze was fixed on the road ahead, the car rumbling forward.

She settled back in the seat and sighed. The kiss was only a friendly gesture, but his hug earlier had felt like so much more. How could a man be so confusing? He was hugging her as if he loved her one minute and getting phone numbers from former lovers the next. She needed to get away from him before he had her heart tied up in knots.

NINE

Reese chatted about the weather while steering into the parking lot. He nosed the car into a space near the entrance, climbed out, and rushed around it. After opening her door, he took Lacey's hand and lifted her from her seat. She stared into his azure eyes, and her mouth dried. Heat filled her cheeks as she inhaled his spicy cologne. What was happening to her?

"I'm starved," Krista's voice announced behind her. "Let's go eat."

Reese held Lacey's hand and followed Tommy and Krista into the restaurant. The line of people waiting for tables coiled out the front door. However, when the hostess spotted Reese Mitchell and Tommy Reynolds waiting, she led the group to a table in a matter of a few minutes.

While weaving through the dining room toward their table, Krista waggled her eyebrows at Tommy. "Sometimes notoriety pays, huh?"

Lacey sank into a chair next to Reese at the square table and gazed across at Krista and Tommy chatting about the weather.

A waitress appeared and took their drink orders. She returned a few moments later with their beverages and took their meal orders.

Sipping her diet cola, Lacey idly wondered how serious Krista and Tommy were becoming. They seemed comfortable with each other while Krista jabbered on about her job and asking question after question about the race team. Lacey swirled her straw in the glass and the carbonation sizzled at the movement. Her thoughts drifted back to the funeral service and a renewed grief washed over her, tying her stomach in knots. She'd laid her father and stepmother to rest, and it just didn't feel real.

When their food arrived, Lacey picked at her chicken parmesan and ate a few bread sticks. The food seemed to settle her stomach a bit, but she still felt under the weather. She longed for a warm bath and a hot cup of tea in the comfort of her father's recliner.

"We're not leaving until your plate is clean, Miss Fowler," Reese whispered in Lacey's ear.

She ignored his comment and glanced across the table. Krista twirled a blond lock around her finger and batted her eyelashes as Tommy discussed his goals for the upcoming ARA race season. Her best friend was flirting in full force. Lacey smiled. Krista hadn't dated in several months, and it was comforting to see her so happy.

"It's good to see that beautiful smile again," Reese said.

Is my smile as pretty as Sandy Webb's? Lacey couldn't help the sarcastic thought. She bit her bottom lip. Reese was leaning so close she could feel his body heat on her arm. Heat swirled in the pit of her belly, despite the knot.

She ate as much of the chicken as her stomach would allow before Reese paid the bill, and they headed out to the parking lot. Lacey stood by the passenger door of Reese's sports car, running her fingers over the cool metal and contemplating her exhaustion. She craved the hot bath and cup of tea more than ever and hoped one of her friends would take her directly home, preferably Krista, who wouldn't insist on conversation or ask how she was. With Krista, she could enjoy a comfortable silence and no pressure for small talk.

"I can take Lacey home." Reese leaned against the driver side and folded his arms.

"Are you okay to stay alone tonight?" Krista jingled her keys and Tommy sidled up to her in front of the nose of the sports car.

"Yeah." Lacey nodded, even though the idea of being alone in her father's eight-bedroom house made her queasy. However, she didn't want to be a burden on Krista, especially if her best friend wanted some time alone to cultivate the spark igniting between her and Tommy.

Krista embraced Lacey in a warm hug. "If you need anything, call me," she whispered.

Lacey's throat constricted at her friend's concerned words. She was so lucky to have Krista by her side. "I will." Her voice wavered. "Thank you for being such a wonderful friend."

When the men began their own conversation about their schedules for their return to Florida, Lacey took the opportunity to question Krista about her flirting. "What's going on between you and Tommy?" she asked.

"I'm not sure, but it's pretty cool." Krista grinned and held onto Lacey's arm. "What about you and Reese?"

She snorted. "Yeah, right."

Reese's arm looped around Lacey's shoulders. "What's so funny?" he asked.

"Nothing." She looked up at him. "Take me home, please."

"Yes, ma'am." He gave her a mock salute.

"Good night, Lacey." Tommy kissed her cheek. "I'm so sorry about your dad. He was a wonderful man."

"Thank you, Tommy." Lacey gave him a quick hug.

"Good night." Reese smacked Tommy's shoulder and hugged Krista.

Lacey stepped over to the passenger side, and Reese opened the door for her. After she was settled in the seat, he pushed the door closed.

She stared out the window during the ride home. He chatted

about the upcoming race at Daytona, and she yawned and nodded, feigning interest when they approached her father's large, brick colonial.

"Do you want me to come in with you?" he asked, nosing the car up to the garage.

"That won't be necessary." She fished around in her purse and snatched her keys from the bottom.

"Really, it's no big deal." He touched her thigh, causing her to jump, and he pulled his hand back. "Sorry. I didn't mean to startle you."

"It's okay." She climbed from the car, and a cool mist of rain sent a chill through her bones. Shivering, she hugged her purse and hurried to the door. She fiddled with the key, but it wouldn't fit in the lock. She jiggled it, cursing under her breath.

"Just go in!" she yelled, her voice quavering with frustration mixed with dismay. She fought with the key, and tears spilled down her hot cheeks.

"Let me try." Reese's strong hand stole the key, which slid into the lock and turned, opening the door.

Wiping her tears, she took the keys back and cleared her throat. "Thanks," she whispered, ignoring the hot embarrassment flaming through her cheeks.

"I'm coming in with you." He hit a button on his keychain, and the sports car's alarm beeped.

"I'm fine." She marched into the house. Stopping by the door, she punched in a code, resetting the alarm. She then kicked off her pumps on her way into the large kitchen.

"Lacey, you were in tears over a door lock. You're not fine." He rested his arms on her shoulders. "I'll stay."

"Stay?" Her heart thumped in her chest while she tossed her keys onto the counter. Was he proposing sex? Was he trying to take advantage of her fragile emotions? How dare he!

He smiled. "I meant to keep you company."

She gasped, cupping her hand over her mouth. He *was* proposing sex! Did he think she was easy? Anger ignited in her gut. Reese Mitchell was more than a ladies' man; he was also a slime-ball!

As if reading her thoughts, he held his hands up in protest. "No, no! Not like that! I meant I'd sleep in the guest room so you wouldn't feel alone."

Her cheeks warmed with renewed embarrassment. "Oh. That won't be necessary."

"But this house is so big, and—"

"And I'm a big girl." She forced a confident smile. "I'll be fine. Thank you."

"Do you want me to pick you up tomorrow and take you to the lawyer?"

"No, thanks. I can drive."

"But it seems silly to take two cars."

"Two cars?" She placed her purse on the counter next to her keys. "What do you mean by that?"

"I'm going too."

"Why?"

He shrugged. "Guess I'm in the will."

"Oh. Really, I can drive myself." She studied his face. He was so handsome with his hair damp from the rain. His dark locks brought out the powder blue of his gorgeous eyes. Too bad he was such a ladies' man.

Not that she was interested.

"Suit yourself. I guess I'll see you tomorrow." He jammed his hands in the pockets of his trousers.

"I guess so."

He paused as if expecting something, and then started for the door. Grasping the doorknob, he cut his eyes over his shoulder to her. "Lock the door behind me."

"I will."

"Good night." He turned the knob and opened it.

"Reese," she called after him.

"Yeah?" He faced her.

Her stomach plummeted at the anticipation in his eyes. "Thank you for dinner."

"You're welcome. Call me if you need anything."

"I will."

He disappeared through the door, and she closed and locked it behind him.

Once she was alone, she wandered through the house, studying her father's and Veronica's things and soaking in the memories. The silence of the house was deafening, and numbness slammed through her, replacing the grief from earlier in the evening.

She stopped in their bedroom and studied the wedding photos. Sitting on the edge of their bed, she stared at the wall. After what felt like a long time, she retreated into the bathroom and took a long, hot shower before collapsing onto her bed for the night.

TEN

Stepping into the office of Boucher and Boucher, Attorneys at Law, the following afternoon, Reese smiled at Lacey. "How are you?" he asked.

"I'm fine, thanks." Lacey straightened her dark blue suit jacket and met Carl's gaze as he stood beside his son. "Hi, Uncle Carl."

"How are you, sweetie?" Carl touched her arm and lightly kissed her cheek.

"I'm okay. How are you holding up?" She patted his arm.

Reese's father shook his head. "It's all so strange without your dad. I go to the shop, and it feels so empty. Something is missing, for sure."

His words spoke volumes for her emotions. Sorrow overtook her, causing her voice to catch in her throat. Speechless, she scanned the formal reception room filled with four leather chairs and two matching sofas. Two dark wooden end tables and a matching coffee table were littered with magazines.

Brenda sat in the corner with her husband. Lacey nodded a greeting and then stepped over to a chair and lowered herself into it.

Reese folded his lanky physique into the chair next to her. She sized him up with her eyes, admiring how his beige Dockers and cream-colored, button-down shirt complemented his lean body.

"You look like you finally slept." His eyes seemed to assess her too.

"I did. I woke up about an hour ago." She fiddled with the strap on her purse to avoid his probing stare.

"Mr. Boucher is ready for you now," a woman called from the far end of the lobby.

Reese stood, took Lacey's hand, and helped her up. She followed him through the door, down a long hallway, and into a large conference room where a middle-aged man in a dark suit stood before a massive table.

"Good afternoon. I'm Charles Boucher." He shook Brenda's hand. "You must be Mrs. Wilkinson. I'm so sorry for your loss."

"Thank you," Brenda said. "This is my husband, Phillip."

He shook the Phillip's hand. "Mr. Wilkinson." He then approached Reese and Lacey. "You must be Miss Fowler. I know how much your parents cared for you. Your stepmother spoke fondly of you the last time we met. Allow me to extend my condolences, and keep in mind we will do what we can to make today go easy for you."

"Thank you, Mr. Boucher." Lacey took his firm handshake.

The lawyer shook Reese's hand next. "And Mr. Mitchell. It's a pleasure to meet you. I'm a big fan."

"Thank you, sir." Reese flashed that sexy smile.

"And the elder Mr. Mitchell." The lawyer shook his hand. "How are you, Carl?"

"I'm managing." Carl's smile was sad.

"Well, please have a seat." The lawyer gestured toward the table. "I'm sorry we have to meet on such a somber occasion. Mr. and Mrs. Fowler were wonderful people. I enjoyed getting to know them." He sank in a chair before a stack of papers at the far end of the table.

Lacey sat next to Reese, who placed his hand on hers. She stole a glance at him, wondering why he was being so attentive.

What was he after? He gave her a bleak smile, causing her heart to thump.

"If it's okay, I'd like to address Mr. Fowler's insurance matters first." The lawyer slipped his half-glasses on his wide nose and studied a stapled stack of papers he'd lifted from the table. "Mr. Fowler had three life insurance policies, totaling two-point-five million dollars. All of these will go to Miss Millicent Doreen Fowler."

He glanced over the papers at Lacey. "We can discuss the monies and your management of them later, if you'd like."

Lacey nodded as a cold, hollow feeling stabbed at her heart. All of the money in the world couldn't make up for her loss. Her daddy was gone forever. A lump constricted her throat, and Reese squeezed her hand as if reading her thoughts.

"As for Mrs. Fowler's insurance," the lawyer continued, "she left five-hundred thousand to you, Miss Fowler."

Lacey cleared her throat. She felt a hand on her shoulder as Reese handed her a tissue. "Thank you," she whispered, dabbing her eyes.

"And now, the wills." The lawyer glanced at Brenda. "Mrs. Wilkinson. Your sister left you a list of items that belonged to your mother." He handed her a piece of paper. "You can pick them up at your convenience."

"Now, Miss Fowler." The lawyer cleared his throat. "Your father left you all of his personal possessions, including his home in Mooresville, some land he owned in Florida, and his vehicles. He also had a sizable amount of stocks, bonds, and mutual funds." The lawyer paused for a moment.

Reese's warm hand found hers again. Although she didn't want to admit it, his closeness sent a surge of confidence through her.

"Now, regarding Mr. Fowler's ownership in Southern Racing Incorporated, there are certain stipulations. I will read them to you," the lawyer began.

" 'I, Gregory Corbin Fowler, shall bequeath my share of Southern Racing Incorporated to my daughter, Millicent Doreen Fowler, with the following conditions. If Millicent Doreen is over the age of twenty-five or married at the time of my demise, she shall have the full share of my sixty percent of the company. However, if Millicent is under the age of twenty-five and unmarried, then she and Reese Douglas Mitchell shall share equally the sixty percent.' " The lawyer paused, put down the papers, and met Lacey's gaze.

Speechless, she studied him, the words swirling in her head. Had she heard him right? Did she have to share her part of her father's company?

No. That's insane.

Reese squeezed her hand. "I guess we're business partners, squirt."

"Whoa." Lacey snatched her hand away from Reese. "Mr. Boucher, please read that again for me." He repeated the words, and Lacey shook he head. "That can't be right." She folded her arms. "He didn't mean that. My age and marital status should have nothing to do with this. His share of the company is mine. End of story. So, what's next?"

"Miss Fowler, the will clearly states you and Mr. Reese Mitchell will share the company." The lawyer slipped his glasses on and glanced down. "And Mr. Carl Mitchell is the new Chief Executive Officer."

"What?" Lacey stood, her voice shaking with a mixture of anger and disbelief. "Are you telling me I don't get my father's full share of the company, and Carl is now the CEO? Is this some sick joke?" A white-hot rage swelled within her. This was crazy! How could her father do this to her?

Reese reached for her hand. "Lacey. Just calm down. You're upset."

"Damned right I'm upset!" Her voice rose. "This is outrageous! My grandfather built that company and passed it on to my father. My father should pass it on to me. That's my company!" She wagged a finger at Reese. "I'm a Fowler, and you're not!"

"Now, Miss Fowler . . ." the lawyer began.

She leaned forward on the table, trying to calm her trembling body. "I want to contest this. What do I have to do?"

The lawyer sighed. "You're talking a lot of money and court dates."

"Let's do it. I'm not going to give this company away without a fight." She tapped her finger on the polished table for emphasis.

"Lacey, your father made me a partner almost twenty years ago." Carl's voice was calm.

"You were never a partner." She cut her eyes to his. "He owned sixty percent, and you only have thirty."

Carl grimaced. "That's not the point. The company isn't only a Fowler company."

"But I'm his *daughter*." She pointed to her chest. "It doesn't make sense that he wouldn't give it to me."

"I think he trusted Reese to help guide you," the lawyer said.

"Why should Reese guide me? We're not related, and we're not married."

"Because he always trusted me." Reese's voice had an edge that caused her to snap her eyes to his. His stare was steady but cold, as if her comment had cut him like a knife.

"Let me buy you out." She ignored the guilt nipping at her due to his stare. "How much do you want?"

"I'm not selling." Reese's gaze was unmoving. "Sit."

"I'm not a dog," she snapped.

Reese gritted his teeth. "Sit now. We'll argue about this later."

"There's nothing to argue about," she said. "You're not getting *my* company."

Reese let out a frustrated sigh. "Lacey . . ."

She lowered herself into the chair and folded her arms across her chest. Her body shook with fury.

While the lawyer finished the reading of the wills, her mind whirled with questions. Why didn't her father trust her to run the company by herself? Why did he want Reese involved? What was he trying to say from beyond the grave? How on earth was Lacey going to work with Reese when his mere presence heightened her pulse along with her frustration?

When the lawyer finished, Lacey stood, hugged Brenda and nodded a goodbye to Phillip. She then glanced toward the Mitchells standing close together and speaking in hushed tones near the door.

Lacey cut her gaze back to the lawyer, who was gathering up documents. "May I speak with you alone, Mr. Boucher?"

"Of course. Follow me into my office." He nodded toward the door at the far end of the large conference room.

Heading toward the door, Lacey heard Reese call her from behind.

She waved her hand without facing him. "Call me when you have time in-between your hot dates and your racing schedule."

"Lacey . . ." Irritation vibrated in his voice.

She stepped into the lawyer's large office, and he shut the door behind her and then walked to his desk.

"Have a seat." He motioned toward one of the large wing chairs. He then sat and folded his hands. "I have to ask. How did you get the nickname Lacey?"

She smiled. "The story I'm told is that my grandmother gave it to me. I was named after both of my grandmother's, and Grandma Millicent always hated her name. She called me Lacey, and it stuck."

"I see." He smiled and leaned back in his chair, which creaked under the weight. "So, I have a feeling you want to discuss the will."

"Mr. Boucher, I don't understand my father's thinking about the company. He never discussed this with me." She took a deep breath, hoping to calm her raw nerves. "Why didn't he trust me? I'm not saying I should run it, but why do I have to share my part with Reese? What does my marital status have to do with my ability to help run the family business?"

"Miss Fowler." The lawyer paused as if choosing his words.

"Call me Lacey." She settled back into the chair, smoothing her suit jacket and taking deep breaths to get her frustration under control.

"Lacey, I knew your father for many years. He was a very smart and savvy businessman. When he and Mrs. Fowler rewrote their wills a few months ago, I, too, was surprised by the provision. However, he told me he had complete faith in you, but you were so young he wanted you to have some guidance."

She shook her head. "My degree's going to be in business. I may not have the experience, but I can learn. I have a good background and a good head on my shoulders."

He sat forward in the chair. "From what he told me and how he bragged about you, I understand that, but I think he wanted you to mature before you took on a company of this size."

She pursed her lips and considered the comment. It still didn't make sense. He should've trusted Lacey and her alone.

"But why Reese?" she asked. "He's a driver. Yes, he's a darned good one, but he's not a businessman. He's not the corporate type. Heck, he'd suffocate if he had to go into an office every day."

"Your father had a great admiration for Reese. He said he was like the son he never had. And he said Reese had been very smart with his investments from his winnings. Maybe he thought you'd make a good team."

Lacey shook her head and stood. "I'd like to talk to you about contesting the will."

The lawyer frowned and grasped a pen from his desk. "You'd probably regret that. It would take a lot of money and time. And it might ruin your relationship with the Mitchell family."

"Still, I'd like to discuss it with you further." She leaned over and extended her hand. "Thank you for your help."

Carl smacked Reese's shoulder while they stood in the lobby of the lawyer's office. "You heading out?"

Reese gazed toward the door leading to the hallway. "Not just yet. I want to talk to Lacey. I can't figure out why she's been so cold to me. It's like she's angry about something, but she won't tell me what it is. It's making me nuts."

"She's just going through a lot. Give her time."

"No, Pop. It's more than that. She's angry with me, not just the situation. Did you see the resentment in her eyes when the lawyer said I got part of the company?" Reese's stomach churned at the thought of those emerald eyes glaring at him. Her hostility stung him like a pack of angry hornets.

"It's about money, Reese." Carl folded his arms. "She's upset that she has to share her inheritance."

"No, it's not just that." Reese rubbed his chin while he contemplated the source of her coldness. "I wish I knew what I've done to hurt her." He couldn't bear the thought of losing her over a business deal. Heck, he couldn't bear the thought of losing her—*period*.

"Just give her time. Let her grieve." Carl glanced at his watch. "I gotta run to a meeting at the shop. Will I see you before you head back to Daytona?"

Reese shook his head. "Probably not. The flight leaves in two hours."

Carl gave him a quick hug. "Then I'll see you tomorrow night, and we can talk about the changes in the company. I'll have to get you and Lacey together at some point. We'll also have to meet with the board."

"We'll figure out the protocol after Lacey calms down." *If she ever calms down.* Reese's schedule for the weekend clicked through his mind while his father headed for the door. "Hey, Pop. Do me a favor."

Carl faced him. "What?"

"Take Lacey to lunch after the burial tomorrow and talk to her. See if you can figure out what's bugging her and then call me."

"Sure." A smile spread on his father's face. "Are you and Lacey . . . together?"

"No!" Reese held his hands up. "Heck, no. I'm just worried about her."

"Sure you are." He waggled his eyebrows. "See you later."

Reese snorted with sarcasm. "Get out of here, old man."

While his father exited toward the parking lot, Reese wondered where his old man got his wild ideas. Reese and Lacey together—there was a recipe for disaster. He could never handle that fiery redhead with her quick temper and stubbornness. She'd drive him to an early grave.

Smiling and shaking his head, Reese leaned against the wall and mulled over the will. He was now part owner of Southern Racing, Inc. Never in his wildest dreams did he imagine he'd be part owner. It was a responsibility he'd take on with care and pride. He'd be sure to honor Greg's memory in every decision he and Lacey made.

Southern Racing was Reese's life. He'd grown up in the shop and at the track. The crew members and race shop employees had been his family. Reese's dream came true the day he became a driver for the company. However, he'd never dreamt that

Greg would leave the company to him and Lacey.

The door to the hallway clicked open, and Lacey stepped out with an armload of papers. Her emerald eyes met his, and she scowled. "Don't you have someplace to be? Like Daytona?"

He almost chuckled at her over-the-top demeanor. However, her expression was pure hatred, and it stabbed him right in his heart. "I stayed to say goodbye. I'm leaving this afternoon, and I don't know when I'll see you again."

"Goodbye." She started past him, but he grasped her arm. "What?" She spun, glaring at him.

"Can we talk?"

She pursed her lips, her eyes boring into him.

"Lacey, I'm not going to let you or your dad down." He released her arm. "I'm honored your dad thought of me. My only goal is to help you now that he's gone. He was the backbone of the company, but maybe together we can help fill some of the void he left."

She narrowed her eyes, which smoldered with disgust. "You have no right to the company."

So, she still wants to play hard ball. He folded his arms, taking her challenge. "Actually, I do. My dad is part owner."

"Part owner." She stressed the words. "My dad was CEO."

Unbelievable. He shook his head. "You want to play 'my daddy is bigger than your daddy'? This is so juvenile." Exasperated, he gestured widely. "How long are you going to carry this grudge against me?"

"I'm going to contest the will. I suggest you get yourself a lawyer."

"Lacey, why are you doing this? I just want to help you." He reached for her, but she stepped away.

Her eyes softened, becoming more exhausted than angry. "Why does everyone think I need guidance? Why can't I just take care of myself?"

So, that was it. She wanted independence. "I'm not saying you're incapable. I just want to help."

"I don't need any help." She turned to go. "Be safe in Daytona. Goodbye."

He couldn't let her go like this. He had to make things right before he left for the airport.

"Lacey!" He rushed after her and pulled her back. "I thought we were friends. Are we competitors now that I have part ownership in the company?"

"Right now, I don't know who anyone is. I don't even know who I am." Her voice quavered, her beautiful eyes filling with tears.

He touched her cheek. "I'm still just Reese."

"I gotta go." Her voice came in a hoarse whisper. She turned and hurried out the door, rushing toward her father's expensive sedan.

He started after her and then stopped. Perhaps giving her space was what she needed and craved. He couldn't force her to forgive him for whatever atrocity she believed he'd committed. His father was probably right—she was mourning and needed time.

Defeated, Reese sauntered over to his sports car. When she motored past him, he wondered when or if he'd ever see her again.

ELEVEN

Lacey stabbed at her salad the following afternoon. Her mind wandered, reflecting on the burial and what it all meant. Her life had changed so quickly in the past week that she felt dizzy. Exhaustion mixed with bereavement pulsed through her.

Carl sat across from her in the restaurant. "Penny for your thoughts." His voice was warm and comforting.

She looked up, marveling how similar Reese's eyes were to his. They were soothing, azure pools. "My thoughts are too complicated to verbalize." She laid her fork on the table.

"Try me." He placed his burger on his plate.

She closed her eyes for a moment and willed her swirling thoughts to slow. Taking a deep breath, she opened her eyes. "I want to come home. I want to drop out of school and concentrate on building my life here."

"Don't." He shook his head. "Honey, you're so close to graduation."

"I can take care of myself." She leaned back in the booth seat. "I need to focus on something. The company was Dad's life, and I want to make the company my life. By running the company, I can get a piece of Dad back." Her voice wavered, and she sniffed back threatening tears.

He patted her hand. "Focus on finishing college and then come home. I'll watch out for the house and the race team. You'll still have a piece of your dad with you everywhere you go. You were his life and his heart."

She considered his comments, but she disagreed. College didn't matter as much as being home. It was more important for her to move back and get what was rightfully hers—Southern Racing.

It was best to be direct with Carl. She picked up a breadstick and cleared her throat. "I want control of the company," she said, keeping her voice even.

Something flickered in Carl's eyes, but she couldn't read it. "Don't worry about the company," he said. "I'll take care of it."

Lacey shook her head. "Why is everyone treating me like a dumb little girl? My grandfather started that company. I want to learn how to run it so I can be CEO someday."

"No one thinks you're dumb." He snatched a fry. "You just need to finish your degree and then learn the company one step at a time."

Biting into the breadstick, she concentrated on his words. "I can finish my degree here."

"But you'd have to transfer credits. You're so close, Lacey. Why start over?"

"This is my home, Uncle Carl."

"It'll still be here when you get back."

Chewing the breadstick, Lacey wondered how she was going to concentrate on school when she returned to class. Grief bubbled up in her throat at the thought of leaving again. Who would bring flowers to her father's and Veronica's grave? Who would sort through her father's office? She was needed here, not at school.

"Why are you so angry with Reese?" Carl asked.

His question startled her. Her stomach flip-flopped at the sound of his name.

"I'm not angry with him." Her cheeks heated with embarrassment. "I'm just upset about everything."

"He thinks you're angry with him, and he's nearly making

himself sick over it."

"He is?" Her cheeks flamed as she sipped her diet cola. How did Carl know Reese was upset? Had Reese talked about her?

"He was really worried about you yesterday when I left the lawyer's office. You're making my boy crazy." A smile tugged at the corners of his lips. "Is something going on between you two? He told me there isn't, but you two seem to be acting different with each other lately."

"Uncle Carl!" She gasped, horrified. "You can't possibly be serious."

Chuckling, he shook his head. "I got the same reaction from Reese." His smile faded and he picked up his burger. "You may want to call him once you're settled. I think he needs to know you're still friends."

She rested her chin on her hand. "I will." *Maybe later. Much later. Like next year, when I get over his obsession with blondes.*

"Honey, just go back to school and put all of this business out of your head." He patted her hand again. "Get that degree. Your daddy was so proud of you for going to college. He'll be smiling down on you when you graduate, and I'll be there to cheer you on."

She sniffed. "Thanks."

Lacey tried to pour herself into her studies over the next few weeks, but she constantly found herself daydreaming about going home. Thoughts of home crept into her mind when she studied for exams, wrote term papers, and attended study groups. She longed to be back in her own house, sleeping in her own bed, and working at the race shop every day.

Carl called her at least once a week to check on her, and she insisted she was fine. But deep down she knew she was homesick, more so than ever. Memories of her father and Veronica tugged at her heart strings and haunted her thoughts and dreams. A melancholy blue colored her days.

Reese tried to call her a few times her first week back at school. When she didn't answer, he left her voicemail messages. She considered calling him, but images of him flirting with Sandy stopped her dead in her tracks. She couldn't stop the thoughts of Reese and Sandy hooking up at the track in his bus. The mere thought of Reese kissing Sandy sent her stomach into a queasy swirl.

However, Lacey longed to talk to Reese because she was haunted by questions about her father's death. She couldn't shake the inconsistencies. Her father wasn't one to take chances. He never drove when he was tired, and he never would've left for a long road trip in the middle of the night. Why would he head back to North Carolina in the middle of Daytona practice? What could've possibly been so important that he couldn't take the team plane home the following morning?

Lacey wanted to bounce ideas off Reese, but she couldn't let go of her pride and call him. She knew she was stubborn, but she was afraid she'd call and find him with Sandy. Or Sandy would answer the phone in his bus. Then Lacey would surely be sick.

The questions surrounding her father's death and her mounting homesickness hijacked her concentration. She couldn't sleep and couldn't study. The only solution was for her to go home.

Lacey flew to Charlotte late one Friday night, rented a car, and drove to her father's house. She'd expected to find the house empty, but the lights in the kitchen were burning when she stepped inside.

"Hello? Anyone here?" Lacey called, letting her backpack, duffel bag, purse, and keys drop onto the floor at her feet.

Stepping into the den, Lacey gasped. Her father's wedding portraits were missing from the mantel and end tables. Someone was working on redecorating the house.

But who?

An icy anxiety slid through her veins.

Lacey moved down the hallway toward the large bedroom suite. "Hello? Is anyone here?"

A slam resembling a metal filing cabinet drawer crashed through the silence.

Carl appeared in the doorway. "Lacey? I didn't know you were coming home."

"Hi." She glanced past him, finding the former guest room converted into an office, complete with a computer, desk, printer, and filing cabinets. "I see you've done some redecorating."

He leaned in the doorway, and she couldn't help wondering if he was blocking something behind him. "I told you I'd take care of the house for you."

She motioned behind her and toward the den. "Where are my dad's wedding photos?" Biting her bottom lip, she studied his face. Was he hiding something or was she overreacting?

"I thought it might make it easier for you if I took them down. I know how hard your father's death has been for you."

"Don't you think it should be *my* decision to take them down? After all, this is *my* house, not yours." She folded her arms in defiance. Who did he think he was, moving into her house and making drastic changes to the décor without her permission?

Grimacing, he shook his head in apology. "You're right. I'm sorry, honey." He touched her arm. "How are you?"

She tried to decipher the computer screen behind him without craning her neck. She spotted spreadsheets but couldn't read them. Was he hiding something?

"I'm fine," she said. "Why aren't you in Vegas with the team?"

"I needed to stay behind and take care of some business for the board."

"What business?"

"Oh, just some boring old accounting things." He placed his hand on her shoulder and led her toward the kitchen. "Are you hungry? I have some leftover baked chicken."

"No, I ate in the airport."

"Have a drink with me."

"No, thanks."

Despite her protest, he hurried across the kitchen and fished two cans of cola from the refrigerator. Why was he in such a rush to get her to the kitchen? She again wondered if he were hiding something displayed on that computer screen in his new office.

"How's school?" He handed her the can and opened his.

"Fine." She opened hers and sipped it. The cool carbonation soothed her parched palette.

"Have you been watching the races?" He grinned.

She shook her head, taking another gulp. "I haven't sat through a race, but I keep up through the web. Our boys have been doing great."

"Fourth and eighth in points. Not bad." He raised his can in a toast.

"No, not bad at all. Reese is still the best." She sighed, wondering how he was. She missed him. A lot. Her heart ached to hear his sexy voice and see his handsome face.

"What brought you home?" He leaned back on the counter and took a long drink.

She placed her can on the island in the center of the large room. "I just needed to get away. Why was my dad on his way home the night he died?"

Carl's eyes widened then quickly returned to normal. "I honestly don't know."

"It doesn't make sense." She lifted the soda, running her fingers through the cool condensation. "He wouldn't drive through the night for no apparent reason. Something was wrong."

Carl nodded and drank more cola.

"You don't know why?" She studied him. Was he hiding something? Did it have anything to do with the spreadsheets? She pushed the thoughts away. How could she mistrust Carl? He'd been like a brother to her father.

He shrugged. "No."

"Why weren't you in Florida?"

"I had some things to take care of here."

"What things?"

"Just business with the team. Half of our marketing department quit."

"Oh?" She took another sip and considered his answer. That was a valid excuse. Someone had to handle the marketing issue. Guilt nipped at her for not trusting Carl.

"I hired Sandy Webb to clean up what's left of the department."

Lacey gasped and her stomach twisted. "You did?"

He looked astonished. "You remember her?"

"Vividly," she deadpanned. How could she forget the rumors of Sandy's and Reese's torrid affair?

"She started last week. I think she'll do a good job."

"Is she in Vegas for the race?" Lacey braced herself for the answer. *Please say no. Please say no!*

He shook his head. "I don't think so."

Thank goodness. Lacey took a deep breath, trying to relax.

"How long will you be in town?" he asked.

"Probably just the weekend. I have an exam next week."

His eyes darted to the clock on the wall. "It's almost one. You probably want to get to bed."

"Yeah." After tossing the empty can into the trash, she crossed the kitchen and picked up her bags. "I'll see you in the morning. Don't stay up too late."

"I won't. Good night, honey."

Carl headed back toward the office while she walked to the back stairs. Trotting up to her room, she wondered what Carl was up to. He didn't seem like himself. Why was he so secretive? Why had he redecorated her house? After grabbing her pajamas, she slipped into the bathroom and contemplated Carl's actions while taking a long, hot shower.

Once dressed, she tiptoed down the hallway, peeking in rooms to see if he had gone to bed. She stopped at her father's room and her mouth gaped at the site. All of his photos had been removed from his dressers and walls and were placed in the open boxes cluttering the floor.

She lifted a portrait of her father and stepmother on their wedding day and studied it, running her fingers over the cool metal frame. What was Carl attempting to accomplish by packing up her parents' memories? Was he truly trying to help Lacey adjust to her life without them? Or was he hiding something or trying to erase something?

But why? He'd been her father's best friend for close to forty years.

Hugging the frame to her chest, Lacey padded toward her bedroom. When she heard footsteps ascending the stairs, she ducked into her room, closed the door, turned off the light, and hopped into bed. Closing her eyes, she held her breath while the footsteps stopped outside her room.

After the footsteps had continued down the hallway, she sat up. Her heart pounding in her chest, she tiptoed to the door and peeked down the hallway. The door to the large guest room clicked closed, and she sneaked down the stairs in the dark, her heart pumping against her ribcage like a marathon runner.

When she reached the office, she slipped in, gingerly closing the door before turning on the small desk lamp. She grasped

Betrayed

the cool handle to the file cabinet and pulled. However, it didn't budge. She yanked harder, but it still didn't move. After a few more tugs, she realized it was locked.

Mumbling under her breath, she sneaked out into the hallway and into the bathroom. Her pulse skittering with alarm, she searched the vanity until she found a nail file and then rushed back into the office.

She rammed the file into the lock, turned it and then tugged on the drawer until it opened with one smooth motion, knocking her onto her rear on the carpet. She knelt before the drawer and leafed through it, reading file names such as payroll, purchase orders, statements, and suppliers. Lacey wondered why Carl would keep these documents in her father's house instead of at the shop. She skimmed the files then placed them back.

She was closing the drawer when something caught her eye—a file named "Greg." Flipping it open, her heart paused in her chest when she saw photographs of a smashed car. Her eyes filled with tears when she recognized her father's favorite leather jacket lying on the ground next to the crumpled black sedan. A sick feeling gripped her stomach, and bile rose in her throat.

She ripped her eyes away from the horrible photo and fished through the file, skimming articles regarding her father's accident and memorial service. Near the back, she found documents concerning the race team.

A thump sounded outside of the office, and she quickly closed the file cabinet drawer and turned off the light. Standing by the door, she thought she heard footsteps. With her heart thumping madly and adrenaline coursing through her veins, she grabbed the file, stole out of the office, rushed through the kitchen, and ran up the back stairs.

Finding the hallway clear, she dashed into her room, closed the door, and jumped into bed. She read the file from front to back by the light of her small bedside lamp and then lay awake all night, wondering what to make of it all.

TWELVE

The following morning, Lacey stayed in bed until she felt the vibration of the garage door closing below her. Then she popped up and hurried down the stairs to the office, adrenaline shooting through her veins like a prowling cat burglar. She idly wondered why she felt like a criminal in her own house. However, Carl's redecorating made her feel like a guest.

Positioning the rolling desk chair up to the file cabinet, she leafed through the files. Yanking out spreadsheets, she studied them.

When a door slammed, she jumped. Her heart hammering in her chest, she folded the spreadsheet and stuffed it in the pocket of her pajamas, slipped the file back in the hanging folder, then slowly slid the drawer closed.

Her hands shook as the footsteps pounded down the hallway. She swiveled the chair around in front of the desk and tapped the spacebar. She stared at the monitor as the door opened.

Carl appeared in the doorway. "Lacey?" he asked.

"Hi." She tilted her head and faced him, hoping to appear casual. "I wanted to check my email, but I can't figure out the login. What's your password?"

Frowning, he stepped into the room. "You don't want to use that computer."

"How come?" She willed her heartbeat to slow to a normal rate.

"It's not working right. I think it's about to crash." He leaned over and clicked the computer off. His eyes darted around the room as if in search of something. "Have you had breakfast?"

"No." She stood and stepped toward the door. "I was heading to the kitchen next. What brought you back to the house? I thought I heard you leave."

"I forgot my wallet."

"Oh." She studied his blue eyes, which darted away from her gaze. What was he worried about? Was it only the information in the filing cabinet?

"I think I might make a few phone calls while I'm here." He lowered himself into the desk chair.

Lacey started into the hallway and then stopped cold. An edgy sensation slid up her spine. Something was wrong. She felt as if the walls were closing in on her. She had to get out of the house. She had to find someone to help her figure out this mystery. Whom could she trust? Should she call Reese? Had he meant it when he said they'd be a team?

She stepped back into the doorway where Carl sat in front of the computer. The login screen appeared, and he logged in with no problem. When he suddenly faced her, she jumped with a start.

"What's up, Lacey?" he asked, blocking the screen with his body.

"I just realized I forgot to bring some of my books home, and I have a big test on Monday. I better head back to school." The fib rolled off her tongue so easily that she surprised herself.

"That's a shame. Come again when you can visit longer." He didn't sound all that disappointed.

"I'm going to pack and see if I can change my flight."

"Be sure to say goodbye before you leave."

Lacey hurried upstairs and packed. She slipped the spreadsheet and the information on her father's accident into her backpack. After dressing, she hauled her bags downstairs, where

Carl met her in the hallway.

"You have a safe trip and call me when you get back to your apartment." He gave her a quick hug.

"I will." She looked up at him. His eyes seemed tired. "Are you okay, Carl?"

He gave a weak smile. "I think I'm going to be fine . . . eventually."

"Take care of yourself." She patted his arm and headed out through the kitchen to the garage.

Climbing into her rented SUV, her thoughts moved to Reese. She needed his help figuring out the mystery of his father's actions and the company secrets. She fished her cellular phone from her backpack, stared at it and then put it down. What would she tell him? How could she possibly apologize for all of the awful things she'd said to him? Would he forgive her and help her figure out this mystery with the files?

Sighing, she steered out of the driveway and drove toward the airport. She'd call him later—maybe after she was back in Maryland.

That evening, Lacey maneuvered into the parking lot of her apartment complex and nosed her SUV into her usual spot in front of her building. She'd spent her entire trip back to Maryland analyzing the information she'd found in the file cabinet and wondering what Carl was concealing. She wanted to call Reese. No, she *needed* to call him.

After putting the truck in park, she scrolled through her address book until she found "Reese Cell." She cleared her throat as the phone rang. When his voicemail picked up, she groaned. She wanted to hear a live voice, not his recorded message!

"Hey, this is Reese," his sexy voice said. "Leave me a message, and I'll call you when I can. Thanks."

After the beep, Lacey stammered through her message. "Hi,

Reese. Um, this is, well, you know who this is." She took a deep breath. "I'm sure you probably hate me, but please listen. I need to talk to you right away. I went home for the weekend, and, well, something's going on with the company, our company. Your dad's been staying at my dad's house, and he's completely rearranged the furniture. He made my dad's downstairs bedroom into an office. I got into the filing cabinet, and I found a file with pictures from my dad's accident."

She shook her head. She was babbling and needed to get the point before her time ran out on the message. "I have a feeling my father's death wasn't an accident." She gripped the steering wheel and her stomach clenched at the words. "I also found some strange files. I think there's something going on. The company's losing money or something." She bit her lip, hoping she made sense. "Look, I'm all mixed up. I need to talk to you. Please call me. Thanks. Bye."

Rolling her eyes, she snapped the phone shut and tossed it onto the passenger seat. He'd probably think she was nuts when he heard the message. She'd have to call him again after he got home from Vegas and explain things a little better.

Reese took off his racing shoes, groaned, and lifted his feet up onto the sofa of his bus later that evening. He was wiped out from a day of practice, meetings, more practice, and media appearances. He gripped the remote and powered up the television. After flipping channels, he settled for an action movie.

Glancing over, he noticed his phone on the counter separating the kitchen area from the den. So that was why he hadn't heard it ring all day—it had been in his bus. Snatching it up, Reese read "4 voicemail messages" on the screen.

He dialed his voicemail and turned down the volume on the television. The first message was from his crew chief looking for him when he overslept this morning. The second was from

Sandy, wondering if he wanted to meet for lunch. He shook his head, glad he'd missed that one. The last thing he needed was to get mixed up with her again. The third message was from Gina, his PR rep, reminding him about the interviews at five. He'd gotten there on time.

When he heard the voice begin speaking on the fourth message, he gasped.

Lacey.

She'd finally called him back. A smile tugged at his mouth, and warmth surged through him. It was so good to hear her voice.

He listened to her message with bewilderment. She thought her father's death might not have been an accident. She'd found some strange files, and she wanted his help. What an interesting turn of events, after she'd pretty much told him off the last time they'd spoken.

Scrolling through his address book, he located her number. However, a knock at his door stopped him from hitting send. Reese crossed the room and opened his door to see his crew chief scowling at him.

"We need to talk about tomorrow," Brett Turner said.

It never ends. Reese sighed and rolled his eyes while gesturing for him to come in.

"We need to rethink our race strategy." Brett stepped in, closing the door behind him.

"Just give me a minute, man. I need to make a call. Help yourself to a beer." Reese stalked down the aisle and into the bedroom, where he lowered himself on the bed and scrolled through the address book in his phone. He stopped at the number for his old friend Danny Brooks, who ran a security company in Charlotte.

Danny answered after two rings. "Hello?"

"Hey, Danny. This is Reese Mitchell."

"Reese! Holy cow. How are you, man? You did great at Daytona."

"Thanks." Reese stared down at the lap of his jeans. "Listen, I was wondering if you could do me a favor. Are you still friends with that private investigator?"

"Yeah." Danny sounded taken aback. "What did you need?"

"Would you give me his number?" Grabbing a pen and notepad from the bedside table, he recorded the number Danny recited. He then thanked him and hung up.

Reese stared down at the number. As soon as he was done talking to Brent, he'd give the PI a call and ask him for help with the Southern Racing mystery. He'd do anything to get Lacey to see she could trust him with her father's company.

THIRTEEN

Lacey hummed while climbing the stairs to her third-floor apartment Monday evening. Her boots scraped the wooden steps while the cool breeze blew her hair back from her face. Pushing the door open, she dropped her purse and backpack onto a kitchen chair. She heard voices coming from the next room and assumed her roommate was watching television.

Opening the refrigerator door, she snatched a can of diet cola, opened it, and turned toward the den.

"Missy, you're not going to believe what happened to me to—" Lacey stopped dead in her tracks when she found herself staring at her roommate and Reese.

"Hi." Reese grinned and folded his arms across his wide chest.

Lacey gasped, dropping her soda, which exploded as it hit the floor, fizzing into a giant puddle.

"Oh, man. I'm such a klutz." Her cheeks burning, she leaned over the puddle. She grabbed the can, hurried back to the kitchen, and tossed it into the sink.

Missy rushed in and fetched the roll of paper towels from the counter. "I guess you didn't know he was coming, huh?"

"I had no idea." Lacey ripped the paper towels out of her roommate's hands.

Missy grasped her arm and tugged her back. "He's hot."

"Yeah and a superstar. Out of your league."

"I know." Her roommate smirked. "I think he only wants you anyway."

Lacey stared at her. "What did you say?"

"He's been asking about you the whole time he's been here. He's concerned about how you're doing." Missy waggled her eyebrows. "I think you'd have yourself a boyfriend, if you let it happen."

"Don't be silly. We've known each other our whole lives. He'd never think of me that way." But could he possibly . . . ? She did a mental head slap. Reese Mitchell only wanted blond, bimbo models. Not normal girls like her who could think for themselves and didn't jump into bed after only one date.

"I think you'll be surprised," her roommate said.

"I have a mess to clean up." Lacey returned to the den where Reese crouched on the floor mopping up the spilled soda with a handful of napkins.

"I got it." He stood.

"Where did you get these?" She took the wet napkins from him.

"Over there." He pointed toward the coffee table, his wide smile disarming her.

Lacey's hackles settled. She felt bad for the way she'd snapped at him when they last spoke at the lawyer's office. How could she have been so hateful to someone she'd known her whole life?

"Oh. Thanks." She gestured toward the couch, suddenly remembering her manners. "Make yourself at home. Can I get you anything?"

"Thanks." He lowered himself onto the sofa, his grin widening. "A drink would be great, as long as you don't spill it on me."

She couldn't help but return the smile. "I'll try my best."

She padded to the kitchen, threw out the wet napkins, and

grabbed two fresh cans from the refrigerator. Returning to the den, Lacey handed him one. When their fingers touched, heat surged up her arm.

Taking a deep breath, she sat in a chair across from him. "When did you get here?"

He opened the cola. "About an hour ago."

"Did you drive?"

He took a drink and shook his head. "Flew."

"But you just got in from Vegas last night."

"I flew here this morning."

He took another gulp, and Lacey studied him. Why would he get up after flying across the country and fly to Baltimore? Had he gotten her message and felt compelled to see her? Did that mean he cared?

Her cheeks heated at the thought. She needed to erase that notion. She knew full well that Reese Mitchell would never think of Lacey as more than his squirt.

"I'm going to the library," Missy called from the doorway behind Reese. "I'll see you later." She winked and gave Lacey the thumb's up.

"All right. Bye." Lacey's cheeks burned with embarrassment.

Reese turned and waved to her. "Thanks for letting me in. It was nice meeting you."

"You, too." Her roommate disappeared through the kitchen, the front door clicking closed behind her.

"This is unexpected," Lacey said. She opened her soda and sized Reese up with her eyes.

He was gorgeous in his tight blue jeans and navy blue Henley shirt. His cowlick of dark brown hair fell into his eye, and he pushed it back.

"I wanted to catch you off guard, so you wouldn't have time to run." His smile faded to a serious expression. "I got your message."

"Oh." She gripped the drink and her stomach clenched.

"I could never hate you." The sincerity in his powder blue eyes made her mouth go dry.

"Why didn't you just call me back?"

"Because I didn't want to risk getting your voicemail and waiting another three weeks for you to call me back."

Guilty as charged. She cut her eyes to the cola. "You did great yesterday. I watched most of the race." She looked up to find him studying her, and something sparked in the air between them. Was she imagining it?

"Thanks." He shook his head. "With all of the problems we had with that car, I still can't believe I finished in the top ten."

She lifted her soda to toast him. "But you're Reese Mitchell. You can take a crummy car to Victory Lane."

He snorted. "You have too much faith in me."

"No, I don't." She placed her drink on the end table next to her. "I know what you're capable of when you're in a car. Like that time at New Hampshire. You were involved in five wrecks and still took the checkered flag."

He smiled, and her heart thumped in her chest. "That was cool, but I just got lucky."

"No, you've got talent."

Taking a drink, he shook his head. "Sometimes I just feel like I'm in the right place at the right time on the track. But thanks for the compliments."

She bit her lip, silently marveling. His championship and his record spoke for themselves, but he was still so humble. She smiled, wondering what to say next. The silence was awkward, making her self-conscious. She straightened her green blouse and licked her lips, watching him take a deep breath.

As if on cue, at the same time they said, "I don't know why this is so difficult."

The sounds of their voices echoing each other caused them

both to chuckle. Boy, she loved that smile. And those lips. She wondered what they would feel like brushing hers.

Lacey pushed that thought aside and tucked a strand of hair behind her ear. "You go first."

"I need to ask you about something." His mouth closed while he examined the soda.

Again the silence seemed to be a weight pulling them into a dangerous pit. She wished she could read his mind. Her breath paused in anticipation of what he'd say next.

"I met with one of the guys in accounting before I left town this morning." He placed the can on the coffee table and steepled his hands.

"Oh?" She waited for him to continue, the anticipation coiling in her stomach. "Who?"

"Ryan Matthews." He paused as if searching for the right words. "Have you ever heard of Racing Industries, Inc.?"

"No. Should I have heard of them?" She shook her head and crossed her legs, resting her right ankle on her left knee.

"No, no, I don't think so." He raked his hand through his hair, pushing his cowlick back from his forehead.

She was losing patience. He had to get to the point, or she was going to go crazy with worry. "Reese, what's going on?"

"I'll show you." He crossed the room, fished through a duffel bag, and brought back a stack of papers. "He gave me this. It's a list of expenses. He said this mysterious company shows up on the accounts every couple of months." He handed the papers to Lacey and crouched down beside her. "See?" He pointed to the paper.

He was so close to her that she could feel his body heat radiating with hers. Awareness tingled up her spine. While she examined the spreadsheet, the aroma of his cologne made her senses spin. He placed his hand on her thigh, and she nearly jumped out of her skin. She tried to concentrate on the words and numbers, but her mind kept turning to Reese's fresh scent and his warm hand resting on her jeans.

"This charge for Racing Industries shows up here, here, and here." He flipped pages and pointed to numbers. "Each time it's for five thousand. But back in July, it was for seventy-five-hundred. Ryan said he had no idea where it came from."

"Oh, my gosh." Lacey cupped her hand over her mouth and leaned back in the chair. She studied Reese while he knitted his brow, still leaning on her thigh. "How did you get Ryan to tell you all of this?"

He shrugged. "I just said I was part owner in the company and had some questions about the expenses. I said I wanted to get familiar with our accounting system and what we're spending on supplies."

"Did he tell you the charges were suspicious?"

"No, no." He stood. "I asked him what Racing Industries was, and he said he didn't know."

"Who authorized these charges?"

"That's what we need to find out." Smiling, he touched her nose and then crossed to the sofa again and sank down onto it. "That might help us figure out what's going on. I can ask the crew chiefs about the suppliers we use." He folded his arms behind his head. "Maybe it's legit, but in all the years I've been hanging around the shop, I've never heard of Racing Industries."

She stared down at the spreadsheets and shook her head. This was bigger than she ever imagined. Anxiety raced through her body.

"So, what did you find, squirt?" he asked.

She met his gaze, and he grinned.

"I'm sorry," he said. "I meant Lacey."

She grimaced. "It's okay. You can't help it if you still see me as ten."

He leaned forward and shook his head. "I didn't mean it like that."

"Forget it." She sighed with disappointment. How could Missy think Reese wanted a relationship with Lacey when he still saw her as a child?

"So, what did you find out?"

Lacey retrieved the file from her bedroom and handed it to Reese. He patted the spot next to him on the sofa, where she sat and explained everything she'd seen in the house. Their thighs touched, sending the pit of her belly into a wild swirl. She'd give anything to kiss him, but she was merely his squirt.

He flipped through the file, shaking his head and frowning while she spoke.

"Your dad seemed really strange. I'd never seen him like that." Lacey folded her legs beneath her and leaned back on the arm of the sofa.

Reese rubbed his chin and flipped to the front of the file, where he stared at the photos of the car. Lacey's stomach twisted while imagining her father and his bride trapped within the crumpled heap of metal.

Why would someone want to hurt her father? He was the sweetest, most loyal man Lacey knew. He had no enemies. Veronica was just as loving and thoughtful as he was. It just didn't make sense. Was she wrong to assume it was more than an accident?

"Do you think someone killed them?" Lacey's question came in a trembling whisper.

Reese's eyes met hers. Comfort shone in his Caribbean blue orbs, but uncertainty still plagued her gut. "I don't know, sweetie. I just don't know."

"But why—? How—?" Her throat constricted, and her eyes welled with tears.

"Hey, it's okay." He turned to her, taking her hands in his.

"We'll figure this out together."

Embarrassed by her display of emotion, she stared down at her thighs, trying to clear her throat. Despite her efforts to stop them, tears spilled from her eyes and down her hot cheeks.

"Look at me." With a finger under her chin, he lifted her gaze to meet his. "We'll get to the bottom of this. If someone caused this, I'll find out who's responsible and make sure they pay. I promise you." His face was full of determination. He cupped her face with his hands and wiped her tears with his thumbs.

His expression softened, and Lacey's heart thundered like a revving V-8. He leaned down, and her breath paused. Was he going to kiss her? Did she want him to?

Yes, yes, she did!

But what would happen if he crossed the line? Everything would change. Did she want it to change? She had to stop him. He closed his eyes and leaned in close. She felt his breath on her lips, and her body tensed with a mixture of excitement and alarm.

No! This was wrong!

She had to stop him before they made a mistake they'd regret later.

"Are you hungry?" Her voice was a little louder than she expected.

"Hmm?" His eyes blinked open.

"Would you like something to eat?" She popped up from the sofa and started toward the kitchen. "I can make us some burgers or order a pizza or make some pasta or something."

"Whatever you want is fine with me."

She turned and found him leaning on the doorframe. Oh, he was so gorgeous. She wanted him for dinner! What if he'd kissed her? But kissing him would've been a mistake, given his reputation as a ladies' man. They were business partners, not lovers.

Pushing those thoughts aside, she opened the freezer. "I have frozen pizza, frozen burritos, bagels, and waffles." She scanned the refrigerator next. "Hot dogs, salami, cheese, and leftover mac and cheese."

His hands on her shoulders made her jump. "Hot dogs are fine." He brushed her hair back from her shoulders, sending shockwaves of chills cascading down her spine.

"Okay." She gulped while grabbing the pack of hot dogs and trying to ignore the heat his hands sent surging through her veins. Moving away from his touch, she grabbed a plate from the cabinet and a knife from the block on the counter. After opening the package of hot dogs, she dropped four on the plate, sliced them, and placed the plate inside the microwave.

"I think there are some chips in the cabinet above the toaster." She started the microwave.

"So, what do you think we should do?" He opened cabinet doors and fetched the bag of chips.

"About what?" She stared at him, startled by the question.

"About the company." He opened the bag and offered her a chip.

She snatched a few and munched on them. "I think we need to be a united front. We need to take control of the company."

He nodded, biting into the chips. "We should meet with the lawyer and find out how to do that."

"We can do it this week." Lacey pulled condiments out of the refrigerator.

"Don't you have classes?"

"I want to drop out." She lined up the condiments on the table.

"No." His answer was firm.

She raised an eyebrow in awe. "Excuse me?"

"Get your degree. No one can take that away from you. I wish I'd gone to college."

She laughed. "Please. You could buy my college."

"That's not the point." He wagged a determined finger at her. "You're so close to graduating. Finish."

"You sound like your dad." She set utensils on the table.

"Well, my pop's right." He fished two more colas from the refrigerator.

"I want to come home. I need to figure all of this out, and I don't want you to do it without me." The microwave beeped, and she grabbed the plate of hot dogs. She brought them and a bag of buns to the table. "I can finish up college later on."

"Lacey . . ." He sat at the table.

"My mind's made up." She sank into a chair across from him. "I want to come home. We can pack up my truck tomorrow and drive it home—unless you plan to fly home."

"We'll drive." He took two hot dogs and then passed her the plate. "Have you talked to Krista?"

"No." Lacey snatched two buns and handed him the bag.

"She's been spending an awful lot of time with Tommy."

"You're kidding!" She grinned.

"They were together at the track this weekend."

"Good for her." Lacey put a dog on a bun and grabbed the ketchup. "So, what's the rest of the gossip at the track? I'm out of touch."

They chatted about members of the team and competitors while they ate. The conversation was easy, and Lacey found herself laughing frequently. Before she knew it, it was eleven, and Missy came through the door with an armful of books.

"Hey, guys." She grinned, closing and locking the door.

"Is the library open this late?" Lacey stood and grabbed the plates.

"I went for a drink with Molly and Lindsey." Her roommate snatched a chip while heading toward her room. "You guys are eating late."

"We've been doing more talking than eating." Reese gathered

up the condiments and carried them to the refrigerator.

Missy grinned at Lacey. "Well, good night. See you in the morning."

"Missy," Lacey said. "I'm going home to Carolina—for good."

Missy stopped and faced her. "You're dropping out?" She placed her books on the table. "Why?"

"Reese and I are going to get to the bottom of the weird things going on with the company. I can finish up school back home."

"Are you sure?" Her roommate shook her head in disbelief. "You've worked so hard."

"I know." Lacey gathered up the utensils. "I just need to do this—for my dad. I'll give you a check for the rest of the year's rent, so you're not left in a lurch."

"Don't worry about the money." Missy hugged her. "I'll miss you."

"I'll miss you, too. But I'll keep in touch." Pulling away from her friend, she glanced at Reese, who was picking up the remnants of dinner. He met her gaze, causing her to smile.

"Would it be all right if I used your shower?" he asked.

"Sure." She pushed a lock of hair behind her ear. "There are clean towels on the shelf in the bathroom."

"Thanks." He nodded and then headed for the bathroom.

"What's going on between you guys?" Missy folded her arms.

"Nothing. We're just making plans to save my dad's company." She leaned against the counter.

"I think he's a good guy."

Lacey nodded. "He is."

A smirk spread on her roommate's lips. "And he's hot."

Nodding, Lacey sighed. "Yes, he is." *But he's totally out of my league.*

FOURTEEN

"The bathroom's all yours." Reese's voice sounded behind Lacey while she stuffed another bag with clothes.

She turned, her breath catching in her throat. He leaned on the doorframe clad in a white t-shirt and boxers with his muscular arms folded across his wide chest. His hair was wet and stuck up slightly, with his cowlick hanging over his eyes. His sinewy, tanned thighs were only the beginning of his long legs.

"You need help packing?" he asked.

"Uh, no. Thanks." She cleared her throat and zipped up the bag. Idly, she wondered if the heat had just clicked on in her bedroom. "I can finish in the morning. It's nearly midnight."

He stood up straight, his long, lean physique filling the doorway. "Well, I can sleep on the sofa. I just need a blanket if you have one."

"No, no. You take my bed. I'll sleep on the sofa." She shoved the bag into the corner of her small room.

He smiled. "I appreciate it, but I'm fine on the sofa."

"It's really uncomfortable."

"I can manage for one night." He walked over to her. "I'll just borrow a blanket."

"You take my bed. I insist." She grabbed the comforter on her double bed and yanked it down. "Go ahead. I'm just going to take a shower. Make yourself comfortable. I'll be back in to get a pillow and blanket."

Lacey grabbed her pajamas and headed out of the room before he could protest. She needed a very cold shower to calm the heat surging through her. Seeing him in his underwear sent her body into overdrive.

After the door to the bathroom clicked closed, Reese sat on the edge of her bed, the mattress creaking under his weight. He scanned the room, taking in her piles of books, CDs, and DVDs. Noticing photos displayed on her dresser, he crossed the room. He found one of Lacey, her dad, and Veronica at the wedding. Lacey's smile was radiant while she posed holding her bouquet and standing next to her father in front of a trellis covered in pink roses.

Another photo featured Lacey and Krista grinning on the beach, both clad in sunglasses and bikinis. He admired Lacey's thin but curvy body in her hunter green string bikini. For a moment, he wondered why he hadn't noticed when she'd become a woman. It was as if she'd blossomed overnight. Or maybe he'd been too focused on himself to see it.

His gaze moved, and a third photo bewildered him. It featured Lacey and him on pit road at a racetrack. They stood before his race car, which bore last year's paint scheme. Upon closer inspection, Reese placed the scenery. It was Bristol, and he'd won the race later that evening. He wondered why she'd displayed that scene prominently on her dresser. Did their friendship mean that much to her?

He glanced around the room and then crossed to her bed. He felt strange climbing into it. It was as if his staying there changed the dynamics of their relationship. However, it seemed as if everything had changed when her father died. At first she was hostile, but that hostility was now gone—at least it seemed to be gone. Lacey was different. Or maybe Reese was the one who'd changed, since he was more aware of her femininity. Heck, he'd almost kissed her when she'd cried earlier, and that troubled him deeply. Where'd this attraction come from, and what did it mean? Was he falling for her?

He groaned while moving under her sheets and lying back on the bed. How could he fall for Lacey Fowler? He remembered the day her parents brought her home from the hospital. She was like family. A relationship with her would be so wrong. But why on earth did it feel so right to touch her and hold her?

He turned to his side and breathed in the citrusy scent of her shampoo emanating from the pillowcase. He had to shake these disturbing feelings before he did something he'd regret later. What if he was the only one feeling this attraction? If he said or did the wrong thing, he could offend her or, worse yet, scare her. He didn't want to risk ruining their friendship, especially when they had the company to consider.

He sighed, contemplating the issues with the company. Something was definitely wrong, and the articles she'd shared with him confirmed he had to do more investigating. He prayed his father wasn't involved. It would kill him to find out his father was skimming money or cheating the company. If his dad were guilty, Reese would have to find a way to protect him. Or should he worry about protecting the company, since he and Lacey owned two-thirds of it? Where should his loyalty lie? Whom should he protect?

A door clicked shut, and he pulled the covers up to his torso. Footsteps on the hardwood floors alerted him Lacey was coming to the bedroom. His eyes widened when she stepped into the room wearing pink satin shorts and a matching camisole top.

His body stiffened at the sight of her milky white arms and legs. Her hair cascaded down her back in wet red waves. And when she bent to pick up a bag, his mouth gaped at her generous cleavage. He closed his eyes and mentally berated himself for these strange feelings. He'd lost his mind.

"Do you think someone killed my dad? I know I already asked you that, but I can't stop wondering." Her question wrenched him back to reality like his car smashing into the wall at Talladega last year.

He sat up. "Honey, I really don't know, but I hired a private investigator to look into it for us. We'll find out. I promise."

"Thank you. That means a lot." She crossed the room and sat on the edge of the bed, crossing one leg under her. "I just don't understand how someone could hurt my dad. Everyone loved him. I don't think he had any enemies."

Her eyes filled with tears, and he pulled her to him. "I wish I could turn back time and tell him not to get into that car."

He ran his fingers down her back, enjoying the feel of her warm, soft skin. She smelled of buttermilk soap and flowery shampoo, and his mind turned to thoughts of easing her down next to him in the bed and making love to her.

Whoa.

"That's what I mean." She pulled away, her emerald eyes serious. "My dad never would've driven home in the middle of the night. He constantly lectured me about being safe and only driving when I was well rested. I wanted to leave at seven one Friday night to come home for the weekend, and he wouldn't let me. He made me wait until eight the next morning."

She grabbed his hands and squeezed them. "There was a reason he left in the middle of the night, and it had to be urgent. He has a team plane, Reese. He could've flown home the next morning. Why did he leave? What happened?"

"You're right." He nodded, ignoring the fire in his belly caused by the touch of her warm, soft skin. An idea flashed in his head. "Did the police give you his personal effects from the car?"

She shook her head. "I never even thought to ask."

"Maybe they have his cell phone. We can find the last call he made. That could give us a clue."

She smiled. "Great idea." Then she reached over and hugged him. "I'm so glad you're here. I knew you'd help me figure this out."

"I'm glad too." He kissed the top of her head, inhaling her scent again.

"Well, I better let you sleep." She stood and grabbed the extra pillow off the bed. "Good night."

"Good night." He sized her up as she headed for the door. *My gosh, she's gorgeous.*

She suddenly stopped and faced him. "Reese, thank you for being here. Thank you for helping me with all of this."

"You're welcome." He shifted under the sheets. "I really don't feel comfortable taking your bed while you suffer on that old, lumpy sofa."

"It's the least I can do after the way I've treated you."

He waved off the thought. "Please forget that."

A strange expression formed on her beautiful face. She bit her lip as if considering something. "Can I sleep with you?"

"What?" His heart lurched, and he sat up like a shot.

"Never mind." She turned and started for the den.

He shook his head with disbelief. Did she just proposition him?

"Wait a minute," he called after her. "What did you just ask me?"

She stopped in the doorway and faced him. "I was wondering if I could stay in here with you. It's a pretty big bed, and I trust you to be a gentleman."

He breathed a sigh of relief. The idea of making love to Lacey Fowler both intimidated and stimulated him. They were partners, and she was like family. As much as they excited him, thoughts of being intimate with her were just plain wrong.

"Oh." He moved toward the wall. "Sure. I used soap, so I

shouldn't stink too bad."

She chuckled, flipping off the light. He loved the sound of her laugh. It was a sweet melody to his ears.

"You smell just fine," she said.

He lifted the covers, and she crawled in next to him. Heat roared through him when she snuggled down with her back to him, her foot brushing his leg.

"I'm really sorry for being such a witch to you," she whispered through the darkness.

"Forget it." He stared up at the ceiling and prayed his body would relax.

"No, I won't forget it." She rolled over and touched his chest. "You didn't deserve it."

He wished she'd stay on her side of the bed and keep her hands to herself. Her nearness was making him crazy.

"It's okay, Lacey. Really. I'm fine. We're fine." *Except I'm imagining you naked and beneath me, and your father would shoot me if he were alive.*

"Well, thank you." She leaned over him, and he held his breath as her soft lips brushed his cheek. "Good night."

"Night," he said in a strangled whisper.

She snuggled up next to him with her head on his arm, and her breathing quickly slowed. He lay awake listening to the sound of her breathing and feeling her heart beat on his arm for what felt like a long time.

When he fell asleep, he dreamt of holding her in his arms and then slowly making love to her, savoring her taste and the feel of her warm, soft skin.

FIFTEEN

Charles Boucher leaned his chair back and folded his hands late Tuesday afternoon. "Let me get this straight. You both think someone's embezzling funds from Southern Racing."

"Right." Lacey glanced at Reese, who nodded, prodding her to continue. "Reese talked to one of the accountants and found some strange payments. I saw files with receipts and a spreadsheet detailing mysterious transactions. I also found one with details of my father's accident."

"You have some definite hunches, but no real, solid proof." The lawyer glowered, glancing at his desk.

She sighed. He didn't believe them. He thought they were crazy. And maybe they were.

"Look, Mr. Boucher," Reese began, "we just want control of the company. We can figure things out from there."

The lawyer looked at Reese. "And you don't trust your father?"

"I don't know what to think." Reese's voice was low.

Lacey studied him, her eyes widening with astonishment. She'd wondered if Carl had something to do with the company issues, but she hadn't expressed it aloud for fear of alienating Reese. She wondered how difficult it was for him to doubt his father when they'd always been so close. Like Lacey, Reese had lost his mother at a young age, but his father had never remarried.

As if reading her thoughts, he met her gaze and gave her a

bleak smile. Her pulse leapt at the warmth of his gaze.

"You want to take control of the company from your father?" Mr. Boucher asked.

"That's right." Reese nodded.

"But you both want control?" he asked.

"Exactly," Reese said.

The lawyer turned his glance to Lacey. "And you don't want to buy him out or contest the will anymore?"

Her cheeks warming with embarrassment, she shook her head. "I need Reese by my side." Her face burned hotter when she realized what she'd admitted.

"If you two want control of the company, that's easy." The lawyer shrugged. "Form your own corporation."

Considering his suggestion, Lacey tilted her head in question. "What are you saying? Give up my father's company?"

"No, don't give it up. Combine your pieces." Mr. Boucher held up laced fingers like a puzzle.

"Combine them how?" Reese asked.

"By combining yourselves. Get married. Then you can be co-CEOs."

She gasped, dumbfounded. "Married?"

"Right. Married." The lawyer nodded.

"Oh." She tried to sound casual, but she was reeling at the thought. Marry Reese? Become his wife? How on earth could she marry a man who had a different girlfriend every week at the track?

Sure her cheeks would spontaneously combust, she kept her eyes on the lawyer to avoid Reese's stare, which she spotted in her peripheral vision.

"Get married, huh?" Reese's voice sounded pensive. "That would do it?"

"It would." The lawyer sat forward in his chair, which squeaked under the pressure. "Think about it. Mr. Fowler left each of you thirty percent of the company. If you combine, you'll have sixty percent, while your father has thirty and the investors have ten. You could take over the company and clean it up. You'd share control. Simple as that."

"Simple." Lacey cleared her throat, staring at the toes of her shoes. This was insane. It would never work. Her heart pounded while she folded her trembling hands.

"But my dad would still have a job, right?" Reese asked.

"Of course. He'd be vice president or whatever you and Lacey decide."

She stole a glance at Reese and found him nodding and leaning back in the chair, as if contemplating the idea with great care.

"But how would I explain our sudden union?" he asked.

The lawyer shrugged. "You two have known each other your whole lives. You could tell everyone that since Mr. Fowler passed away, you and Lacey have realized how much you mean to each other. Life's too short, so you want to be together before it's too late."

"That sounds reasonable." Reese smiled at Lacey, and she quickly looked away, anxiety skittering through her veins at the thought.

How could Reese even consider this? Marriage would cramp his style and ruin his playboy image. No one would believe he'd fallen for Lacey. She wasn't his type of girl. She was too straight-laced, too serious and boring, and she was still a virgin. She'd be the laughing stock of the track, sitting in his bus and staring at her wedding ring while he'd cat around with his leggy, blond models.

"You two could straighten things out with the company and then divorce," the lawyer continued. "You could say things didn't work out. It happens all the time."

"It happens all the time," she whispered. "Right. Just get

divorced." She'd have a broken heart while he walked away, the ladies' man looking for a new bimbo.

"You okay?" Reese touched her hand.

"I'm fine." She pulled her arm away and stood. "I better go. I need to unpack my truck, and—"

"Don't you want to discuss this?" Reese looked confused.

"No, I don't." She turned to Mr. Boucher. "Thank you for your time."

"It's the only way to save your dad's company. Isn't that what you want?" Reese asked.

She met his stare, his blue eyes pleading with her. "I didn't want to do it this way." Picking up her purse, she headed for the door. "I'll talk to you later."

While anger and hurt whirled in her gut, she stalked through the office and out to her SUV sitting next to his sports car, which they'd picked up on their way to the lawyer's office. She hit the unlock button on her keyless remote, opened the door, threw her purse in the passenger seat and climbed in.

As she started the engine, Reese loped across the lot toward her SUV. She considered slamming the truck into gear and jetting through the parking lot to avoid another hurtful conversation about a casual marriage, but she couldn't do it. An invisible magnetic force kept her frozen in the seat.

Reese motioned for her to lower her window when he approached, and she lowered the window and killed the engine.

With his eyebrows knitted together with concern, he leaned on the door. "Wait a minute. Talk to me. What's going on?"

"Nothing's going on." She tried her best to sound calm, in spite of the indignation swelling in her heart. "I need to go unpack this stuff in the back of my truck." She nodded toward the clock on the dashboard. "You need to get to the race shop for your team meeting."

He shook his head. "Don't change the subject. Why did you

go ballistic when Mr. Boucher said we should get married?"

"I didn't go ballistic, Reese." Her tone was smooth, even though her hands were trembling.

"You stomped out of the office like someone insulted you." His blue eyes studied hers. "What's going on? Don't shut me out, like you did after the funeral. *Talk* to me."

The determination in his voice wrenched something deep in her soul. Did he really care for her?

"I told you nothing's going on. I have to go." She started the truck again. "I'll call you later."

"Uh-uh." He reached across her and snatched the keys from the ignition. "Not so fast." He stuck the keys in his pocket and backed away from the truck.

"Hey!" She opened the door and climbed out. "Gimme my keys."

He folded his arms in defiance. "Not until you talk to me."

She grunted. He was impossible! "I am talking to you!" She held out her hand. "Reese Douglas Mitchell, give me my keys this instant."

He shook his head. "Nope."

She studied him, wondering how he could be so sexy and so darned irritating at the same time. "I just don't think it's a good idea. *Now, give me my keys.*" She enunciated each word.

"Not good enough." He leaned against his car. "Why isn't it a good idea?"

She sighed. "Okay, let's be honest with each other."

"That's a fabulous idea," he deadpanned.

"Don't be such a smart aleck." She narrowed her eyes.

"But I'm so good at it." His smirk infuriated her.

"I thought you wanted me to talk." She threw her arms up.

"Okay, okay. I'm sorry. Go ahead."

She leveled a glance at him. How could she be honest when the truth was she loved him and couldn't bear the thought of being his wife and then his ex-wife?

"The idea of you and me is just plain crazy," she said. "No one would believe it."

"Who cares what anyone else thinks? We'll just act like a married couple in public. It would be a business deal."

The words stabbed her like a knife. She swallowed. "A business deal."

He stood up straight. "Right. We'll get married, get control of the company, fix it, and then go our separate ways."

She folded her arms to shield her heart. "Like nothing happened."

"Right." He stopped, holding his hand up. "Well, no. I don't mean we won't be friends anymore."

"Reese, no one will believe you fell for me."

"Why not?" He looked confused. "You're beautiful and smart, and I've known you my whole life. It makes perfect sense to me."

"No, it doesn't make sense. You'd go from your latest blond model bimbo to me, boring old Lacey Fowler." She gestured wildly with her arms for emphasis. "Every racing gossip column would pick us apart. Maybe you could handle that, but I don't think I could. I want to be respected in this industry, like my dad was."

He stepped toward her and placed his hands on her shoulders, sending warmth to the pit of her belly. His eyes were serious while studying hers. "I don't care what people think or what they say. Please marry me, Lacey."

Her throat constricted as images floated through her mind. She saw herself standing at the altar with him and then crawling into his bed. She would be his wife, his partner, his lover. It would be a dream come true.

She mentally shook herself. But it was only a fantasy. A ruse. A facade.

A business deal.

They'd be divorced, and her heart would be broken before the ink was dry on their marriage certificate.

"No." Her voice was hoarse.

"Why?" He stepped back.

"How would your latest girlfriend feel about you marrying me?"

His lips formed a thin line. "Lacey, I don't have a girlfriend."

"What about Sandy?"

He lifted an eyebrow in surprise. "Sandy? Sandy Webb?"

She wagged a finger at him. "I saw her give you her number at my dad's funeral. That's why I was so angry with you. You said you didn't bring a date, and then you wound up getting one anyway."

He shook his head and jammed a finger in his chest. "She gave me her number. I didn't ask for it."

"But you hugged her!" Her voice trembled, and she hated the sound. Why did she let him get to her? Why did the idea of him with another girl make her so crazy?

"I didn't hug her. She hugged me!" He threw his hands up, frustration clouding his handsome face. "I don't ask women to throw themselves at me. It just sort of happens."

She shook her head. "Don't you see, Reese? I'd be the joke at the track. Guys would point and say, 'Look at poor, stupid Lacey Fowler. She married Reese, and he's still out getting lucky every night with pit lizards.' "

"I would never cheat on you." His eyes looked sincere, causing the lump to swell in her throat.

"It just wouldn't work. I'm sorry." She held out her hand. "Please give me my keys."

"Fine." He smacked the key ring into her sweaty palm. When his fingers brushed hers, electricity sparked between them.

Ignoring the intensity of the moment, she climbed into her

truck and started it. "I'll see you later."

He leaned on the door. "Would you at least think about it? We'd be honoring your father's memory. Remember at the wedding when he told us to take care of each other? We could take care of each other and the company."

Grief bubbled up in her chest, and a tear spilled from her eyes at the memory of her father's words. "I gotta go," she whispered.

He stepped back, and she put the truck in gear then sped through the parking lot.

Sixteen

"Man, are you all right?" Brett Turner asked over the swirl of air guns and banging of hammers in the race shop two hours later.

"Yeah." Reese sank onto a stool. He glanced up at his crew chief, who hugged his clipboard to his chest and studied him. He'd been deep in thought about how to convince Lacey to marry him ever since she'd driven out of the lawyer's parking lot with tears in her eyes.

"You've been out of it since you got here. Did you hear anything I said in the meeting?"

Reese smiled. "You told me to win next week."

His crew chief shook his head. "I didn't think you were listening."

"You don't want me to win?" Reese feigned confusion.

Brett slapped his arm with the clipboard. "You're a smart aleck."

"Funny. Someone else just called me that a little while ago."

His crew chief raised his eyebrows in question.

"Never mind." Reese scanned the shop while his mind clicked with questions about Lacey. He didn't understand her reaction to his proposal. Why wouldn't she marry him? Why did she think he'd make a fool of her? Why was she crying when she left? He was worried about her. He wanted to help her, even though he had no idea why he was so determined to convince her to say yes.

When he spotted Krista and Tommy across the bay, hope swelled within him. Maybe Krista could talk some sense into stubborn Lacey.

He cut his eyes to Brett. "Can I go now?"

"I don't know, since you completely blew off my pep talk and instructions for Atlanta."

"Yeah. Whatever." He stood and smacked Brett's shoulder. "See you later, man."

He hurried across the shop and approached Tommy and Krista. "Hey." He turned to Krista. "Can I talk to you a minute?"

She gave him a confused expression. "Uh, sure."

"Out there." He nodded toward the open bay door.

"I guess so." She gave Tommy a sideways glance.

"I just need to ask her advice," Reese said. "I'll bring her right back."

"You better," Tommy gave him a feigned glare.

Reese and Krista filed past the mechanics making last minute changes on his race cars. Stepping out into the parking lot, they passed the tractor-trailers where crewmembers were loading supplies for Atlanta. He sauntered onto the grass in front of the large, open field behind the shop and leaned his back against a tree.

"What's goin' on?" Krista folded her thin arms. "You look upset."

"Is it that obvious?" He grimaced. "Lacey's driving me crazy."

She guffawed and then covered her mouth with her hand. "I'm sorry. I wasn't expecting that."

"It's okay." If he weren't so frustrated, he'd probably laugh along with her.

Her expression changed to a look of concern. "She called me and said she was back in town and heading to the lawyer's to discuss taking over the company. What happened?"

"The lawyer said we should get married. I proposed, and she said no."

"What?" Her voice rose over the rumble of a race engine in the shop behind them. Her eyes were wide with shock. "She turned you down?"

"That's what I said." He wished she'd lower her volume before the whole shop heard the news that Reese was a loser who couldn't get a girl to marry him!

Krista shook her head, her brown eyes glistening with disbelief. "Is she crazy?"

He shrugged. "I don't know."

"Why would she turn you down?"

"That's what I'd like to know." He didn't see himself getting any insights from her. He decided to take the direct approach. "Would you talk to her for me?"

"Wait." She touched his arm. "Slow down. Tell me everything."

He recounted the story of their visit with the lawyer and the plan for the company. He explained how Lacey stormed from the office and then turned down his proposal in the parking lot.

Krista shook her head. "I don't get it. I figured she'd jump at the chance to marry you."

His eyebrows careened toward his hairline. "Really?" he asked, nonplus.

"Absolutely. I'll talk to her for you," she offered.

"That would be great."

"I'll let you know what she says." She turned to go, but he grasped her arm.

"I have one more favor. Would you give me advice on what kind of ring she'd like? I've never bought a diamond before."

A grin grew on Krista's lips. "I'd be honored."

Later that evening, Lacey carried the last box into the garage.

Huffing and puffing under the weight, she slowly made her way into the house and up the back stairs. She stopped in the doorway of her bedroom and dropped the box with a loud thump.

Surveying her room, she found it cramped with boxes and bags. She'd spent all afternoon unpacking and organizing. Although she was going through her personal belongings in the room in which she'd lived since she was a girl, it felt strange to be home. The house was too big and too empty without her father and stepmother.

She flopped onto her bed and stared up at the ceiling, wondering if she'd made the right choice in coming home instead of graduating. However, a deep longing for home had inundated her soul. She belonged there and not in school wondering what would become of her father's company now that he was gone.

She'd prowled around the office Carl had set up in the downstairs bedroom and found the filing cabinet replaced by a newer, empty one. She'd tried to log into the computer but had no luck guessing the password. Defeated, she concluded she'd have to go into the shop tomorrow and start snooping there.

Lacey had tried all afternoon to immerse herself in thoughts of unpacking and moving home, but Reese's proposal tore into her concentration like a freight train. She kept seeing those eyes pleading with her to say yes. He looked so sincere, so genuine, and so darned sexy.

He drove her crazy!

She wanted him, needed him. She knew she could never have his whole heart, but she would give him hers willingly.

Sighing, she stood, grabbed the box flap, and yanked. Instead of moving, the flap ripped off, sending her backward, where she landed on her bottom with a thud. She stood and muttered under her breath while glaring at the box.

The shrill ring of the phone cut through the silence of the house. Lacey kicked the box, dove onto her bed, and snatched the cordless receiver from the cradle. "Hello?"

"I've been ringing the doorbell for twenty minutes. Are you going to let me in or what?" Krista's impatient voice crackled over her cell phone.

"How are you, Krista?" Lacey snapped back at her while popping up and heading out to the hallway.

"I'm fine, thanks. Now let me in."

Lacey chuckled and bounced down the stairs, her loafers scraping on the hardwood. "You never were one for pleasantries. I'm hanging up now."

She turned off the phone and placed it on the little table by the door. She then unhooked the chain, flipped the deadbolt, and wrenched the door open.

"It's about time." Krista smiled and hugged Lacey. "How are you?"

"I'm okay." Lacey motioned for her to come in.

"You're a liar. You're not okay." Her best friend dropped her purse onto the floor and shucked off her coat.

"All right." Lacey folded her arms in defiance. "If you know so much, then tell me what's wrong with me."

"You're moping because you turned down Reese's proposal today." She pushed a finger in Lacey's collarbone. "You know you made a mistake, so you're hiding out in your house trying to deal with it."

Speechless, Lacey's eyes widened with shock. Krista was a professional at getting to the point and getting into Lacey's business.

"You got anything to drink? I'm thirsty." Krista pushed past her toward the kitchen.

Lacey ran after her, annoyance surging through her. "Wait a minute! Did he send you here to talk me into it?"

When Lacey reached the kitchen, Krista handed her a can of diet cola. "You look thirsty, too."

"You might as well give it up, because I'm not going to marry him." Lacey jammed a hand on her hip. "I'm offended you're helping him and not listening to my side of the story."

"Go ahead and talk. I'm listening." Her best friend sat at the kitchen table, opened the can, and took a long drink.

Lacey sat across from her and watched her drink. She shook her head, bewildered. How could Krista be so casual at a time like this?

"What?" Krista asked.

"I can't believe he sent you here."

"He didn't send me here. He asked me for help."

Lacey studied her friend. Why was Reese going to such great lengths for this? Was he that determined to control the company? Hope radiated through her. Or could he possibly feel something for her—maybe just something small? Then the hope faded when she remembered that he'd called it a *business deal.* Scowling at the reality of the situation, Lacey opened her can and took a drink.

"I'm waiting . . ." Krista sang. "Spill it, Fowler. Why did you turn down his proposal?"

"Because I love him." Lacey examined the logo on the can to avoid her friend's probing stare.

Krista's laughter sounded in a burst, and Lacey glared at her.

"Okay, Lacey, let me get this straight. You're in love with Reese. But he proposes to you and you say no."

"Exactly." Lacey took another drink.

"That makes no sense!" Her best friend slammed her hand on the table, causing Lacey to jump. "Are you listening to yourself?"

"Did he tell you the whole story?" Lacey snapped. "It's a business deal. It's not love."

Krista shrugged. "So?"

"So, he's going to divorce me once the company is back on its feet!" Her voice vibrated with frustration at her friend's lack of sympathy for her situation.

"You don't know that."

Lacey nodded with emphasis. "Yes, I do."

"No, you don't."

"He doesn't love me, but I love him. He'll move on to his next bimbo, and I'll be drowning my sorrow in diet cola and staring down at my wedding band." She saw a smile twitch on Krista's face, and her scowl deepened.

"He wants to marry you," Krista said. "He looked really upset when I saw him. He may not know it yet, but he's nuts about you."

"No, he isn't." Lacey couldn't risk her heart by holding onto the hope in Krista's voice. *She's wrong. Dead wrong.*

Her friend grinned. "Yes, he is. Right now he thinks he's doing it to save the race team, but in his heart, he's doing it for you."

Lacey groaned with confusion and covered her face with her hands. "Why did my dad have to leave me with this mess? I'm so mixed up that I'm losing my mind." She felt a hand rub her arm.

"I'm sorry, Lace, but I think this is going to work out. Just give him a chance."

"Why should I?" Lacey dropped her hands to the table. "He's the biggest playboy around, and I'm not his type. He'll hang around long enough to get the company back on its feet to save his ride, and then he'll bolt for the next hot model that comes along and shakes her big, fake boobs at him."

Krista laughed. "You're so dramatic."

"I am not!" Lacey moaned, dropping her head into her hands on the table. "I'm totally crazy about him. He smiles, and I turn to mush. I can't marry him. I'll fall even more head-over-heels, and then you'll have to have me committed when he leaves."

"He won't leave. Trust me."

Lacey sat up, grimacing. "You honestly think he loves me."

"Are you kidding? I could see it in his eyes at the memorial service. He was trying everything in his power to console you."

"Yeah, and he also got Sandy Webb's phone number." Lacey lifted her can and took a drink.

"Sandy Webb is an idiot. He only has eyes for you, Lace. He just needs to realize it."

Lacey pondered Krista's words, questions swirling in her mind. Did Reese really love her and just not know it? Would he stay with her after the company was back in line? Did she want to take the risk of losing her heart? But he didn't say he loved her. He said it was a business deal.

Lacey studied Krista. "You and Tommy are in love, right?"

Krista's cheeks glowed pink. "I think so."

"I'm really happy for you." Lacey reached out, putting her hand on Krista's. "Don't take this wrong, but I think you're all caught up in Tommy. You think Reese feels the same way for me, but he doesn't."

Krista shook her head. "You're wrong. He loves you. Marry him."

Lacey sighed with disappointment. "I can't do it. I just can't."

"Yes you can, and you should. Marry him. Seduce him. Make him see how awesome you guys are together."

"Seduce him?" Lacey's voice rose to a squeak. "What do I know about seduction? I'm a virgin!"

"It comes naturally. You'll figure it out." Krista winked. "Trust me."

"Did you . . . ?"

Krista's cheeks glowed a deeper rose.

"Oh, my gosh!" Lacey leaned forward with her chin on the palm of her hand and grinned. "Tell me all about it."

SEVENTEEN

Reese stared across the parking lot the following morning. "She said no." He repeated Krista's words, running his thumb over the small velvet box in his hand.

"I'm sorry." Krista touched his arm. "I tried, but she's afraid."

"What exactly is she afraid of?" He shoved the box back into the pocket of his leather jacket. He could tell Krista was struggling to form her answer and he hoped she'd tell the truth, no matter if she'd hurt his feelings or not.

"I can't tell you everything she said, because I don't want to lose her trust. But she's mostly afraid of, well, getting hurt."

"I would never hurt her. She's been like family to me my whole life." He shook his head and scanned the parking lot, absently watching traffic whiz by on the highway in front of the shop. He had to figure out how to win her trust. "What should I do?"

"Kidnap her."

"What did you say?" Bewildered, he looked down at her grin.

"You heard me. Kidnap her. The only way to get stubborn Lacey Fowler to do something is to force her." She glanced at her watch. "It's almost eleven. Tell her you're going to an early lunch and take her to City Hall. Tommy and I will tag along as witnesses."

"Don't you have to get back to work?"

"Nope. I took the day off." She grabbed his arm and yanked

him. "Let's get you hitched, Romeo."

Lacey rubbed her eyes and leaned back in her high-back, leather desk chair. Her head was pounding with a roaring migraine from staring at spreadsheets. She hadn't made heads or tails of anything, despite hours of studying them. She'd been searching through files all morning, trying in vain to locate the ones she'd seen at her dad's house.

Carl must've hidden them at his house or in the office. He hadn't visited her dad's house since she'd gotten back to town, and she hadn't seen him in the shop either. She planned to hunt him down later in the afternoon—after her headache subsided.

When Lacey had arrived at the shop that morning, her father's secretary insisted she take his office. Lacey had wondered why Carl hadn't moved into it as the new CEO.

She scanned the office, taking in the memories her father had captured in photos on the walls—photos of his race teams, drivers, and friends over the years. There were photos of her dad in Victory Lane twenty years ago, grinning with his first champion, Joe Clay. He looked so young, so happy.

She tried to ignore the sad reminiscence twisting in her gut while she crossed the room to take a closer look at the gallery. Her gaze settled on a photo of Reese in Victory Lane at Homestead-Miami Speedway when he accepted his championship trophy last year. He held the large trophy high over his head while their fathers looped their arms around his waist and grinned with pride. Lacey hated missing that race. She wished she could've been there to hug him in Victory Lane and celebrate the occasion Reese had dreamt of his whole life.

Reese.

Her heart thumped at the thought of him, and she shook her head while viewing more photos. She'd almost called him several times last night, but she couldn't bring herself to pick up the phone. Plus, she didn't know what to say.

Despite Krista's best efforts, Lacey refused to budge on the marriage issue. It just didn't make sense to put her heart on the line like that. She refused to go into a marriage without giving her whole self. That was why she'd "saved" herself and didn't want to lose her virginity or her heart until it felt right. She'd had plenty of boyfriends who wanted her, but she knew all they wanted was sex, not her love.

Maybe if she could convince herself to keep her eyes on the prize—saving her father's company—she could consider the marriage. She surveyed the wall of photos and smiled. This is what she wanted to save. This was what her father had worked his whole life for—his team, his surrogate family. His first love was racing.

The door to the office slid open with a whoosh across the plush carpet, and Lacey jumped. Reese, Krista, and Tommy bounded into the room, all grinning as if they knew a wonderful secret they weren't going to share.

"Hey, boss." Reese approached, taking her hand in his. "We're taking you to lunch."

"Lunch?" Lacey cut her eyes to the checkered flag clock on the wall. "It's not even twelve."

"It's close enough, and we're kidnapping you." Krista came up behind her, handed Lacey her purse from the floor, then nudged her toward the door.

"But I have a meeting at one." Lacey tried to pull her hand back from Reese, but he continued to grip it and ease her toward the door.

"You can reschedule," Tommy chimed in, slipping through the door ahead of them. "I'll tell Betsy to clear the rest of your day." He approached the young brunette behind the desk in the lobby. "Please cancel Miss Fowler's afternoon appointments."

"Okay." The brunette looked confused while Lacey moved past her with Reese pulling and Krista pushing.

"Miss Fowler is going to get married." Krista's grin was wide.

"Krista, what are you talking about?" Lacey gasped.

"You're getting married?" Betsy stood, raising her voice with excitement. "You're getting married *today?*"

"That's right." Reese pulled a small velvet box from the inside pocket of his jacket.

"Reese, what are you doing?" Lacey's face burned with a mixture of embarrassment and anger as a throng of employees gathered around them.

He smiled, dropping to one knee and opening the box. "Will you marry me, Lacey?"

"Reese, get up this instant!" She gritted her teeth, trying to ignore the chorus of sighs, oohs, and aahs rising around them. "We need to talk about this in *private.*"

She shot a glance at Krista, who folded her arms and gave a victorious smile. Lacey narrowed her eyes. *The rat!* Krista and Reese had set her up! How could Lacey turn him down when she was surrounded by a knot of her friends and coworkers cheering her on?

Reese took her left hand and slid something cool up her finger. Lacey glanced down, and her breath caught when she found a beautiful diamond ring shimmering on her finger. The emerald cut stone sat surrounded by a cluster of smaller diamonds lining the gold setting. Tears filled her eyes, and she cupped her mouth with her right hand.

Her gaze collided with Reese's blue eyes. "Would you do me the honor of being my wife, Lacey?" He folded her left hand in his and pulled it to his chest. Then he lowered his voice. "I promise I'll never hurt you."

The chorus around them grew louder with more employees joining the clapping and sighing. Reese had created a circus at

Southern Racing.

Thoughts whirled in Lacey's mind. Should she risk her heart? But it was for her father's memory and for his pride and joy—his company.

She could do this for him, and she should do it.

"Yes." Lacey's voice trembled with a mixture of excitement, love, and panic. "I'll marry you."

The cheers around them swelled. Reese jumped up and grabbed her hands. Before she could stop him, he put his arms around her waist and pulled her close. His lips brushed hers, and electricity skittered through her veins, causing her knees to wobble. She wrapped her arms around his neck to stabilize her weak legs and pressed her lips to his.

Closing her eyes, she savored his sweet, warm taste and heard herself moan as his lips probed the recesses of her mouth. Was she dreaming? Was Reese Mitchell really kissing her the way she'd imagined since she was a teenager? When he stepped back, she was breathless and light-headed. She held onto his arm for balance.

"Well, let's go do this before you change your mind," his voice was husky in her ear. He took her hand and led her to the exit while the knot of employees clapped behind them.

Still reeling from the kiss, Lacey gripped his hand for dear life, afraid her rubbery legs would cause her to fall on their way out to the parking lot.

"We'll take my truck." Reese led them to his new, four-door, hunter-green pickup parked in the back of the lot.

"Were you surprised?" Krista sidled up to Lacey, looping her arm around her neck.

"Yeah." Lacey stared down at the gorgeous ring.

It seemed as if he'd read her mind when he chose it. It was so beautiful that her eyes filled with tears every time she looked at it. And that kiss. Holy cow! She'd never experienced anything like it. Was it all a dream—a cruel, horrible dream that would haunt her when she woke?

The pop of the door locks wrenched her back to reality. Looking up, she found Reese flashing that sexy smile and holding the door open for her.

"Your ride, milady," he said.

"Thanks." She climbed in and studied the ring some more.

"Do you like it?" He was leaning in the truck so close she could feel his body heat mix with hers. His spicy cologne permeated the air around her.

"I love it," she whispered, her voice hoarse with affection. *And I love you.* She stared into his eyes. If she leaned slightly, their lips would brush again. Oh, how she craved the touch and taste of his sweet lips.

"Wait until you see the matching band." He slammed her door before she could respond.

Her eyes widened while she processed the words. *Matching band? This is really happening!*

Krista thumped the back of Lacey's seat. "You made the right choice."

Lacey faced her best friend. "I can't believe you set me up."

Krista's smile was smug.

Reese climbed into the driver's seat and slammed his door.

"Where are we going?" Lacey asked.

"It's a surprise." Tommy chimed in from beside Krista.

"You guys are a dangerous trio." Lacey settled into her seat and fastened her safety belt.

"We'll take that as a compliment." Reese waggled his eyebrows and he started the truck.

Lacey spent most of the ride deep in thought, unaware of the conversation bubbling around her. She contemplated her ring, internally debating her acceptance of his proposal. He had her right where he wanted her by proposing in front of their coworkers. She was sure the rumors were flying already about their marriage by now. She'd bet someone had called the media. Maybe Gina had already sent out a news release. By tomorrow morning, the whole world would know Reese Mitchell had proposed to his late team owner's daughter. And what would the rumor mill say? Would folks assume he'd gotten Lacey Fowler pregnant and had to marry her?

Lacey groaned at the thought. The whole world would call her a slut. Great! She was a virgin, but everyone would call her easy.

But would she still be a virgin tomorrow? Her stomach clenched at the thought of spending the night with Reese. Did he expect her to sleep with him? And would she live up to his expectations when she'd never . . . ?

"Well, we're here," Reese announced, nosing the truck into a space in front of the city hall complex.

Lacey met his gaze, her body trembling with fear of her wedding night.

Wedding night.

She swallowed, hoping to wet her parched throat.

He raised an eyebrow. "You okay?"

She gave a tentative nod.

He faced the couple in the back. "How 'bout you guys go find out where we get the license, and we'll meet you in a bit."

"Will do," Tommy said.

Lacey felt Krista touch her shoulder while she climbed from the truck. When they slammed their doors, Lacey jumped.

"You've got a deer-in-the-headlights look." He wrenched his keys from the ignition, unfastened his belt, and moved closer to her. "Talk to me."

"I don't know what to say." Lacey wished her body would stop trembling in panic.

"Don't shut me out. I can't stand when you do that."

Her eyes moved to the ring while confusion rose in her throat. She was his fiancée. Did that mean she should tell him what was in her heart and on her mind? Should she trust him?

With a finger under her chin, he moved her eyes back to his. "I'm sorry for putting you on the spot like I did, but I didn't see any other way. This marriage makes sense."

She swallowed again, her throat bone dry. His azure eyes were so sincere that her heart swelled with a mixture of awe and love. Whether she wanted to admit it or not, he had already stolen her heart.

"Don't think about this as marrying me," he said. "Just think of this as a way to save your dad's company and find out why your parents died."

She blinked. So, he didn't think of this as a marriage? Her hope sank. He might have had her heart, but she certainly didn't have his.

"Lacey, I want the same thing you do. I want to save our race team." He took her hands in his. "Let's just do this, and we'll have it annulled as soon as we find the people responsible for this mess Southern Racing is in."

"Okay." Her voice sounded foreign to her. How could she even think about an annulment when she wasn't even married yet?

It's a business deal. That's all it is. She sighed and then mustered all the strength she could find in her soul. She could do this. She had to do this for her father.

He leaned over and hugged her. "Let's go get hitched."

EIGHTEEN

Three hours later, Lacey gazed down at a complete wedding set on her ring finger while she sat in a booth at Tony's Restaurant. The matching diamond band fitting snugly next to her engagement ring must've brought her finger close to two karats. The set was breathtakingly gorgeous, and she couldn't believe it was on her finger. She had to be dreaming. How did she go from no ring to a wedding set in just a few hours?

Her stomach fluttered at the memory of the events of the afternoon. They'd bought their marriage license and then sealed their union through a short civil ceremony in the magistrate's office, complete with another mind-blowing, knee-weakening kiss from Reese. Tommy and Krista had signed off as witnesses and then it was done. She was now Lacey Mitchell. Legally, she was Millicent Doreen Fowler Mitchell, but Lacey Mitchell sounded better.

It all felt so surreal.

Lacey moved her stare from her rings to her seafood linguine while Tommy and Reese continued to chatter about their trip to Atlanta the next morning.

Lacey felt a sharp kick in her shin under the table and winced when she looked at Krista. "What was that for?"

"You're a total space cadet. Are you okay?" her best friend asked.

Lacey grimaced. "What do you think? I wasn't planning on getting married when I got up this morning."

"You need to celebrate!" Krista lifted her fork from her lasagna. "We have to have a party. You need a reception."

"That's a great idea," Reese chimed in. "We'll have it in my basement tonight."

Lacey shook her head. The idea of facing the rumor mill sent dread coiling the pit of her stomach. "I don't know . . ."

"Oh, come on." Tommy lifted his glass of cola. "Don't be such a party pooper."

Lacey took a deep breath. She could make it through this, as long as Krista was by her side. Besides, most of the folks they knew were out of town, so it wouldn't be a big party. Her stomach eased a bit at the thought.

"But who will we invite?" she asked. "The crew left for Atlanta last night."

"We have other friends," Krista said. "I'll make some calls."

"I'll get a few cases of champagne and order some food." Reese lifted his glass in toast. "Here's to our new marriage."

"Hear, hear!" Krista sang.

Lacey touched her glass to his, panic nipping at her. The world was going to find out that she had married Reese. She'd hoped no one would ever find out it was merely a business deal. Had she just made the biggest mistake of her life?

Lacey touched Reese's arm when he threw the truck in park in front of Southern Racing later that afternoon. "Can we talk for a minute?" she asked. "Alone?"

"Sure thing." He turned to Krista and Tommy. "See you guys later, okay?"

"Do I hear a list of honey do's coming?" Tommy snorted.

Krista nudged him with her elbow. "They've been married for only a few hours. I guess this is where the hen pecking begins."

Lacey rolled her eyes. They thought they were so funny.

"Hey, we do need to talk." Reese grinned. "I've sort of taken over her life today. I expect she has a few questions."

Krista winked at Lacey. "I have a gift for you. I'll catch up with you later after I plan your reception."

"See you guys later. Congratulations." Tommy hopped down to the pavement.

Krista met Tommy in front of the truck before they walked hand-in-hand toward the bay doors leading to his team's shop. Lacey shook her head, reflecting on their budding love affair. That was the way it was supposed to be—dating first, falling in love next, and marrying later. Getting married without falling in love first was the wrong way to go about it.

"What's on your mind?" Reese touched her hand.

"We have so much to talk about." She unfastened her seatbelt and faced him, her body trembling with anticipation of what was yet to come in their new life together.

"Start talking." He undid his belt and faced her, leaning back against the door.

"If we're going to give the appearance we're really married, don't we need to live together?"

"Move in with me." He shrugged as if it were an easy solution.

"But my dad's house . . ." Her heart flipped in her chest. He expected her to move into his house. This would change everything. They'd truly be a married couple.

"You'll keep it. Remember, this is temporary."

"Right." She sighed. *Temporary.* She needed to keep reminding herself of that and stop the fantasies. "I need to pack up my things and move in. When should I do that?"

"Whenever you want." He held up his keychain and wiggled off a key. "Here. You can have the master suite. I'll move into one of the guest rooms."

That answers the sex question.

"Great idea," she whispered. She slipped the key into her purse. "Now, your wife should be with you at the track. Should I meet you in Atlanta?"

"Yeah." He sat up, shoving his keychain into the pocket of his tight jeans. "I thought about that. I guess you can fly out Friday night and stay in my bus." He quickly added, "I have an extra bed there too."

Her cheeks heated at the word *bed*. She felt a mixture of relief and disappointment at his disinterest in sleeping with her. He must really consider her his sister. But those two kisses seemed real enough. Maybe only she was the one who felt anything when their lips touched. Too bad.

Not that they were really married. Not that she really *wanted* to be married to him.

Lacey sighed. Why was she so darned confused?

"Anything else?" he asked. "You look confused."

Whoops! How'd he know that? "I think that's it." She ran her fingers over the hem of her suit jacket in order to avoid his probing stare. The way he read her expressions was disconcerting. "So, we're having a reception tonight?" she asked.

"Yeah, I figured we'd have some people over and celebrate our news." He sat up.

"I would imagine the gossip is spreading like wildfire." She gathered up her purse. "Do Tommy and Krista know to keep the truth a secret?"

He nodded. "We can trust them."

She glanced toward the race shop entrance and spotted Reese's PR rep staring toward the truck and tenting her hand over her eyes to block the sun. Lacey's stomach clenched. The moment of truth.

"There's Gina," she said. "I bet the news release has gone out already. Let the circus begin."

"Don't worry," he said, patting her hand. "We can handle

this. We're a team, remember?"

They climbed from the truck and crossed the parking lot.

Gina ran up to meet them, her eyes wide with shock. "I heard a rumor you two ran off and got married at lunch time. Is that true?"

"Yup." Reese pulled Lacey to him.

"Was this a spur-of-the-moment thing?" Gina looked back and forth between them.

"Sort of," Reese said. "We'd been talking about it for a while, and it just felt like the right time."

"I didn't even know you were dating." Gina studied Lacey, her brown eyes boring into her.

"We kept it a secret." Lacey prayed she sounded sincere, despite her trembling hands. She despised lying. "You know how rumors fly." She gave Reese her best loving look, hoping to help make her answer authentic.

Gina grabbed Lacey's hand and gasped. "Wow. Those are some gorgeous rings."

"Thanks. Reese has fabulous taste," Lacey said.

"That's why I married you," he said.

Lacey looked up, ready to roll her eyes at his over-the-top sentiment, but when she found him smiling, she changed her mind. His eyes were genuine, and warmth roared through her stomach.

She mentally shook herself. She needed to stop fabricating this feeling of a real marriage. He'd already said they'd get it annulled once the company was straightened out. Kidding herself into believing he really loved her would only break her heart when it was over.

"Where's your ring?" Gina asked Reese.

"Oh." He looked stumped. "Well, I—"

"It's okay. I'll tell her." Lacey touched his chest, and he raised an eyebrow in question. "It's my fault, Gina. I dropped it off to have it sized, and the jeweler still has it. I plan to bring it to Atlanta with me Friday."

"Oh. Okay." Gina shrugged. "So, can I send out a release with the news?"

"Absolutely." Reese grinned, embracing Lacey. "We want to tell the world."

Lacey took a deep breath. The world would now know she was Lacey Mitchell, wife of the ARA superstar and champion. Her life would never be the same.

Lacey was glad to sneak out of the office at four. Her marriage was the latest news. Visitors stopped by to gawk at her rings, and her phone never stopped ringing all afternoon. A few nosy callers had the nerve to ask if she was pregnant! Although she was appalled, Lacey's calm answer was, "Not that I know of."

Sneaking out unnoticed, Lacey sped to her house to gather what she needed to take to Reese's. It felt strange to pack up again, and it felt even stranger to pack to go to Reese's house.

Because we're married.

She examined her finger for what felt like the hundredth time to make sure the rings were still there. She absently wondered how much a wedding set like that cost. He'd sure spent a lot of money to make the deal look authentic.

Lacey jammed another pair of jeans into her bag and then carried the two bags down to her truck, throwing them into the backseat next to her favorite suits and blouses she'd picked out for work. She liked the idea of going to work at her dad's shop every day. She just wished he were there, too.

Sighing, Lacey wracked her brain, trying to figure out if she forgot anything. She walked back into the house and checked the doors and windows. After flipping on a small light above the stove, she set the alarm and headed back out to her truck.

Driving to Reese's house, Lacey reflected on the day and

wondered how many people would show up for their reception. When she was a little girl, she'd imagined her wedding like a fairytale. She would wear a beaded, sequined gown with a long train and a tiara on her auburn hair. Her groom would look handsome in his traditional black tuxedo. They'd declare their love before the altar of her childhood church, dance the night away at the local country club, and then jet off to Hawaii for a week of passion and romance on the golden beaches.

She frowned at thoughts of her wedding earlier today. Never in a million years did Lacey fantasize about running to the magistrate's office on her lunch hour to get married in her navy blue suit.

Lacey was relieved that the long, winding driveway was empty when she pulled up to Reese's house. At least she could move in without a crowd of people asking her what the rush was and if she was pregnant.

Pregnant.

She chuckled at the thought. No, that wouldn't have been possible, unless if it were Immaculate Conception.

She stopped her truck in front of his six-bay garage that housed part of his car collection, including his two trucks, two sports cars, and two classic muscle cars. As if on cue, one of the garage doors opened, revealing him standing in his tight jeans and a button down blue shirt that made his eyes even more striking.

He wore a wolfish smirk that made her nerves prickle when she climbed from the truck. She wondered if he was rethinking his stance on their sex life. At least, that gleam in his eye looked almost . . . sexual. Heat swirled in the pit of her belly, and she pushed the thought from her mind.

"What's going on?" She gave him a tentative smile while hitting the button to open the tailgate of her truck.

"My dad just called my cell. He's insulted I didn't tell him we were getting married. The old man feels left out." He snickered.

She stared at him, her eyes wide with alarm. "You didn't call him after the ceremony? How could you do that to him, Reese? That's so hurtful."

His smiled faded. "Lacey, haven't you even considered that my dad is part of the reason we're in this mess?"

Mess? The marriage is a mess?

She blinked. "What do you mean?"

"Let's be honest here. Don't you think my dad's guilty of something underhanded? It's not easy for me to say, but I've been thinking about it."

"Well, I . . ." Her voice trailed off. Yes, she'd thought it, but didn't want to hurt Reese by saying it out loud.

"I've thought it, too." He rested his arms on her shoulders, and that heat in her belly swirled faster, nearly taking her breath away.

His eyes gleamed with an intensity that caused her body to stiffen. Was he going to kiss her again? Boy, she hoped so. And after the kiss, they could revisit that sex decree. Her breath paused in anticipation and excitement.

Whoa. She was losing her mind and her heart to Reese Mitchell, and it scared her to death.

"Welcome home, Mrs. Mitchell." He dropped his arms and sauntered to the back of her truck. "Let me show you to your room."

Ignoring her disappointment, she joined him at the back of her SUV and snatched up the bags he hadn't grabbed.

"I thought you'd like to take the master suite, so I picked up a little bit." He put a bag down and slammed the tailgate. He nodded toward the bay. "Tomorrow I'll move my truck out, and you can park there. I'll give you a garage door opener too."

He flashed his smile while starting toward the house. "Of

course, you're welcome to drive any of my vehicles. Don't be afraid to take the Camaro out for a spin. I know you always loved that car."

"Cool." She couldn't help but grin. She did love that car and cherished the memories of their driving lessons behind the race shop when he taught her how to drive a manual transmission.

She followed him through the kitchen of his gorgeous, five-thousand-square-foot house and up the sweeping, open staircase toward the master suite. It was difficult to believe this was now her home with its beautiful high ceilings, polished tile floors, plush carpet, and antique furniture. Well, at least, it would be hers for a short time—until the annulment.

She bit her lip as she entered his large master suite. The king-size bed sat in the center of the room. Two dark wooden armoires lined one wall, and a matching triple dresser lined the other. A large, flat screen television, complete with surround sound, hung across from the bed.

"Everyone should be here in about an hour or so." He placed her bags on the bed and then crossed the room. "There's room in the big dresser for your clothes." He opened the door to the walk-in closet, which was the size of her bedroom in her apartment in Maryland. "I made room in here too."

Entering the closet, she spotted a rack of empty hangers on the far wall. "Thanks."

"You know the bathroom's over here." He crossed the room again and opened the door to the large bathroom, which was bigger than the closet and contained a garden tub, glass shower stall, a long vanity with two sinks and a linen closet.

"Towels are in here." He opened the closet. "And the hamper's here for dirty clothes. Rosa comes on Thursdays to clean and do laundry." He closed the door. "I think you'll be comfortable. Make yourself at home."

"Are you sure you want to give this up?" she asked.

"I can still use it. I just have to knock before I enter." He touched her nose and then padded from the bathroom. "Go ahead and unpack. I'll be in the basement getting things ready."

Biting her lip, she watched him go. She was moving in with Reese. Why was he really doing this? Did he care about her as more than a sibling?

"Reese." She spoke his name before she could stop herself. Her cheeks burned with embarrassment.

"Yeah?" He faced her, smiling.

Boy, he's sexy. She cleared her throat in order to try to stop the attraction radiating through her. "I know you're doing this for my dad. Thanks."

He folded his arms across his wide chest. "You know I'd do anything for you."

Lacey sighed while he disappeared through the doorway. Oh, she wanted him. If only the marriage were real. She bit back the regret in her heart and moved over to the bed and started to unpack.

She was hanging clothes in the closet when she heard the bedroom door click closed. Stepping into the bedroom, she found Krista holding a small pink gift bag in one hand and a garment bag in the other.

Krista gestured with disgust toward Lacey. "How do you expect to seduce Reese in jeans and a Southern Racing sweatshirt?"

"I wasn't planning on seducing him," Lacey snapped. "Remember, this is a business deal."

"Business deal, my big toe. Take off your clothes. I brought you something better." Her best friend dropped the gift bag on the dresser and unzipped the garment bag, revealing a skimpy little black dress with spaghetti straps.

"Oh, Krista." Lacey crossed the room and held up the dress. "This is awesome."

"What do you say?" She smirked.

"Thank you, Krista." Lacey smiled.

"And this is for later." She shoved the gift bag at Lacey.

Lacey laid the dress on the bed and took the bag. She gasped, pulling out a short, white frilly nightgown with a matching G-string. Her cheeks ignited with embarrassment again. "I can't wear that!"

"Sure, you can." Her best friend nodded toward it. "You'll look great."

"Thanks, but take it back." She tried to hand the bag to Krista, but she wouldn't take it. "I'm serious. I won't wear it. Reese made it perfectly clear that we won't, well, you know!"

Lacey gestured toward the bed, her stomach plummeting. "Reese said I'll sleep here, and he'll stay in the guest room. He also said there's an extra bed in the motor coach, so there won't be any of that. He doesn't want it, and I've accepted that. We're not really married. This is just a way to take over the company and fix whatever is going on."

Krista snorted. "Please. He's a red-blooded American male. He'll want to."

"Well, maybe I won't." She dropped the bag on the bed.

"Oh, yeah, right." Her best friend's voice simmered with sarcasm. "With the way you two ogle over each other, I'd be shocked if you make it through the party tonight. You'll probably sneak out early and get it on before midnight."

"Krista, you're not listening to me!" Lacey'd had enough of her contradictions. "He said he doesn't want to."

Her friend shook her head. "All right, fine. Now, let's get you ready for your wedding reception. Put that dress on and get out your makeup."

NINETEEN

Rock music blared through the speakers in the four corners of Reese's finished basement, while he scanned the crowd for his bride. She was nowhere to be found. He spotted a small group of his buddies sipping beer while playing pool and a throng of race team employees leaning on the bar, drinking. Another group of women stood in a tight circle by the basement stairs chatting, probably gossiping about him and Lacey.

But where on earth is Lacey?

Reese gripped his beer, glancing at the clock and trying to ignore the alarm in his gut. The party had been in full swing for nearly an hour, and he was starting to worry that she'd changed her mind and bolted.

He took a long drink, gazing toward the stairs. He knew he shouldn't have forced her into it. It had sounded like a risky idea when Krista posed it, but he was desperate.

Why was he so darned desperate? Heck, he didn't know.

But he'd had to convince her to marry him. He'd had a burning desire to make this plan work and save the company. At least, that's what he told himself.

"Reese, I can't believe it," his father's voice said behind him. "You're a married man."

"Pop." He turned into his father's hug. "I'm glad you made it."

"I just keep wondering if I would've been invited to this party if I hadn't heard the rumor. Why didn't you call me?" His father's blue eyes were full of hurt while he held up his beer.

Reese sighed, guilt nipping at him. He couldn't tell his father the truth. He couldn't say the words, "Because I'm not sure if I should trust you."

"I'm sorry," Reese said. "We just didn't want a big fanfare."

His father's expression was pensive. He grasped Reese's arm and steered him into a far corner, away from the loud voices and music. "Is she pregnant?" he asked, his blue eyes gleaming with concern.

"No! Heck no!" Reese shook his head, trying not to laugh. *She'd better not be anyway.* The thought of her with another man made his stomach sour.

As his father continued to study him, Reese longed to crawl under the pool table on the other side of the large basement to avoid his accusing eyes. "Then why did you two run off and get married? It all seems so sudden."

"We felt like it." Reese shrugged and took a drink of his beer. He hoped he looked as casual as he tried to appear. "You know me . . . I'm impulsive!"

"I'm not buying it, son. Girls love that frou-frou wedding stuff." He made a sweeping gesture with his hands. "When I married your mother, she planned our wedding for almost a year. She was so wrapped up in details I think she forgot about me at one point. All I heard about were dresses, flowers, food, and invitations. I think she enjoyed the preparations more than the honeymoon."

Boy, the old man was intuitive. "Lacey's not like that," Reese said, shrugging again in order to appear apathetic.

His father grimaced. "She's a girl. They're all like that."

"Look, Pop," he said, smacking his dad's shoulder. "Lacey and I decided to do something crazy. We're married now. I'm sorry you weren't in on our little secret, but we wanted to keep it quiet. Just be happy for us."

"Oh, son, I am." His smile was wide and proud. "I'm happy you two finally figured out you belong together."

"We do?" He didn't mean to ask it, but the words slipped out in his confusion.

"I always told Greg you two were made for each other. It just took you kids a while to figure it out." His old eyes surveyed the crowd. "Where's that beauty anyway?"

"I was just wondering that myself." Reese lifted his beer, almost dropping it when he spotted her.

Like some clichéd chick flick, it was as if time stood still while she descended the stairs. He didn't hear the music or the clamor of voices around him. He forgot anyone else existed. It was just Lacey and him.

And she was absolutely dazzling.

Her soft red hair was pulled up in a twist with only a few curls framing her face. Her makeup accentuated her emerald eyes. His pulse raced like his car roaring down the front stretch at Atlanta Motor Speedway while his eyes raked over her body. The dress hung only to her mid-thigh, and her legs were long and shapely in those tan stockings, finished off with sexy, strappy black heels.

Her milky white shoulders were naked except for the thin straps. The dress dipped down into her cleavage, showing just enough of her soft, ivory skin to cause his jeans to feel too tight and his mouth to run as dry and the Sahara Desert.

"She's beautiful," his father whispered, his words echoing Reese's thoughts.

"That's an understatement." Reese's answer was a hoarse whisper.

"Go kiss your bride, son." His father smacked his shoulder, nudging him forward.

Reese started across the room, only to be stopped by Sandy. "Hey, you." She jammed her hands onto her small hips and threw her long blond hair over her shoulder. "What's this crap about you gettin' married? You said you were single a month ago."

"I was, but I'm now not." Reese started past her, but her hand on his forearm stopped him.

"Whoa. I'm not done. How did you wind up with Lacey? I never even heard you were dating her, and I checked around." Her blue eyes assessed him.

"Maybe I kept it a secret because it was none of anyone else's business." He put his hands on her arms and gently moved her. "Excuse me. My bride's waiting for me."

"Maybe you're full of it." She pursed her lips.

"Excuse me?" He shook his head in disbelief of her direct words. *What the heck is her problem?*

Her eyes moved down to his hand. "Where's your wedding ring?"

"If it's any of your business, it's being sized at the jewelers."

She glanced at his trousers and then back up to his eyes. "She's not your type. I'm your type. Plus, you're not the marrying kind, Reese. I know you."

"No, you knew me four years ago. Now, if you'll excuse me—"

Sandy raised her manicured eyebrows. "Is she pregnant?"

Why did people keep assuming that? Reese gritted his teeth in irritation. "No, she's not."

"Did she trap you?" Sandy's assumption infuriated him further.

He folded his arms, staring at her. Part of him wanted to rip her a new one, but another part of him wanted to blow off her rude comments. He mentally debated how to handle her, knowing full well anything he said would be broadcast through the race shop and then through the pits at the track.

"She did, didn't she?" Sandy's smile was smug while she ran a long, red finger over his chest and stepped close enough for him to inhale her overpowering sweet perfume. "I thought so. Well, when you decide to give up on her, my door will always be open to you."

He grabbed her wrist, and her eyes widened in awe. He then leaned down to her ear. "If you ever speak about my wife that way again, I will tell the entire team about how you cheated on me with three of my competitors and then ran off to California like the cheap floozy you are."

While she huffed at him, he let her wrist go and started across the room where Lacey scowled while speaking to Krista.

"Who invited her?" Lacey snipped over the blare of the music, watching Sandy run her finger over Reese's chest.

"I think the whole team was invited," Krista said with a shrug. "Don't worry about her. Reese only has eyes for you. Did you see the look on his face when you made your grand entrance?"

"If she doesn't get her talons off my husband, I'm going to break them." Lacey's stomach twisted while Sandy moved closer to him. She felt sick with jealousy and fury.

Krista made a noise similar to a meow and then snickered.

Lacey scanned the room of people, amazed by how many had come. There had to be close to fifty. A throng swayed and bopped on a makeshift dance floor in the center of the large room. A group of men played pool in the corner, and more stood by the bar drinking beer and eating snacks.

Lacey's eyes found Reese again, and he held Sandy's wrists while he said something in her ear. She prayed he was telling her off and not making plans to meet her later. From his expression, he looked upset, but she didn't trust Sandy as far as she could throw her. Her body tensed with animosity.

When Sandy looked at Reese, Lacey saw a deep, serious attraction, and it made Lacey very, very nervous.

"See?" Krista asked. "He pushed her away and here he comes.

I told you he only has eyes for you."

Lacey hoped Krista was right while Reese maneuvered through the crowd toward her. Her heart hammered in her chest, watching a smile form on his sexy lips.

"You look amazing," he told her, taking her hands in his.

"You don't look so bad yourself."

"Would you join me in a toast?" He held out his arm.

"I'd be honored." She looped her arm around his.

Lacey relaxed while she and Reese chatted with friends, toasted their marriage with champagne, and danced. The few hours the party lasted flew by at lightning speed. Around midnight, the guests began to leave, congratulating Reese and Lacey on their way to the door.

By twelve-thirty, only a few friends remained. While Reese escorted the last of the revelers to the door, Lacey and Krista picked up the cans, bottles, and plastic champagne flutes scattered about the room, filling large trash bags.

"You made out like a bandit," Krista said, handing Lacey a stack of envelopes.

"What's this?" Lacey dropped the last beer bottle into the bag and took the cards.

"Your wedding gifts, silly." Krista gave Lacey a confused look while picking up her purse.

"Oh." Lacey stared at the cards. "This wasn't necessary."

"Of course it was. You get married, you throw a party, and you get gifts. That's the tradition." Krista smirked. "Like sex on your wedding night."

Lacey's cheeks flushed as she scanned the room, relieved to find it empty. "Drop the sex issue."

Her best friend grinned, heading toward the basement stairs. "You should go slip into that negligee before he gets upstairs."

"I will do no such thing." Lacey shook her head with emphasis while they ascended the stairs. "In fact, let me get it for you, so you can return it. I'm sure it wasn't cheap." She wasn't going to try to seduce Reese after he'd made it perfectly clear that they were going to stay in separate rooms. She wasn't going to turn into a slut overnight.

"I won't take it back, and you'll wear it. Trust me. It may not be tonight, but you will."

"Why are you so sure?" Lacey faced her best friend at the top of the stairs.

"I'm telling you that man is crazy about you. It's written all over his face."

"It's all an act. We're giving the appearance we're this happy couple that just realized we're in love. But it's a facade. And if I allow myself to fall into his arms, I'll be that much more heartbroken when he leaves and gets it annulled."

"You're too stubborn for your own good, Lacey Mitchell." Her friend wagged a finger at her as if she were chastising a child. "Believe what you want. But if you let him slip through your fingers without even trying, you'll be even more heartbroken."

Lacey shook her head while they moved through the kitchen toward the front door. Krista was wrong, dead wrong. If Reese wanted to have a real marriage, then why did he give her his bedroom and move down the hall? Why did he promise her a separate bed at the track? He kept telling her they were together to solve the mysteries at Southern Racing.

There was no love, no romance—just mutual respect and friendship. Along with a truck full of attraction and lust—at least on her part. Lacey sighed with disappointment. She did want a real marriage with him, but it wasn't going to happen. Trying to seduce him wouldn't create it, either.

"Call me tomorrow, okay?" Krista asked, heading into the hall.

"Yeah. Thanks for every—" Lacey stopped and gasped when

they stepped into the foyer, where Reese and Sandy stood talking at the front door.

When Sandy reached up and touched his chest, Lacey's stomach roiled. Jealousy roared through her veins.

Lacey's eyes narrowed at Krista. "If he only wants me, then what's that called?" She jammed her hands on her hips.

"I think that's a desperate slut trying to steal your husband." Krista stalked toward the door.

Lacey tugged her arm. "What are you doing?"

"I'm going to interrupt them." Krista yanked her arm back, marching toward Reese and Sandy who were engrossed in what looked like a deep conversation.

Lacey stayed back, out of their line of sight.

"Well, good night." Krista's voice was little too loud. "Congratulations again, Reese." She gave him a quick hug, and he thanked her.

Krista shot Sandy a very sweet smile. "Don't Reese and Lacey make the cutest couple?" She winked at Lacey then opened the door. "Good night!"

Sandy spotted Lacey and shot her a glare before talking to Reese. Disgusted, Lacey hurried back through the kitchen and up the stairs to the master suite, envy and hurt souring her stomach.

TWENTY

Lacey dropped onto the bed and stared at the little gift bag holding her skimpy lingerie from Krista. She briefly contemplated pulling it on and meeting Reese at the door. But what if he rejected her, saying he wasn't attracted to her? What if he thought she was a slut, since they'd never been involved before? Heck, he'd only kissed her for the first time this morning, so would she be a slut for falling into bed with him?

But they were married! How was she a slut if they were married? They had a license to do it!

Confused, Lacey groaned and flopped onto her face on his pillow. She inhaled the musky scent of his cologne while rolling onto her side. She wondered what it would be like to lie next to him with his arms wrapped around her all night long. She'd bet it would be paradise.

Her eyes moved down the bed to the cards and, sitting up, she snatched them. Kicking off her shoes, she folded her legs under her and opened each card, reading the words and trying to block the uneasiness she felt every time she thought of Reese and Sandy and their secret conversation.

She read the sentiments about brides and grooms, silently marveling how she didn't feel like a bride. Each card had a gift certificate or cash. Most were for department stores, and one was for a wine store.

She shook her head while staring down at her rings. It all was so surreal.

"Penny for your thoughts," Reese's voice said, wrenching her back to the present.

Her eyes darted to the door, where he stood leaning on the frame, his arms folded across his wide chest, and his cowlick falling over his eye. He was so gorgeous that her breath caught in her throat, and she couldn't speak for a moment.

"I didn't mean to startle you." He stepped into the room and crossed to the bed.

"That's okay. I was just looking at our gifts." Suddenly self-conscious, she sat up straighter and smoothed her dress over her thighs.

"What'd we get?" He lowered his long, lean physique on the corner of the bed.

"Gift cards." She handed the gift certificates and greeting cards to him and smiled. "I guess we can go buy a toaster oven."

He chuckled, flipping through the cards. "Cool. You can think about what you want to get."

I want you. "Yeah."

"I think the party went well." He placed the cards on the bed next to him.

"It did." Her heart thumped wildly in her chest.

"I think we have everyone convinced." He sat so close that their legs touched, sending tendrils of heat racing up her thigh.

Trying to ignore the wanting burning in the pit of her belly, she nodded toward his left hand. "I just need to get you a ring."

He waved off the thought. "No big deal. I'll pick one up."

"No." She touched his hand and liquid heat surged through her. "I want to get it. You got my rings."

"Okay." He smiled. "I talked to my dad."

"Was he upset?"

"He's happy we're together, but he was disappointed he wasn't let in our little secret wedding."

"At least he's happy."

"Try ecstatic."

"Really?"

Reese grinned. "I think this made him happier than my championship."

"I doubt that. He cried at the awards banquet."

He glanced across the room toward a photo of him and his team posing in front of his championship car last year. "I guess you're right. But he was happy." Reese stood, yawned, and stretched. "Well, I guess I better pack for Atlanta."

"You haven't packed yet?"

"No. I need to steal some things from here. You can go shower or whatever you need to do." He gestured toward the bathroom door. "I won't come in unless you want me to." His wolfish grin caught her off guard.

She licked her dry lips and her cheeks glowed with embarrassment.

His smile vanished, replaced by a panicked expression. "I was just kidding. I didn't mean anything—"

"It's all right." She stood.

"I didn't mean to scare you."

"It's okay. Really." She cleared her throat. "What time does your flight leave tomorrow?" she asked, changing the uncomfortable subject. His sexual jokes struck a chord in her, filling her with a mixture of excitement and anxiety.

"Eight." He rolled his eyes. "I have to leave here insanely early." He disappeared into the closet. "Are you going into the shop tomorrow?" he called from the closet.

She stood by the door while he filled a duffel bag with shirts and jeans. "Yeah, I'm going to meet with the accounting team and try to figure out what's going on. I guess we'll meet with the board next week and tell them about our plans to reorganize?"

"Sounds good. Are you coming down to Atlanta?"

"I figured I'd fly out Friday sometime."

"Good." Slinging the bag over his shoulder, he stepped toward her. "You'd think I'd just leave some clothes in my bus, but I never do that."

"I'll have to organize the bus for us."

"That's a good idea." Stepping past her, he headed to the armoires and added socks and boxers to the bag.

Lacey glanced at the gift bag from Krista and then back at Reese, who was busy packing. She wondered if the idea had crossed his mind, but she was too nervous to ask. She wanted him, but she was scared he didn't want her. Her gut filled with anxiety and longing for him.

"Well, I guess I'll shower." She fished her favorite silky green pajamas from the dresser and then headed toward the bathroom.

"Lacey," he said.

"Yes?" She spun, facing him.

"Thank you."

"For?" Her stomach plummeted with anticipation at his voice.

"Marrying me." He stepped over to her, and she held her breath.

He cupped her face in his hands and looked deep into her eyes. He leaned down, and she closed her eyes. She could feel his breath on her lips, sending chills through her, momentarily causing her breath to pause and her heart to skip a beat.

She let her mouth go slack. His lips brushed hers, and she melted at his touch. His hands moved down her arms, sending shockwaves of electricity through her. She gazed up at him, and he smiled.

"Good night." He stepped back.

She studied him, her eyes opened wide with doe-like innocence and lips swollen from his kisses. She closed the door with a click.

While he finished packing, he tried in vain not to imagine her undressing on the other side of the door. He wanted her so badly that his body ached for her touch. She'd been more beautiful than ever at the party. He couldn't take his eyes off her. He was so darned proud she was his wife.

So then why was he packing his things and going to sleep in the guest room? They were married, right?

But they weren't *really* married. It was just a business deal to get control of the company. She didn't really love him, and he didn't really love her. He had to force himself to put intimate feelings for her out of his mind and think of her as his "squirt."

But she wasn't a squirt. She was a grown, beautiful, sexy woman who made his body tighten and his heart pound in his chest every time they kissed. And, darn it, he loved kissing Lacey more than any woman he'd ever kissed, and he'd kissed quite a few. Lacey was different. She stirred things in him he'd never felt before.

And that bothered the crap out of him.

He'd known Lacey since she was born. How could she have such an effect on him? Was that natural? Was it sane? He didn't know the answers to those questions. All he knew was he wanted to kiss her—often. It seemed that she liked kissing him too. She opened to him, allowing her lips to savor his taste while he savored hers.

He studied his bed while turning toward the door. He wanted to kiss her there, in that bed. He wanted to make love to her. It was their wedding night, so it seemed like a natural progression.

He heard the water running from the shower in his master bathroom. Sighing, he pushed away fantasies of her gorgeous body under the stream of water while he sauntered out into the hall.

Shaking his head, he stepped into the guest room. He had to let go of these crazy sexual feelings for Lacey and remind himself they weren't really married. They were friends who were going to work together for a common goal of saving her father's company and solving the mystery of his and Veronica's death.

Reese tossed his bag onto the floor and stripped down to his boxers before turning off the light and climbing into the bed. Rolling onto his stomach, he groaned and punched the pillow. Why did he have to spend his wedding night alone when his beautiful wife was just down the hall?

Lacey tried to push Reese and his incredible kisses out of her mind while pouring through file after file on her desk Thursday afternoon. She'd spent all morning in meetings, learning everything she could about the company and how the accounting and marketing departments were run.

She stared down at the spreadsheets and forced herself to concentrate on the numbers, but her mind kept defying her. Within a matter of seconds, she was lost in memories of Reese in his jeans and leather jacket hugging her goodbye in the kitchen earlier this morning, his cologne filling her senses while he told her he looked forward to seeing her Friday night.

Stop it!

She threw her pencil down and buried her face in her hands. She had to quit torturing herself. So what if he hugged her and gave her a quick kiss? That didn't mean her loved her. He was just going through the motions, practicing for their public performances at the track this weekend. They had to behave like a married couple, so his affection was merely an act.

The loud ring of her desk phone cut through her thoughts and brought her back to reality.

"Lacey Fowler Mitchell," she said, balancing the receiver on her shoulder and organizing the papers on her desk.

"You're doing the hyphenated last name thing, huh?" Krista asked, snapping her gum.

"No." Lacey leaned back in her chair. "I just automatically

say Fowler. I figured I better add on Mitchell and get used to it."

"So, how'd he like my little gift last night?" Her best friend's smile emanated through her voice.

Annoyed, Lacey rolled her eyes. Leave it to Krista to cut to the chase. "He didn't get to see it."

"You chickened out." Her gum smacked.

Lacey sighed. "Not exactly."

"What does that mean?"

"He wasn't interested."

"Did you even model the lingerie for him?"

Lacey frowned. "No."

"So, how do you know he wasn't interested?"

"Because of his body language. He kissed me, said good night, and left."

"He was probably waiting for you to give him a sign that it was okay."

Lacey's gaze collided with the photo of Reese standing in Victory Lane with his championship trophy last year. She studied his face. "I didn't push him away. I figured he'd take that as a hint that I wouldn't have stopped him."

"Men are stupid, Lace. You gotta hit 'em with a brick." The gum snapped again.

"And when did you become such an expert?" She absently twisted the phone cord around her finger while examining her desk.

"When I fell for Tommy."

Lacey grinned. "Is that so?" It was so good to hear Krista was happy after the losers she'd dated.

"Yup. You gotta hit him over the head and make him realize he wants you as much as you want him."

"Well, maybe in Atlanta." Despite disagreeing with Krista, she told her what she wanted to hear. Lacey shook her head.

She couldn't fathom forcing herself on Reese. "I didn't get a chance to thank you for the lovely party," she said, changing the subject.

"You're welcome." Krista chewed loudly. "So, are you sitting down?"

"Yeah. What's up?" Lacey sat up straight.

"Can you boot up the Internet?"

"Sure." She cut her gaze to her computer and smacked the mouse, bringing the screen back to life. "What am I typing?"

"Try *racinggossip.com*. Brace yourself. You're going to be shocked."

While her stomach clenched with anxiety, Lacey typed in the URL. A website popped up with *All Racing Rumors Fit to Whisper* emblazoned across the top. Her mouth gaped when she read the headline smack-dab in the middle of the page—*Champion Reese Mitchell marries owner's daughter.*

She gasped as she skimmed the article, which offered questions on why "known playboy" Reese would suddenly marry—was he after the company, was he after her father's money, or was she pregnant?

There was no mention of the possibility of love. She and Reese had their work cut out for them if they were going to convince the public that they were truly a happy couple.

"Oh, no!" Lacey's voice rose. "How can they say this about us?"

Krista sighed while chewing. "I know. I hated to tell you about it, but I figured you should hear it from me before you faced the media frenzy in Atlanta. I talked to Tommy earlier, and he said the reporters were cornering Reese all morning."

"Great." Lacey closed the website window and shook her head, dread gripping her stomach. "This was a mistake. They're disrespecting my father's memory."

"No, they aren't." Her friend's words were emphatic. "This

will pass. Some driver will do something stupid on the racetrack or make a stupid comment about someone else, and the gossip mongers will turn to him. Just ignore what people say. You and Reese will rise above this. When they see you two together, all of their vicious rumors will pass."

"Until we get divorced."

"You won't get divorced."

"Krista, please don't start."

"Look, I gotta run. My boss is calling me into a meeting. Call me later."

"Okay. Bye." Lacey dropped the phone into the cradle and blew out a long sigh before turning back to the spreadsheets. She tried to push the vicious rumors from her mind, but they still continued to peck at her.

TWENTY-ONE

Lacey hugged the accordion file to her chest while loping through the secured parking area at Atlanta Motor Speedway late Friday night. Her plan to arrive by nine was ruined when she stayed at the office past seven to delve into more files.

Since her bags were packed in her car, she managed to get a nine o'clock flight. Reese had called her cell four times to check on her and offered several times to meet her at the airport, but she insisted she could catch a cab. Lacey smiled to herself, recalling his concerned voice. Hope swelled within her. Maybe he did care after all.

Glancing at her watch, she pushed the thought aside. It was just past midnight. She was happy to see the lights inside the motor coach still burning and the reflection of the large television flickering through the blinds. Her boots clicked up the metal steps, and she lightly knocked on the door.

The door opened with a whoosh, causing her pulse to quicken at the sight of Reese in boxers and a t-shirt. He smelled of soap and his dark hair was wet, evidence he'd recently showered.

"Hey there. I started to get worried and considered calling the highway patrol out to find you." He took her hand and helped her up the last step.

"Traffic was awful." She dropped her bags by the sofa and slapped the file onto the counter separating the den from the kitchen area.

"Thirsty?" He stepped into the kitchen and fished two colas

from the refrigerator.

"Thanks." She took the soda and opened it.

"How's work?" He popped his can and gulped a drink while leaning on the other side of the counter.

"Busy." She shook her head and sipped from the soda. "I think I've taken on more than I can handle, though."

He raised an eyebrow. "You? Lacey Fowler not handle something? Ha."

"Lacey Fowler Mitchell." She smirked.

"How could I forget?" He raised his cola to toast her. "I'm sorry, Mrs. Mitchell."

She snapped her fingers. "That reminds me. I have a present for you." She fished a small box from the pocket of her jacket.

"Oh?" He placed the can down on the counter.

"I'm sorry this is late." She handed him the box and bit her lower lip, hoping he'd like it.

Reese opened the box. Lifting the simple gold band, he slipped it on his ring finger.

"Does it fit?"

"Perfectly." He came around the bar and embraced her. "Thank you."

Lacey held her breath and excitement raced through her. Oh, how she'd missed him the day they were apart. How dumb was that?

"I guess we're really married now, huh?" He smiled down at her, pushing a lock of hair from her face.

"Yeah," she whispered, wishing she had enough confidence to kiss him. Thoughts of the rumors slammed through her mind, deflating her fantasy. "So, how bad have the reporters been?"

He grabbed his drink and gestured toward the sofa. "Not too bad. They've asked me if it's true we're married. I've said 'yes.' That's about it." He lowered himself into a chair.

She followed him to the den and sat on the sofa across from

him. "Tommy told Krista you'd been cornered constantly."

He shook his head and took a drink. "Not that bad."

"Have you seen the gossip on the Internet about us?"

"Nope, and I don't care what people say."

"They're saying you must've married me for my dad's company, for my dad's money, or because I'm pregnant."

He shrugged. "Screw what they say."

"It doesn't bother you?"

"Nope." He took a long drink.

"Why not?"

"Because it's not true."

She gripped the cool can in her clammy hand while irritation bubbled within her. "But you did marry me for the company, Reese."

"Not entirely."

"What do you mean?" She studied his blue eyes, wishing she could read his thoughts.

"We got married to save the company and figure out why your father passed away. I didn't marry you to steal the company from you. We're a team, right?"

"Right." She took another drink, glancing at the gold band on his hand. It looked strange, even out of place, but she loved seeing it there. Knowing he was wearing the band gave her a twinge of confidence that they'd make it as a team.

"I heard from the private investigator."

Her gaze snapped to his. "What'd he say?"

He raked his hand through his hair. "He's working on getting cell phone records, but he knows our fathers talked the night your dad died."

"Oh."

"So, it looks like there's a possibility that my dad may be . . . well, guilty."

"Not guilty, Reese." She shook her head. "I don't think he

could ever do anything as awful as kill someone."

His glance was skeptical.

"However, I do believe he's involved somehow," she added.

"What've you got?" He nodded toward the file.

"Not a whole lot yet." She picked up the file and, crossing the room, sat beside him, inhaling his fresh scent of soap mixed with spicy aftershave. "I can tell you that payments have been made to Racing Industries, Inc., for over fifteen years." Pulling out the papers, she smacked them on her lap.

"Really?" Placing his cola down on the end table, he picked up a spreadsheet.

"Yeah, it's so strange." She leaned over and pointed to numbers, their thighs touching and her hand brushing his. Her pulse raced and her cheeks heated. Pushing sensual thoughts aside, she tried to concentrate on the numbers. "See how the payments were made every month for a while and then bi-monthly? Then it was every few months."

He nodded.

"And the payments were weird," she said. "They were for five hundred, then seven-fifty, and then twelve-hundred. I went through receipts, and I can't find any for that company. I can't find anything on the Internet either." She leaned closer, placing her hand on his thigh, sending more heat roaring through her veins.

"I asked around, and none of the guys have heard of the company." Reese put the spreadsheet down on his lap. "So, what do you think?"

"I think I'm in over my head." She sighed, leaning back on the sofa. "I think I should go back to school and sign my part of the company over to you. Or I can be a silent partner."

"Nope, not gonna happen. I won't let you."

She looked up when he touched her hair. "Reese, I've been in the office a total of three days, and I'm stressed out and confused. I have no idea what I'm doing, and the board is going to find out. I'm way out of my league."

"No, you're not." His eyes were reassuring. "We're in this together, remember?"

"Yeah, but you need to concentrate on driving, not this crap. I can't drag you away from the track to help me figure out what all this means."

"But you can meet me here, and we can stay up all night talking about it."

"No, we can't." She sat forward and pointed to the clock on the stereo system across the room. "It's almost one. You need your sleep for tomorrow."

"I've been known to get three-hour's sleep and win races. I won Bristol after only two hours."

"What were you doing up all night?" She regretted the words as they came out. She held up her hand, wishing she could take them back. "Forget I asked." She didn't want to hear about Reese with other women. The mere notion made her stomach sour.

"Why?" He raised an eyebrow in question.

"Because I don't want to hear about your sexual escapades."

"Why do you assume I was up all night with a girl?"

Her cheeks immediately heated. "I didn't mean to imply . . ." She stopped speaking and closed her eyes. "I'm sorry."

He laughed. "It's okay. I actually had the flu that night."

Her eyes flew open. "You did?"

"You don't remember?" His blue orbs studied hers. "You had a picture of us on pit road on your dresser in your apartment. Don't you remember that day?"

Lacey gasped, recognition flashing in her mind. "That's right. You were so sick you couldn't keep one of those sports drinks down, but you wouldn't let anyone else drive your car."

He nodded. "Right, and I somehow won that race."

"Because you're the best." She felt like a lovesick fan after the words escaped her mouth.

"Not really." He shook his head. "But I guess it's okay if my wife believes that." He grimaced. "And I hope my wife knows I'm not the ladies' man everyone says I am."

"Reese, I didn't mean—"

"It's okay. Forget it." He waved off the thought. "So, back to this low self-esteem issue you have. We can do this together. You'll be the one at the office while I'm investigating things at the track."

"Right." She took the papers from his lap and put them back in the file.

"So, who approves the payments to this company?" he asked.

"Ryan Matthews couldn't really tell me. He said they've been automatic for so long that he didn't know. He promised to check on it." She dropped the file on the floor and then sat back. "Until I find that out, I'll just keep searching the files. I want to know why my dad's dead."

He took her hands in his. "We'll figure this out. I promise you. It just might take longer than we'd hoped."

He stared into her eyes, and she felt intensity spark between them like fireworks on the Fourth of July. She had to get away from him before they did something she might regret later.

"I better let you get some sleep." Tugging her hands back, she stood. "I'm sure you have a full day tomorrow."

Sighing, he stood, towering over her. "I've got practice, sponsor appearances, meetings, and all that jazz." He placed his drink on the counter. "Let me show you to your room. I changed the sheets for you."

But I love sleeping in your scent. "Thanks." She followed him down the aisle to the bedroom area.

"Here you go." He made a sweeping gesture toward the area containing a king-size bed and counters with built-in drawers.

"You can put your clothes in the drawers or the closet over here."

"Where will you sleep?"

He nodded toward the den area. "The sofa's really comfortable."

"But—"

"It's okay." He touched her shoulder. "The bathroom is over here. Towels are in the little cabinet in there. Just yell if you need anything."

"Will you wake me when you get up?"

"Sure thing." He leaned down and his lips brushed her cheek. "Good night."

"Night." She watched him saunter down the aisle, and Krista's words echoed in her head. Should she hit him with a brick and invite him to stay with her? But what would the consequences be? Would they regret it in the morning and ruin the friendship they'd cherished throughout their lives?

But they were married. Didn't that alone change everything?

Regret gnawing at her, Lacey closed the curtain separating her room from the aisle and opened her bag. Her eyes immediately focused on the negligee from Krista. Her inner voice had told her to pack it. She picked it up. The white lace was soft and delicate, and so, so revealing, leaving very little to the imagination. She wondered how ridiculous she'd look in it. Would he laugh at her and tell her she'd always be a squirt and never a real woman to him?

She shook her head while burying the lingerie in her bag. Who was she kidding? She didn't know the first thing about seducing a man. How could she seduce a man she'd loved from afar for most of her life? The idea of undressing in front of Reese scared her to death. It would be awkward and embarrassing.

Grabbing her bag, she retreated to the bathroom. She quickly showered, dressed in her pajamas, brushed her teeth, and opened the door.

Glancing down the aisle, she found the lights were off. She assumed Reese was already asleep. Sighing with disappointment, she stepped back into the bedroom area and crawled into bed. Snuggling down, she fantasized about having Reese next to her as she fell asleep.

Twenty-Two

"Dude, you can't get married without a bachelor party." Brett Turner tapped his clipboard with his pencil while leaning on the fender of the 89 Ford in the garage the following evening. "That's sacrilege."

"Well, I did, so just drop it," Reese snapped over the roar of an engine in a neighboring stall.

"Nuh-uh." Brett turned to the crew milling around the stall and working on the car. "Don't y'all think we need to take Reese out and celebrate his nuptials? We weren't good enough to go to his wedding or his reception, so we at least owe him a trip to Jug's."

His crewmembers traded hoots, hollers, high-fives, and claps.

"Jug's?" Reese stole a glance at Lacey chatting with Krista and Tommy at the other end of the garage. She wouldn't appreciate him going out drinking with the guys tonight. Her low self-esteem would lead her to believe he didn't want to spend time with her, and that would lead to their first argument as newlyweds. He didn't want to ruin their first weekend together.

Reese grimaced, looking at his crew chief. "I don't think so."

"What? Now that you're an old married man you can't go out for some hot wings and good scenery?" asked Brett with feigned innocence.

"Look, we've got a race tomorrow, and I don't think—"

"How about we go out early?" His crew chief surveyed the crew. "You guys want to head out to Jug's at, say, seven? Eight?"

179

The throng of men in matching uniforms gave approval with more claps and nods.

"I think it's been decided for you, brother. Go tell your old lady you're going out with the guys for a few hours. She can hold down the fort for you while you're gone." He stepped closer, waggling his eyebrows. "I bet she'll even get a little bit of time to miss you."

Reese inwardly groaned. Lacey wouldn't be happy with the idea of his going to a restaurant where the waitresses were hired based on their bust size and how they looked in tight denim.

With the crew working on his car, Reese's eyes darted back to Lacey. She was a vision in that hunter green sweatshirt and tight jeans. All day long he'd had a difficult time taking his eyes off her.

She'd seemed more beautiful lately. He didn't know how he'd kept his hands to himself last night. When she'd stepped into his bus, he was beside himself with relief that she'd made it safely. She gave him the ring, and he felt another rush of warm affection for her. Reese cut his eyes to his left hand. That silly piece of metal meant the world to him.

When they'd sat together on the sofa and talked, he wanted to pull her into his arms and kiss her. He'd stayed awake a good part of the night thinking about her and wishing he were in bed with her. Maybe he was losing his mind, but the attachment he felt for her had grown by leaps and bounds in the past few days. Was it the marriage or was it something else?

Or maybe it was a combination of things?

Whatever it was, it was driving him crazy! The idea of leaving her to go out with the crew for a few hours seemed so undesirable. He wanted to cherish every moment they had together.

Yeah, he was losing it all right.

The day had flown by for Reese. The morning had been full of practice, meetings, and more practice. During the afternoon,

Lacey had accompanied him to the souvenir trailer, where he'd signed autographs for a few hours. Then they went to a sponsor appearance, where he spoke to reporters and hobnobbed with some of his sponsor's VIPs. From there, it was another practice session. He'd been looking forward to a quiet evening with Lacey in the bus. So, maybe Brett was right, and Reese was an old married man.

"Did you hear a word I just said?" His crew chief's question startled Reese back to the present.

"Huh?" Reese looked at him.

"Quit staring at your wife and listen to me."

Reese frowned, folding his arms. Was his attachment to his bride that obvious?

"We need to finish talking about this hunk of junk you call a race car," his crew chief said. "When we're done, you can kiss your bride goodbye, and we'll go out and drink some beers at Jug's."

"You sure you're okay with me going out tonight?" Reese combed his wet hair in front of the bathroom mirror.

"It's fine." Smiling, Lacey stood in the doorway, her arms crossed over her chest. "I can go through the files while you're gone."

He combed the front back again, but no matter what he did, his hair wound up in his eyes. He groaned with annoyance. "I hate this cowlick. Maybe I should shave my head."

"Don't you dare." Her gaze challenged him in the reflection.

"Why not?" he asked.

"It's adorable. If you shave it, I'll divorce you."

He raised an eyebrow. *Adorable? She thinks I'm adorable?*

"When do you think you'll be home?" She tilted her head, and he couldn't help but think she was adorable, too.

Putting down the comb, he gave up on the cowlick. "I'll try

to be back by eleven. These guys get kinda rowdy, but I'll watch the time."

"You don't have to watch the clock. I was just wondering. Just don't bring home any of those waitresses, okay?" She wagged a finger at his reflection in the mirror.

He shook his head. "Don't you worry about that. None of them can hold a candle to your beauty."

"Yeah, but I can't compete with their cup sizes." Her cheeks flushed a bright crimson, and her gorgeous emerald eyes widened. "Did I just say that out loud?" She cupped her mouth with her hands.

Grinning, he faced her. "I think yours are perfect."

Her eyes looked as if they were going to pop out of her head and the cute red of her cheeks deepened. "I'm going to go get a drink."

He chuckled while he finished getting ready. When he walked out to the kitchen, he found her sitting in front of the television, flipping through the accordion file. Her gaze met his, and she immediately blushed again. Yup, she was adorable.

"Well, I'll see you later. Call my cell if you need me," he said.

She nodded and smiled. "Have fun."

Reese and his team took over the far corner of Jug's. The guys chatted and laughed while consuming pitcher after pitcher of beer and more hot wings than he could count. The waitress recognized Reese immediately and all but threw herself at him. He was flattered by her enthusiasm, but his mind wasn't on the buxom blonde in the tight jeans and low-cut halter top. His thoughts were with the lovely redhead waiting for him back at his bus.

It seemed that with every glass of beer, he concentrated more on Lacey and warmth roared through his veins. He wasn't sure if the alcohol was clouding his mind or opening it up.

"I was surprised you went off and tied the knot without telling me, but I don't think you could've done any better than Lacey," Brett said, pouring himself another glass of beer.

Reese studied his crew chief over his glass, contemplating his words. What was Brett getting at? He wasn't one to discuss his personal life often.

"Lacey's head and shoulders above those chicks you'd been dating," Brett continued.

"Yeah, like Sandy. Oh man, what a hose bag." Tim, a pit crewmember, rolled his eyes.

"She's all but stripped and thrown herself at you in the shop," Rob added with a snort.

Reese nodded and took another drink. The guys did have a point.

"But Lacey's got class. She's pretty and smart as a whip. Here's to Reese finally growing up and finding the right woman." Brett raised his glass.

"Hear, hear," Tim chimed in.

The team raised their glasses and toasted Reese. He took a long drink and then stared down at the empty mug before him. They were right. Lacey was special. And she was beautiful, intelligent, and, well, perfect.

And then it hit him like a ton of bricks.

He loved her.

He absolutely *loved* her.

With all his heart.

All his soul.

"Holy cow," Reese whispered.

I'm not crazy.

I'm crazy about her.

His heart raced in his chest. Reese glanced at the clock on the wall. Eleven-thirty. He had to get back to the bus and tell her so before she fell asleep. He turned to his crew chief.

"You okay, man?" Brett asked.

"I'm great." Reese smiled. "Look, I'm really tired. Would you take me back to the track?"

Brett studied him, his eyebrows rising with suspicion. "Sure."

"Great." Reese stood. "Let's go." He started to turn and stumbled.

"Whoa, brother." His crew chief jumped up and reached for him. "You okay?"

"Never been better." Grinning, Reese grabbed the table for balance. "Come on. Let's go."

Lacey yawned, gazing at the clock. Eleven-forty-five. She stood and stretched. She'd wanted to stay up and wait for Reese, but her eyes were starting to burn with exhaustion. She closed her laptop and placed it on the table by her paperwork. She'd been staring at the files all evening, except for the short break when she showered.

Yawning, she padded down the aisle, her fuzzy slippers slapping the linoleum. She flipped off the hall light, closed the curtain, and crawled into bed. Staring at the ceiling, she wondered when Reese would be back. She hoped he'd arrive home safely. The idea of those guys out drinking and driving made her uneasy.

She was just falling asleep when the door to the bus clicked open and then closed. Rolling to her side, she heard footsteps coming down the aisle and assumed Reese was heading to the bathroom.

"Lacey?" his voice asked outside her room.

"Yeah?" She sat up, looking toward the curtain in the dark, the only crack of light shining from beneath it.

"Can we talk?" His voice was urgent.

Her pulse jumped with worry at his tone. "What's wrong?"

"Can I come in?"

She held the sheet up to her chest. "Of course."

He whipped the curtain back, and she squinted while her eyes adjusted to the light. "I realized something tonight, something that's been staring me in the face for a long time."

"What's that?"

"I love you."

She sucked in a breath and her stomach somersaulted with shock. Was she dreaming or was this a cruel joke?

"I've always loved you, but I never realized it until now." He stepped toward her. "I've been a fool. I've taken you for granted, and I'm so sorry."

"Don't, Reese. Please don't do this." She shook her head, her heart thundering in her chest.

"Do what?" Flabbergasted, his eyes widened. "I'm telling you the truth. I love you."

"No, you're just caught up in the euphoria of being married. You only love me like a sister. That's why you've always called me squirt. I've been your little sister since—"

"No, no!" He rushed to the side of the bed. "I used to think that. But now I know I love you, and I want to be your husband. I mean *really* be your husband."

She swallowed a groan of disappointment. So it was about sex. He wanted to have sex with her to get another notch on his dashboard. Her heart pounded harder in her chest. "It's late, and you're racing tomorrow. Good night." She fought to keep her tone even, despite her irritation.

"Please listen to me." He sat on the edge of the bed, taking her hands in his.

Heat shot through her body at his warm touch. His aftershave permeated the small room and sent her senses spinning. Wanting rose in her soul, and she fought in vain to suppress it.

"I love you," he whispered. "I kept telling myself I was determined to marry you to save the company. The truth is I'm saving myself along with the company."

She stared at him, her eyes widening. "You've had too much beer," she whispered, her voice quavering with love. "You're drunk and confused. Please go to bed."

"Do you love me? If not, then say so, and I'll leave you alone."

Her throat constricted, desire drowning her like a tidal wave. "Reese, I've loved you since I was a kid." Her voice trembled. "You were just too blind to see it."

Running a fingertip down her cheek, he smiled. "I want to be your husband. I want to live like a married couple."

"I can't." She shook her head and shivered from the contact of his touch.

"Why?"

"Because I'd never measure up to the other girls you've been with."

"What do you mean?"

"I've never . . ." Her voice shook. She struggled to find the right words, but they all felt stupid and immature.

"You're a virgin?" His voice was soft and his blue eyes were full of understanding.

Unable to speak, she nodded.

"Lacey, you mean more to me than any woman I've ever known. They'd never measure up to *you.*"

Was he telling the truth? Was it just a line to get into her bed?

Lacey studied Reese's gorgeous azure eyes. They were genuine. She wondered who'd hit him with the brick. Had he run into Krista on his way home?

He leaned forward, his hands cupping her face. She closed her eyes just as his lips brushed hers. She wrapped her arms around his neck, and she couldn't miss the musky smell of him as he pressed her closer. The kiss sent the pit of her stomach into a wild swirl.

"Lacey," he whispered, and she tingled at the sound of her

name on his lips.

No, this isn't right.

She pulled back.

He stared at her, his eyes wide. "What's wrong?" he asked.

"Hold that thought." She popped up from the bed and hurried around it.

"What are you doing?"

"You'll see." She grabbed the negligee from her bag and headed to the bathroom.

Once inside, she locked the door and lowered herself to the lid of the commode. Was she making a mistake? Did he really love her? Lacey groaned and covered her face with her hands. But it felt so right. Being in his arms was—well, it was heaven just like she'd imagined.

She stripped and pulled on the negligee. The top clung to her breasts, making her cleavage seem more plentiful. The thong was very uncomfortable. No wonder Krista once called it butt floss. But she figured she could suffer with it, since she wouldn't have it on for long.

Her body quaked at the thought. Reese Mitchell, the man of her dreams, was going to pull off her clothes and make love to her. A strange mixture of fear and excitement filled her. She checked her reflection and ran a comb through her hair.

Why on earth did she care about her hair when it was going to be mussed in just a few minutes? Taking a deep breath, Lacey opened the door and stepped into the aisle.

Reese's gaze collided with hers, widening with awe. "Lacey?" he asked in a hushed whisper.

She grimaced. "I look ridiculous, don't I?"

"N-no." He stood, shaking his head. "You look *spectacular.*"

She approached him, and in one forward motion, she was in his arms. He kissed her, and she parted her lips, allowing his tongue to enter her mouth. As their tongues moved in a seductive dance, she slowly unbuttoned his shirt and slid it off his arms, allowing it to fall to the floor. She then pulled his t-shirt up and over his head. Liquid heat slid through her veins.

His lips seared a path down her neck then her shoulders, causing her to groan with pleasure. She ran her fingertips down his wide, ribbed chest.

"I love you, Lacey," his voice was husky in her ear. "I always have."

Smiling, she climbed onto the bed, took his hand, and tugged him toward her. As he moved over her, she closed her eyes . . .

TWENTY-THREE

Lacey snuggled down onto Reese's hard, bare chest while his fingers drew circles on her back, chills spiraling down her spine.

Feeling completely relaxed for the first time in weeks, she smiled up at him through the dark. Making love to him was more wonderful than she'd ever imagined. He was warm, gentle, loving, and so, so passionate. Her toes curled at the thought of the ecstasy he'd given her.

She was one-hundred-percent crazy about him.

Sighing, she rested her cheek on his chest and closed her eyes, enjoying the musical rhythm of his heartbeat.

Life was good.

No, life was perfect.

"Whatcha thinkin' about?" his voice rumbled from his chest below her.

"You," she whispered.

"Have you really loved me since you were a kid?"

"Yes."

"Why didn't you tell me?"

"Because you were too busy with your flavors of the month to notice me." She cuddled up to him while his fingers caressed her hair. "I was wicked jealous of all of your girlfriends."

He was silent for a moment. "I'm sorry."

"It worked out anyway."

"Yes, it did." He smiled to himself.

If anyone had told him two weeks ago that he'd be in bed

with Lacey Fowler, or Lacey Fowler *Mitchell,* he'd have said the person was crazy. But here he was, naked with Lacey, and he felt like a million bucks. Making love to her had been amazing. It had been better than anything he'd ever experienced with any other woman. It was real love.

Lacey was so responsive to him. When he touched her, she trembled. And when she reached that peak, it was as if the earth really moved beneath them.

He was nuts about her. And he was happy, really happy. Shoot, he was happier than he'd ever been.

How had he missed this for so long? Why hadn't he ever noticed her feelings for him? He'd been a complete dunce for years.

Relaxing, her breathing deepened. He ran his fingers down her back and grabbed the covers. Pulling them up to her neck, he rubbed her bare arms. Lacey sighed in her sleep and wrapped her arms around his waist.

Reese leaned down, kissed her head, and closed his eyes. Within minutes, he fell into a deep sleep.

"Oh wow, Lacey! You finally did it!" Krista's grin was wide while they stood on pit road the following afternoon.

Lacey's cheeks flushed. "How did you know?"

"It's written all over your face." Her best friend hugged her. "I'm so happy for you!"

"Thanks." Stepping back, she cut her eyes to Reese standing by his car and talking to his team before the pre-race ceremonies. He looked so sexy in his fire suit. "I'm happy for me, too."

"So, how was it?"

Lacey's cheeks burned more.

"That good, huh?" Krista smirked.

"Try amazing, mind-blowing, earth shattering." Lacey chortled.

Tommy walked up behind Krista and wrapped his arms around her waist. "What are you girls talking about?"

"Wouldn't you like to know?" Krista looked up at him, and their lips brushed.

Tommy glanced between Lacey and Krista. "It's time for opening ceremonies."

Krista turned to Lacey. "See you in a bit."

"Good luck," Lacey said to Tommy.

"Thanks." He smiled, embracing Krista.

Lacey maneuvered through the crowd of fans, officials, crew-members, and reporters toward Reese. When his eyes met hers, he smiled, and her heartbeat quickened at the memory of their lovemaking last night. She approached and he yanked her into his warm hug.

"I was wondering where you were," he whispered in her ear.

"I was talking to Krista." She glanced up at him, and he brushed his lips against hers, sending chills dancing through her body.

The Master of Ceremonies came over the loudspeaker and welcomed the fans. Reese's team lined up beside him as a minister from a local church gave the Invocation. Reese grasped her hand, running his thumb gently over the side of her palm. A country singer Lacey had never heard of belted out the National Anthem before four Air National Guard jets thundered above them.

While the pit crew traded high-fives, Reese steered Lacey over to the car. "Well, this is it. I'll see you in a few hours." He rested his hands on her shoulders.

"You be safe." She smiled up at him.

"I will. I love you." He pressed his lips to hers, and she drank in the sweetness of his kiss.

When their lips parted, she wrapped her arms around his neck. "I love you, too," she whispered in his ear.

"All right, you two," Brett said as he approached. "Let's break it up. You can continue your honeymoon tonight after the race." He smacked Reese's shoulder. "Climb in the jalopy, brother."

"Yes, Mom." Reese gave his crew chief a mock salute.

Lacey silently admired Reese's rear as he climbed into the race car. She stood by the quarter panel, and Brett leaned in to help him into his safety belts.

When Brett was done, he turned to Lacey. "He wants to talk to you before I close the net."

Lacey leaned in the car. She smiled down at him and felt self-conscious while a television cameraman stood nearby, focusing on them. "Hi."

"I just wanted one more kiss for good luck."

"You don't need luck, Reese. You're the best."

His grin was wolfish while he waggled his eyebrows. "That's what you said last night."

She shook her head. "You have a one-track mind."

"Absolutely, when it comes to you. Kiss me."

She brushed her lips against his. "Good luck. I'll be listening from the box."

His expression was serious. "I love you, Lacey."

"I love you." She stood up and stepped to the side and Brett moved forward.

She watched him fasten the net in the window. Through the net, she could see Reese put in his earplugs and then pull his helmet over his head. She weaved through the crowd to Reese's team's pit stall.

Approaching, she spotted Carl and team manager Rod Smith having a heated discussion behind the large toolbox, known as the war wagon. Both were glaring and gesturing wildly as they spoke. She wondered what they were discussing and why they were so angry. Her stomach clenched, and a feeling of foreboding washed over her. She made a mental note to mention it to

Reese after the race.

She climbed the ladder to the top of the war wagon and sat on a stool. Pulling on a headset, she tuned into the team's channel. A few minutes later, Brett sat on the stool next to her. When the command to start the engines blared over the loudspeaker, the forty-three cars before her on pit road roared to life, sending adrenaline jetting through her veins. She loved the sound of those engines and the smell of the racing fuel permeating the air.

She silently prayed Reese would finish the race safely. She then held her breath, waiting for the cars to head out for the pace laps.

Lacey stood up and screamed when the 89 Ford crossed the finished line, taking the checkered flag first. She jumped into Brett's arms and continued to cheer. Her heart thundered against her ribs.

Reese won!

Her hands had been clenched for the past thirty laps when Reese took the lead. She'd watched his Ford swing low, maneuvering past lapped traffic with only five laps to go. The cars had whizzed by, and Lacey's hair sprayed across her face while her hand lifted, dragging it from her eyes. He was going to do it!

Lacey held her breath for a couple more laps, not realizing she was standing until the car roared over the finish line.

And then . . .

REESE MITCHELL WON!

Her heart soared with a mixture of excitement, love, and pride. She climbed down the ladder and traded hugs and high fives with members of the crew. A reporter shoved a microphone in front of Brett's face, signifying the start of the media frenzy.

The thunder of an engine drew her eyes to the start/finish

line, where Reese's car tore into a noisy, smoky burnout while the crowd cheered him on. Lacey laughed and clapped as Reese spun victory donuts through the grass along the front stretch.

When his car motored around the track to pit road, Lacey headed toward Victory Lane with the crew. The crew lined up on the stage and continued to cheer, and Lacey stood off to the side until the car rumbled into the center of Victory Lane.

She weaved through the crowd, stopping short of the car. Brett removed the window net, revealing Reese pulling off his helmet and taking a long gulp of a sports drink. He looked so sexy with his wet hair and lopsided smile.

He pulled a baseball cap advertising his sponsor over his sweaty head. He laughed when Brett said something to him. The Sports Channel reporter spoke to him and then Reese heaved his long, muscular body through the window of the car.

Tears filled Lacey's eyes when he stood on the door and pumped his arm in the air while his team cheered. A lightning storm of flashbulbs erupted, and he jumped down and hugged Brett. He scanned the crowd. His eyes stopped on Lacey, and with his smile broadening, he took her arm, dragged her to him, and kissed her.

"Congratulations," Lacey said. "I'm so proud of you."

Stepping back, he grinned. "I love you, Lace."

"How does it feel to win again, Reese?" The reporter pushed his microphone into Reese's face, and the cameraman focused on him.

"Awesome, just awesome." He looped his arm around Lacey. "My car was great all day, and my pit stops were perfect. We just had a great day all around." He took a long drink.

"I want to thank my sponsors." His voice breathless with exhaustion, he rattled off the long list. "And I'd like to dedicate this race to the memory of my car owner and friend Greg Fowler and his wife Veronica." He looked down at her, the gleam in his blue eyes making her breath catch in her throat. "And to my lovely bride, Lacey."

Overwhelmed with pride and love, she wiped a tear and smiled at her husband.

"It seems like you're still in championship mode from last year. Do you think you can do it again this year?" the reporter asked.

He nodded. "I think that's possible."

The team behind him hooted and hollered.

The reporter turned to the camera. "There you have it. The 89 is still a force to be reckoned with. Back to you on pit road, Bill."

"All right, let's take some photos," the photographer barked. He walked behind the car and ordered the team members to line up.

"Time for the hat dance," Reese said, removing his baseball cap and catching the ARA hat a series official tossed to the team.

During the "hat dance," the team posed for photographs wearing hats from their various sponsors.

He caught another hat and handed it to Lacey. "Join me with my trophy."

"I'd be honored." She posed with her husband and the trophy while the photographer snapped several photos. In between shots, she scanned Victory Lane for Carl, and she wondered why he would miss such a momentous occasion.

"Have you seen your dad?" she asked.

"You read my mind. I was just wondering where he was."

She looked up at her husband. "I saw him arguing with Rod before the race. He looked pretty upset."

Reese's face was concerned. "I tried to talk to my dad this morning after our driver's meeting, and he was really distracted. It was like he was only listening to half of what I said." He shook his head. "Something's up with him. I'm starting to get worried."

Lacey sighed, the dread from earlier returning. She'd been thinking the same thing but didn't want to worry Reese.

"Quiet, everyone!" the photographer hollered over the chatting. "Smile pretty. Everyone say, 'Victory bonus!' "

Reese's pickup eased into the garage later that evening. Snuggling down in the passenger seat, Lacey yawned while the garage door hummed closed.

"I guess I can forget about celebrating my win with you, huh?" He rubbed her neck, sending currents of desire down her spine.

"Oh, I don't know." She smiled up at him. "You can try to wake me up."

"I can think of a few ways to wake you up." His mouth slowly descended to meet hers, and she felt a dreamy intimacy between them. His lips parted hers in a soul-reaching massage. When he moved back, he left her mouth burning with fire.

She was completely awake now. She ran a fingertip down his shirt. "Let's take this inside."

"Yes, ma'am." He raised his eyebrows while pushing open his door.

After grabbing their bags, they headed into the house.

Crossing the kitchen, she glanced toward the answering machine's red light blinking at hyper-speed. "Looks like a lot of people want to congratulate you on your win."

He dropped his bags. "They can wait."

"Don't you want to know who called?"

He shrugged and wrenched open the refrigerator door. "You can listen if you want. Thirsty?"

"Sure." She hit play, while he retrieved a bottle of champagne left over from their reception.

"Hey, Reese," a sultry female voice said. "Remember me? I just wanted to say good job today. And how could you go and get married? I miss you, baby."

Lacey gasped, her stomach boiling with jealousy.

Reese rushed over to the machine, and she tugged him back when another female voice sounded, also voicing her congratulations for his win and disappointment on his nuptials. When a third similar message started, Lacey stomped from the kitchen and up to the master bedroom, white-hot rage throbbing through her body.

"Lacey! Lacey!" Reese called after her. "Lacey, wait!"

"Leave me alone." She slammed and locked the door before flopping onto the bed. Angry tears threatened her eyes.

"Lacey?" His voice was muffled by the door. "Lacey, please let me in. Don't shut me out. We're married now. Talk to me." A sharp knock sounded on the wood. "This is ridiculous. Why are you angry with me about this? I can't control who calls me. Lacey? Lacey!"

"Go away!" She buried her face in her pillow and the tears spilled from her eyes.

She silently chided herself. How could she believe she could tame Reese Mitchell? He was always known as a playboy, and that image would never fade. She was a fool for dreaming they could have a real marriage.

A pop sounded, and the door clicked open, causing her to sit up with a start.

"We need to talk. This is crazy." Scowling, he crossed the room and sank onto the edge of the bed.

"Yes, the idea of our marriage is completely insane." She swiped the tears from her hot cheeks. "It was a mistake."

"That's not what I meant." Grimacing, he shook his head. "I meant that this"—he gestured between them—"situation is crazy. I didn't encourage those girls to call me."

"But they all seem to think that by calling, you'll have an affair with them."

He wiped an errant tear from her cheek with his fingertip, and the gentleness of his touch warmed her heart.

"They can think whatever the heck they want, but I won't ever cheat on you. You're my *wife,* and they're a distant memory."

"Last night was a mistake. We never should have slept together." Her voice trembled with regret.

He flinched, hurt clouding his blue eyes. "You don't mean that."

"I do. I never should have . . ." her voice tailed off.

"You never should have what?"

"Let you in my heart," she whispered, more tears escaping her eyes.

He pulled her to him. "I let you in mine, completely. I love you, Lacey. You're the only one who matters to me. You have to trust me."

She wrapped her arms around his neck, pressing her face in his chest.

"I love you, Lacey, and only you." His voice was husky in her ear.

Should she believe him? Being in his arms felt so right. But did he mean it? Would he ever hurt her? She didn't know, but she knew she wanted to be with him and only him.

She looked up at him, and his mouth covered hers with hunger. Kissing her devouringly, he eased her down onto the bed and desire shot through her veins like molten lava. He showered kisses around her lips and along her jaw, while she ran her hands through his soft hair. He started to unbutton her blouse, his fingers icy but the palm fiery hot. She grabbed the hem of his shirt and yanked it up and over him.

He slid her blouse off her shoulders and down her arms. His fingers moved beneath her bra, the gentle massage sending currents of wanting through her. Her thoughts fragmented while his hands and lips continued their ravenous search of her body . . .

Twenty-Four

"So, how are you?" Krista sat across from Lacey at a restaurant near the race shop a month later. "I feel like we haven't talked, I mean really talked, in forever. How's married life?"

"It's great." Lacey leaned back in the seat, wishing the headache and queasy feeling in her stomach would pass.

"You don't look like you feel so great."

The server appeared and asked for their orders. Lacey ordered a salad and glass of ice water, and Krista ordered a diet soda, burger, and fries.

Krista raised her eyebrows after the server had left. "A salad and water? You feeling okay?"

"No." Lacey rubbed her temples. "I haven't felt okay in a while now." Her stomach twisted at the whiff an unpleasant, sweet smell. "What perfume are you wearing?"

Krista looked confused. "What I always wear."

"It's making me sick." Lacey covered her mouth with her hands while a smile spread on Krista's lips. "I'm going to be sick, and you think it's funny?"

"What else is bothering you, Lace?" Her best friend leaned forward in the booth.

"I can hardly keep anything down, and my head's pounding." She leaned forward, wincing when her chest touched the table. "And my boobs are kinda sensitive. I nearly screamed when Reese touched me the other night."

Krista's smile widened. "Girlfriend, you're pregnant."

"I am not!" Lacey wailed.

"When was your last time of the month?"

Lacey gasped. "Gosh, I don't remember. It was around my dad's funeral, I guess." She stopped. "No. Wait. Maybe just before the wedding."

Krista folded her arms and gave a knowing nod. "My sister had all of those same symptoms when she was pregnant with Alyssa."

A feeling of dread washed over Lacey while the server brought their drinks. She took a sip, considering Krista's words. "I can't be pregnant," she whispered when the server was gone.

"Are you on the pill?"

"I haven't had a chance to see my doctor. It's been kinda hectic."

"Have you used any other protection?"

Lacey grimaced. "No."

"Have you been having sex?"

"Try every night we're together. He's an animal." Her cheeks heated with embarrassment.

Krista shrugged. "Well, there you have it."

Lacey covered her face with her hands. "Oh, no."

"Let's go buy a test after we eat. Then you'll know for sure. Those things are super accurate, at least my sister says so."

Lacey felt Krista's hands on her arms.

"Hey, it's not so bad," her best friend said. "You're married and in love. You'll be fine."

"This isn't the right time." Lacey sighed, meeting Krista's gaze.

"It's never the right time. At least, that's what Jenna says. Alyssa wasn't planned, but she's the apple of Jenna's eye. A baby is a blessing, no matter what."

Lacey muffled a groan. She wasn't in the mood for Krista's lectures. "But things are so stressful at the shop. I feel like I'm losing my mind. Reese is constantly on the road. He went to test at Dover yesterday and then flew right to Phoenix today. I won't see him until tomorrow night."

She covered her face with her hands again while desperation filled her. "I wish he were here to help me figure out what to do. Talking on the phone's not the same." Her throat constricted. Why was she so darned emotional? All she wanted to do lately was cry.

"So go see him tonight." Her best friend rubbed her arms. "Fly out there and talk to him. He's your husband. He loves you."

Lacey sniffed. "I just don't know how to tell him I think his dad's embezzling money from the company."

"What?" Krista's eyes widened.

"I found some receipts last night. I waited until Carl left and then snooped in his office because he's been acting so strange lately. He's really high-strung, and he loses his temper at the drop of a hat. He even yelled at me last week about something stupid."

"Is he still upset you and Reese took over the company?"

"Maybe. I don't know." She shrugged. "I thought we'd moved past that. He was really angry when we told him we were taking over as co-CEOs. But then he seemed to accept being Vice President for Team Operations. Now he's back to being stressed all the time. He's like a time bomb waiting to go off. I feel like I'm walking on eggshells every time I see him."

Lacey took a deep, cleansing breath, hoping to stop herself from sobbing. "Anyway, I found the paperwork in his safe. He'd left it open. All of the receipts are signed by him. They go back twenty-three years."

"Twenty-three years?"

"Yeah." Overcome by sadness and anxiety, Lacey wiped a tear. "They start after Reese's mom died." Her voice trembled.

"And they stopped a month before my father died."

"What do you think it means?"

"I don't know. I wish Reese were here." She choked on the last words her tears flowing.

"It's okay." Krista patted her hand. "I'll come to work with you, and we'll sort this out. I promise we'll get through this."

Lacey swiped away her tears and dabbed her nose with a napkin. "We can't go through the receipts today. Carl's in the office."

"So go out to Phoenix and tell Reese everything. Maybe he'll want to approach his dad alone and find out what's going on, man to man."

Lacey nodded, lifting her glass. "I might just do that. I just can't figure out why my dad was rushing back to the shop. The company went into the red for payroll last month, so maybe that had something to do with it." She took a long drink of water, hoping to cool her parched throat.

"How short was the payroll?"

"Fifty-thousand."

"Oh, my goodness." Krista gasped.

"Something weird is going on. It's like I'm only scratching the surface."

"Have you told Reese?"

Lacey shook her head. "No, I just pieced this all together yesterday. When we chatted last night, it was really brief. I've been so tired I can barely keep my eyes open when he calls me."

"You can't go through this alone." Krista thumped the table with her finger as if for emphasis. "You need to get Reese involved, especially in your condition."

Lacey frowned. "You don't know for sure."

Her best friend smiled. "You're tired, your chest hurts, you're sick all the time, and the smell of my perfume makes you nauseated. Lacey Mitchell, you're pregnant."

Lacey groaned. "Can things get any worse?"

Krista wagged a finger at her. "Don't tempt fate like that."

Lacey glanced out the window, noting dark clouds flooding the azure sky and mirroring her mood.

"Hey." Krista rubbed Lacey's arm again. "Let's eat lunch and then go by the drug store. We'll get at least one of our questions answered."

"I don't know if I want that answer." She turned back to her best friend just as the server appeared with their food.

"Eat. You need your strength for the baby."

Lacey rolled her eyes and sighed.

"What do two blue lines mean?" Lacey yelled through her master suite bathroom door, holding the test in her hand while examining it.

"It means you need to buy a crib," Krista answered from the other side of the door.

"Oh, my gosh." She lowered herself on the lid of the commode and slapped the stick onto the counter.

The door squeaked open and her best friend opened her arms to her. "Give me a hug! I'm going to be an auntie again."

"I can't believe it . . ."

"Come on." Krista stood with her arms extended. "You'll be more excited when you see that grin on your proud husband's face."

Lacey hugged her. "Ouch! Don't squeeze so hard."

Krista let go and continued to smile. "So, are you going to call Reese?

"No. I want to tell him in person. I have the receipts to show him too." She blew out a sigh, staring down at the stick on the counter, the blue lines seeming to smirk up at her. "Would you help me pack and take me to the airport?"

Reese glanced at his watch for the fifth time in the past fifteen minutes while standing in the team hauler later that evening. He'd tried to call Lacey at least ten times during the past hour but kept getting her voicemail. He'd tried the house, the office and, her cellular phone, and he'd left messages on each line instructing her to call him. It wasn't like her not to call back. His body tensed with worry.

Where the heck was she? Was she okay?

At first he'd assumed she was busy, but a strange feeling had come over him that morning. Something wasn't right, but he couldn't put a finger on what it was.

"Have you talked to your dad?" Rod's voice rammed Reese back to the present.

"No, man, I haven't." He folded his arms and leaned against the counter.

"Is he planning on ever acting like he's in charge?" Rod's glare made Reese uneasy.

"Technically, Lacey and I are in charge. He's VP for Team Ops now."

"Is that why you married her?"

"Excuse me?" Reese's eyes narrowed in defense. *How dare he!*

"Let's face it, Reese. You two never had much interest in each other, and then you suddenly married her a month after her dad died. It did seem kinda sudden." The older man hugged his clipboard to his chest, his stare boring into Reese.

"I married Lacey because I love her and want to take care of her, but I don't think I need to explain that to you or anyone else." Reese stood up to his full six-foot-two, towering over the middle-aged man. "And as for my father, I think he's supposed to fly in tomorrow. You can call him and ask him yourself."

"If you talk to your old man, tell him I'm still waiting for an answer."

"An answer for what?"

"He knows what I mean." Rod stalked out of the hauler, slamming the door behind him.

Reese shook his head and wondered what that was about. Rod had always been a quiet man, never talking about anything except racing. He'd seemed happy working as the team manager, and he'd held that job for nearly twenty years. He was an expert with a car but had never married or settled down.

But lately, Rod changed. He rarely smiled or chatted and always appeared angry. The transformation had occurred around the time of Greg's death. Reese absently wondered if there was a correlation. If so, what was it?

Pushing thoughts of Rod from his mind, Reese fished out his cell phone. The door to the hauler opened and then slammed shut while he dialed Lacey.

When her voicemail picked up, he cussed under his breath. He waited until the beep and then said, "Lacey, it's me. Where are you? I'm worried sick. Call me. Love you. Bye."

Snapping the phone shut, he shoved it into his pocket. A flood of worry soaked through his soul. He hoped she was okay.

"Why are you wasting your time on her when you know only I can satisfy you?" A sultry voice spoke behind him while hands moved up his back.

Reese turned just as Sandy wrapped her arms around his waist.

Dodging increasing raindrops, Lacey trotted through the infield of Phoenix International Raceway toward the team trailer. She shivered and chastised herself for not putting on a jacket as the rain soaked her purple blouse.

When she didn't find Reese in the bus or the garage, one of

his crewmembers suggested she try the hauler. She'd turned off her phone hours earlier in order to avoid hearing his voice and pouring her heart out to him over the phone. She had so much to tell him and only wanted to do it in person

She couldn't wait to see him and wrap her arms around his neck. She wanted to feel his strong arms and hear his warm voice telling her everything would be okay. Her pulse raced with anticipation while she approached the hauler.

"Get off me," Reese snarled, wrenching his body away from Sandy. "What's your problem?"

"You're my problem." Her blue eyes sparkled while she stepped toward him. "Seeing you in that uniform makes me hot."

He stepped backward and rammed into the supply counter. She reached up for his uniform zipper and began to pull it.

"Knock it off!" He swatted her hand away. "I'm not interested in you." He stepped to the side, and she blocked him.

"Not so fast, hotshot." Tossing her blond hair over her shoulder, she grabbed his hands. "We have some unfinished business."

"Sandy, we have *nothing*. I've told you that more than once." He snatched his hands back. "You need to wake up and realize I don't love you, and I don't want to sleep with you."

"You still want me." She licked her ruby lips. "I can see it in your eyes."

"I love my wife, not you."

"Prove it." Encircling her arms around his neck, she yanked him to her.

As her lips pushed against his, the door clicked open and then a loud gasp sounded. He moved Sandy away, his eyes meeting Lacey's in the doorway.

The blood drained from Lacey's angelic face, her eyes rounding with shock. She made a sound similar to a moan while her hand covered her mouth.

"Lacey." He stumbled forward to her.

"You bastard." Her emerald eyes smoldered with rage. "You lying, cheating *bastard!*"

He flinched, regret and anger flowing through him. "Lacey, no! It wasn't what you think."

"Tell her the truth, Reese." Sandy's voice was sultry.

"Lacey, wait." He reached for Lacey, but she jumped back, shaking her head. His heart sank at the hurt in her eyes.

"Stay away from me." She ran out the door into the pouring rain.

He started for her, but Sandy dragged him back.

"Let her go. You're better off without her." Sandy pressed her voluptuous body to his back.

"Stay away from me and my wife." Reese glared at her, rage slamming through him. "You're nothing but a cheap whore."

Reese started out the door, finding Brett and his pit crew walking toward him. He stopped and faced Sandy.

Despite his body shaking with fury, he took a deep breath. "And as co-CEO of Southern Racing, I can say you're fired." He pushed past his crew and trotted down the steps and into the rain.

"You can't do that!" she hollered after him.

"I can, and I just did," he retorted, waving his hand in the air while Brett and his crew stared, their eyes wide with astonishment.

Twenty-Five

Lacey's boots sloshed through the mud on her way to Reese's bus. Her body quaked with anger, rage, and hurt as the cold rain drenched her body. Images of Reese and Sandy kissing made her feel sick. It looked as if Lacey had caught them just before their clothes were going to fall off. His fire suit was even partially unzipped.

She groaned. How could she have been so stupid? She should've known Reese Mitchell would cheat on her! His reputation was the reason why she didn't want to marry him in the first place.

She'd known he'd hurt her. *She'd just known it!*

And now she was *pregnant!*

What was she going to do?

Lacey sighed. She was going to do what any mother would do—raise the baby alone. She had the financial means. She'd just have to find the emotional strength.

She missed her dad. Why did he have to leave her?

Sobs choked Lacey as she approached the bus. After fumbling with the keys, she unlocked the door and climbed in, thankful for the warmth that greeted her. She was heading back for a towel when the door slammed behind her.

"Lacey, listen to me." Reese's voice was urgent.

"Save it!" She held a hand up to his face. "I don't want to hear any of your lame excuses. At least now I know what you've been doing at the track without me."

"That's not it. Just listen to me." His blue eyes pleaded with her. "Sandy came on to me."

"Oh, right!" Lacey made a sweeping gesture with her arm. "It's never your fault, Reese. You *never* do anything to encourage these women. Just like the endless string of messages we get at the house. They all fall at your feet without any encouragement and assume you'll have sex with them."

"Look, I—"

"I don't want to hear it. I'm over it." She folded her arms, hoping to shield her heart. "This is why I didn't want to marry you. I knew you'd hurt me. I knew you weren't capable of being loyal to one woman." Her body shivered with the hurt coursing through her.

"That's not true." He shook his head, his eyes turning an icy blue.

"Spare me the song and dance. We have bigger problems."

"What?"

"I came here to tell you your dad has been robbing the company blind for twenty-three years. I didn't know what to do, so I figured I'd come and talk to you in person."

He looked confused. "I don't understand."

"I'll show you." She snatched her briefcase from the floor, pulling out an accordion file and slapping it on the table. "It's all there in black and white."

He slowly flipped through the receipts. "Where did you find these?"

"In the safe in your dad's office." She took a long, cleansing breath, but the hurt and anger still boiled through her. "He left it open last night before he left. It was as if he wanted me to find them. They go back to a month after your mother died."

"What does this mean?" He lifted his gaze to hers, his eyes full of hurt, wrenching something deep in her soul.

She pushed her longing for him aside.

He cheated on her.

He hurt her.

He made a fool of her!

"I was hoping you had some idea." She hugged her arms closer to her chest when a wave of nausea gripped her.

"Are you okay?" Reese reached for her. "You look really pale."

"I'm fine." Lacey stepped away from him. She couldn't let him touch her. If he did, she'd fall into his arms and do something stupid—like forgive him.

He sighed, his shoulders drooping. "So, it's my dad."

"Everything points to him. I don't know what to do now. I'm so lost." Her voice trembled with her emotional turmoil.

"Lacey." He reached for her again.

"Don't touch me." She shook her head. "I don't want your sympathy. I just want your help figuring this out. Then I want a divorce, and I want your piece of the company." Her words cut her to the bone, but she had to say them. She had to defend herself and her father's company.

His expression hardened. "No. I'm not giving up on you or the company."

"You gave up on me the minute your lips touched Sandy's. You made a mockery of me and this so-called marriage." She stalked down the hall toward the bathroom.

"Lacey! Don't shut me out!"

Hearing his heavy footsteps, she ducked in the bathroom and locked the door.

"I love you," he called.

"Sure you do!" she screamed at the door, her voice quavering. "I trusted you. I gave you everything." She buried her face in her hands while sobs overtook her.

"I didn't cheat on you," he hollered through the door. "I told you I'd never hurt you, and I won't. You're my life. You're my . . . everything."

Liar! She shook her head while crying. She heard his cellular phone begin to ring, and she absently wondered if it was one of his girlfriends.

"Hello?" he asked, his voice moving away from the door.

Overcome by curiosity, Lacey stood close to the door.

"Yes, this is Reese . . ." he said. "Oh my—" His voice was filled with urgency. "When did it happen? . . . Where is he? . . . I'll be there as soon as I can." The phone snapped shut.

She threw the door open. "What's wrong?"

"I have to go." He rushed around the bus as if searching for something.

"What happened?" She followed him into the bedroom area.

"I have to go." He picked up a bag and started throwing clothes into it.

"Reese, tell me what's going on."

He kept packing without looking up.

Walking over to him, she took his hands in hers and looked into his eyes. "Talk to me."

Embracing her, he rested his cheek on the top of her head. He was holding her so close her breasts stung from the contact. But his body was warm, comforting. Oh, she'd missed him.

"Reese?" she whispered. "Please tell me what's wrong." She looked up into his eyes. She could've sworn she saw tears in his deep pools of blue.

"My dad's in ICU."

She gasped. "What?"

"He had a heart attack."

"Oh, no."

"Jeannie from Marketing called. She said he collapsed in the parking lot on his way out to his car this afternoon." His voice quaked. "He hasn't woken up, and he's barely hanging on." He held her close, and she closed her eyes while rubbing his back.

"Let's go."

He stepped back, studying her. "You'll go with me?"

"Of course I will."

He gave her a look of disbelief.

"He's still my father-in-law." She started down the aisle. "Let's go."

While Lacey slept beside him, Reese's mind swirled with thoughts of her, Sandy, and his father during the seemingly endless flight from Phoenix to Charlotte. He was furious with Sandy, distraught with Lacey's demand for a divorce, and sick with worry about his father. He wished he could sleep. He needed some relief from the emotions rioting within him.

His fury boiled at the thought of Sandy. How dared she come onto him and then act as if they were having an affair in front of Lacey! Sandy was delusional. He'd told her more than once that he wasn't interested. She'd tried twice to come onto him at his wedding reception, and both times he told her to get lost in no uncertain terms.

But she wouldn't give up. The woman refused to take no for an answer, and now he'd hurt the person who was the most precious to him—his wife, his lover, his best friend, the love of his life.

Lacey.

He groaned, settling back in the seat. Lacey wanted a divorce, and his father was hanging on to life by a thread. Things couldn't get much worse.

But they already had. Lacey had proof his father was stealing from the company. How would Reese ever explain that to the stockholders? If his father survived, he'd most likely go to prison.

But why was he embezzling the funds? His father had made a nice salary since he came to work for Southern Racing twenty-five years ago. Why did the money start disappearing a month after Reese's mother died? It didn't make any sense.

Reese looked down at his wife curled up in the seat beside him. He ran his fingers over her cheek, and she sighed in her sleep. She looked so sweet, so angelic.

His heart swelled. Oh, how he loved her.

He couldn't lose her. He refused to. He was going to fight for her, for their marriage. He'd never let a woman like Sandy come between them.

He closed his eyes, silently hoping he'd make it through this somehow with his father and his wife by his side.

"I'm sorry, but only one person at a time can go into ICU." The portly, middle-aged nurse behind the desk at the hospital glowered. "And visiting hours are over. One of you can come back tomorrow morning at nine."

Lacey glanced at Reese, his pained expression making her want to cry. She leaned on the counter and swallowed the frustration nipping at her. "Ma'am, we just got in from a very long flight. We left Phoenix as soon as we heard the news about my father-in-law. There was no way Reese and I could've gotten here sooner."

She lowered her voice, staring into the woman's brown eyes. "Can you find it in your heart to let my husband see his father? If his condition is that fragile, I think my husband would appreciate any time he has left with him."

The nurse looked back and forth between them. "Make it quick," she snipped.

Reese's expression softened some. He stepped away from the desk, and Lacey followed. When they reached the doorway leading to the hallway, he looked at her. "Thank you."

"I can't believe Nurse Ratchet treated you like that. I wanted to take her head off." She shook her head, folding her arms. "You take all the time you need. Ignore that witch."

"I love you." His smile was tentative.

"Don't." She shook her head. "Not now."

"Lacey, I didn't—"

"Shh." She put a finger to his lips and ignored the heat that the touch sent bubbling through her body. "Just worry about your dad right now. We'll figure us out later."

"Are we still an us?" His eyes were hopeful, and she'd never seen him look so defeated, so unsure of himself. Reese, the champion, was gone and replaced with Reese, the man. And she still adored him.

Her heart wanted to reach for him, hug him, and tell him it would all be okay. But her pride stopped her. He'd cheated on her and made a fool of her. She needed to keep her emotions in check and push him away.

"I don't know," she whispered. "We'll talk about it later."

He glanced toward the nurse's station. "I wish you could come back with me."

"I was going to run to the shop."

"Why?" His expression became suspicious. "It's almost midnight."

"I want to look in your dad's office while no one is around. I want to prove I'm wrong. We both need that closure for your dad's sake."

He shook his head, concern clouding his handsome face. "I'm not comfortable—"

"I'm a big girl." She touched his arm. "Call my cell when you want me to come get you."

"Be careful." Sighing, Reese watched her head toward the automatic doors to the parking lot.

He wasn't going to allow her to go into the race shop alone at midnight. Over his dead body. She might be stubborn, but he was too.

Knowing cellular use wasn't permitted in the hospital, he scanned the area and found a sign for the restrooms. Moving through the lobby, he slipped into the men's room and pulled out his phone. He found Krista's number in his address book and hit send.

"Hello?" she sounded startled.

"Hey, it's Reese." His voice echoed off the lime green tile walls.

"Oh, hey." Her voice brightened. "What's going on? You guys celebrating?"

"Celebrating what?"

"Oh, uh." She sounded as if she regretted her words. "Nothing, nothing." She quickly corrected herself.

"Krista, what are you talking about?"

"Oh, dear. I didn't say anything." She cleared her throat. "How can I help you?"

"I'm sorry for calling so late, but I'm at the hospital."

"Hospital?" she yelled in his ear, and he held the phone away from his head. "Is Lacey okay?"

"Lacey's fine." He leaned against the counter. "My dad had a massive heart attack, and he's in ICU."

"Oh, Reese. I'm so sorry."

"Thanks." His throat constricted with worry. "Listen, I need your help."

"Anything. You name it."

"Lacey's heading to the shop right now to investigate some receipts she found. Would you please go meet her there and either talk her out of it or stay with her? I'm uncomfortable with the idea of her sneaking around alone at night."

She sighed. "That sounds just like our Lacey. I'll get dressed and run out there."

"Thanks." Reese paused. He longed to ask for her help convincing Lacey he'd never cheat, but he decided against it. He needed to keep this between him and Lacey.

"Reese?" she asked. "You still there?"

"Yeah." He stood up straight.

"Call me if you need me."

"I will. Thanks." He snapped his phone shut and headed out to the lobby. As he made his way down the hallway to his father's room, he wondered what Krista meant when she asked if they were celebrating.

What would they celebrate? Why did she assume Lacey was in the hospital? What was Lacey hiding from him? He'd have to get to the bottom of that after he dealt with his father.

Reese's heart sank when he entered the room and found him lying in bed hooked up to several machines that clicked and beeped as they ran. His father's skin was a strange tint of gray, and his hair seemed a darker brown than usual.

His eyes filling with tears, Reese stood by the bed and touched his hand. "Don't die on me now, Pop," he whispered. "I need you."

Twenty-Six

Lacey rolled her eyes at Krista waiting at the front door of the race shop. "Let me guess," she deadpanned. "My wonderful husband sent you to baby-sit me." She snatched her card key from the front pocket of her purse.

"It's nice to see you, too," Krista quipped. "Yes, he was worried about you, so he asked me to come and talk you out of this expedition or go with you."

Lacey slipped the card in the slot, and the door unlocked with a click. "Did he also ask you to help save our marriage?"

"Save your marriage? What are you talking about?" Krista looked confused.

Lacey wrenched the door open then held it for her to walk into the lobby. "Oh, so he didn't tell you. My surprise visit went over like a lead balloon. I caught him making out with Sandy in the team hauler." A renewed fury slammed through her at the memory of her husband with that bimbo. Trying in vain to push the thought aside, she locked the door behind them.

Her best friend's eyes nearly popped out of her head. "You're kidding!"

"Wish I were," Lacey muttered.

They started down the long hallway toward the executive offices, their shoes clicking on the polished tile.

"What did you do?"

"After I screamed at him, I told him I want a divorce. Then I told him about the receipts implicating his father." She shuddered at the words, but clung to the belief that she was making the right choice.

"What about the baby?"

"What do you mean?"

Krista stopped in her tracks, grabbed Lacey's arm, and stared at her, her pretty face clouded with shock. "You didn't tell him?"

"What for?" Defensive, Lacey jammed her hand on her hip. "I'm not going to raise my baby in a marriage full of lies." She moved her hand to her stomach. "I'll raise my baby myself. We'll be okay. Somehow." Lacey ignored the lump welling in her throat while stalking down the hallway.

"Wait a minute!" Krista jogged after her. "How do you know he was cheating on you with Sandy?"

"Their lip-lock kinda gave it away," Lacey snapped.

"But how do you know he was a willing participant?"

Sighing, she approached Carl's door. "They were kissing, Krista. She had her paws around his neck, and his fire suit was unzipped about five inches. Looked like they were about to get it on."

"You don't know that," her best friend challenged.

"Please drop it. I suspected he was going to have a problem being faithful, and I was right." She pushed the door open then flipped on the lights. "I knew in my heart he was going to hurt me. So I got what I deserved. I never should've slept with him. That sealed my fate."

"But he loves you!" Krista stomped her foot like a three-year-old in the midst of a temper tantrum. "I know he does."

Lacey crossed the office and stood behind Carl's desk. "I guess sometimes love isn't enough." Disappointment slid through her gut.

"That's crap, and you know it!" Krista stood before the desk, wagging a finger at her.

"Would you please drop it?" Lacey pleaded with a defeated sigh. "I have enough stress right now. His dad is hanging by a thread. If we lose him, it'll destroy Reese."

Her best friend's smile was condescending. "You love him."

"I know," she whispered as she glanced at a framed photo sitting on Carl's desk. It showed her and Reese holding up their champagne flutes at their wedding reception. "That's the problem." She rummaged through drawers. "Help me search for evidence."

"Where do you want me to look?"

"Anywhere." She nodded toward the filing cabinet in the far corner. "That's the cabinet Carl had at my dad's house. See if you can jimmy the lock."

Krista shook the drawer.

Lacey pulled a nail file from her purse and tossed it to her. "Try this."

"Thanks." Her best friend slid the file into the lock. After a few grunts and groans, she turned it, and the drawer slid open. "Did Carl move out of your dad's house yet?"

"He moved everything out a couple of weeks ago. I was going to start cleaning it out to put it on the market, but I guess I'll need it for the baby and me." Sorrow rose in her throat and she swallowed a lump. She despised the idea of living alone in that huge house with a baby.

"Lacey, don't give up on Reese."

"I asked you to drop it," she snapped. The comment came out nastier than she'd intended. "I'm sorry. I just can't handle the idea of another woman touching him. I want him all to myself."

"I feel the same way about Tommy." Krista smiled. "But I believe Reese loves you. When the time comes, listen to him. Maybe Sandy attacked him, and you walked in before he put her in her place."

Lacey shook her head. She believed in her heart that Krista was dead wrong. "It looked consensual."

"Looks can be deceiving."

Lacey rifled through the files on the desk, and they searched in silence for what felt like a long time. Lacey was deep in thought and worry about Carl's health and Reese's emotional state when Krista suddenly gasped.

"Lacey," she said. "Come here!"

Lacey dropped the files, rushed over to Krista, and sat cross-legged next to her. "Whatcha got?"

"Look!" Her friend's eyes were wide as Lacey examined a stack of papers.

Resembling ransom notes, the words were created from letters cut out of magazines. She flipped through them, and read messages such as *You better pay up, I know what you did, You are guilty as sin, Where's my money,* and *I will hurt your son if you don't pay what you owe.*

A chill raced up Lacey's spine.

Carl was *blackmailed!*

"Who would do this?" Krista asked.

"I don't know," Lacey whispered.

"We have to tell Reese."

"No!" She touched Krista's arm. "We can't. Reese has too much on him right now. He might have a breakdown if he finds out about this."

"You can't figure this out alone. Not in your condition."

"I'm pregnant, not dying."

"Let me help you." Her friend touched her shoulder. "We'll figure this out together."

An hour later, Lacey walked into the lobby at the hospital. She waited until the nurse behind the desk walked away and then made a beeline for the hallway leading to ICU. Once in, she slowly moved past rooms until she spotted Reese slumped in a chair next to his father's bed.

Lacey's eyes filled with tears as she entered his room. Carl looked so pale, and the machines surrounding him clicked and hummed as if they were working hard to keep him alive. She said a silent prayer he'd somehow make it through. She couldn't bear the idea of losing Carl after losing her father and Veronica.

She squatted in front of Reese and studied him as he slept. He looked so tired and yet so handsome. Reaching out, she pushed his cowlick back from his gorgeous face. Her heart swelled with love and disappointment.

How could he cheat on her? They could've been so good together. They could've been a *family*. She frowned. But he had to throw it away on a stupid trollop like Sandy.

Reese snorted, blinking awake. Leaning back, he stretched. "Hey," he said through a yawn. "What time is it?"

"After one." She gestured toward the bed. "Has there been any change?"

He shook his head.

"What's the prognosis?"

"All I've gotten the nurses to tell me is he's been unconscious since he got here. They won't make any promises one way or the other." His expression was grim.

"I'm sorry." She bit her lip, holding back her threatening tears.

"How did it go at the shop?"

She shrugged. "Okay."

"Did you find anything?"

"No." She hated herself for lying, but she had to shield him from the hurt that the truth would cause him. "Thanks for sending Krista to protect me." Her voice dripped with sarcasm.

"Don't mention it." He smiled, and her heart fluttered in her chest.

"You need your sleep. Let me take you home." She stood.

He shook his head. "I'm going to stay just in case . . ." He paused. "I don't want him to be alone."

She nodded, understanding what he meant. "I'm going to stay at my dad's."

"Why?" His eyes rounded.

"Because of things between us." She folded her arms as if to shield her heart from more hurt.

"Lacey, please don't do this. Not now. I can't handle any more stress right now. I'm at my limit."

"Maybe you should've thought of that before you screwed Sandy." The words escaped before she could stop them.

Shaking his head, he groaned. "I didn't screw Sandy or anyone else. I've only been with you."

She studied his blue eyes. Was he telling the truth? She didn't know. He sounded genuine, but could she believe him? She grimaced. That kiss between him and Sandy sure looked real enough.

"Just stay with me until I get through this with my pop." His gorgeous pools of azure pleaded with her. "Please, Lacey. *Please.*"

She sighed, feeling like a witch for picking a fight with him while his father lay in such a fragile state. "We're going to have a long talk after we get through this."

He threw his hands up in defeat. "I agree. We'll talk about it later."

"Well, I'm going to head out. Are you sure you want to stay?" She started for the door.

"Yes."

"Call me tomorrow."

"I will." He folded his arms.

"And Krista sends her love."

"Thanks."

They stared at each other, and Lacey could feel the intensity sparking between them. So much left unsaid. After a moment, she spoke. "Do you want me to call Brett and tell him you're not racing this weekend?"

He nodded. "I'd appreciate that."

She stood in the doorway. "I'll call him."

"Thank you."

"Good night." Lacey's shoes clicked on the floor while she headed out to the lobby. She felt guilty for not telling him about the ransom notes, but he had enough weighing on his mind. She exited through the automatic doors and as she approached her SUV, she fished her cellular phone from her purse and dialed Brett.

He answered on the second ring. "Lacey?"

"Brett, hey. Have you heard what happened?" Unlocking her truck, she climbed in.

"No. What's going on?"

"We're back in Charlotte. Carl had a massive heart attack. He's in ICU."

"Oh, no. Is Reese with him?"

"Yes. I can't get him to leave Carl's side." Starting the truck, she motored toward the exit.

"I'll find a relief driver and tell everyone the news. Don't you worry about a thing. Just take care of Reese. Call me tomorrow and let me know what's going on."

"I will. Thank you." Lacey snapped her phone shut and sighed while merging onto the highway. She had to clear her mind to concentrate.

Who would blackmail Carl and why?

She pondered that question the whole ride back to Reese's house. After stopping to get the mail at the end of the long driveway, she parked her truck in the garage and struggled to carry their bags and the mail.

She dropped the bags on the floor with a thud and smacked the mail on the counter with a thwap. Flipping through the envelopes, she found bills, except for one envelope addressed to Reese with a preprinted label and no return address. She stared at it and then dropped it on the counter.

Exhaustion drowned Lacey as she slowly marched up the stairs to the master suite. She collapsed into bed with her clothes on and fell asleep immediately.

TWENTY-SEVEN

Sunday evening, Reese sat across from his father's bed and flipped pages of a muscle car magazine. The words didn't register as he glanced at the photos of the shiny restored classic cars. He cut his eyes across the room and sighed. His father's condition hadn't changed since he arrived at the hospital Thursday night. His heart sank. He wished his father would wake up.

The door clicked open, and Reese stood when a man in a white coat walked in. Reese placed his magazine on the chair. "Hi. I'm Reese Mitchell."

"I'm Dr. Freeman." The doctor extended his hand. "It's a pleasure to meet you. I'm a fan."

"Thanks." He shook the doctor's hand then jammed his hands in the pockets of his jeans. "So, how's my pop?"

The doctor sighed, lifting the chart from the base of the bed, and Reese's stomach clenched.

Bad news.

Real bad news.

The doctor flipped through the chart, closed it, and then held it to his side. "As you know, your father's condition hasn't changed."

"That's not a good sign." Reese finished his thought.

"I'm afraid it's not."

"Is he going to die?" His voice vibrated with the hollow sorrow building in his soul.

The doctor paused for a moment, collecting his thoughts. "It's hard to say."

Reese cleared his throat, examining his father. This had to be some sick dream. It couldn't be happening. Losing Greg and Veronica was bad enough.

He felt the doctor's hand on his shoulder. "I wish there was more we could do."

"Me, too," Reese whispered. He cleared his throat again. "How long do you think he has?"

The doctor put the clipboard back in the slot at the end of the bed. "I would guess a few days."

Feeling numb, Reese nodded as if it were good news.

"Do you have any other questions?"

Reese shook his head. "Not that I can think of."

"If you need me, don't hesitate to have the nurses page me. I'm sorry I couldn't do more." Dr. Freeman started toward the door.

"Thank you."

Reese heard the door click closed while he watched his father, wishing he'd sit up and say, "Surprise! I'm okay!"

"Pop, Pop." Reese touched his father's hand. "It's me, Reese. Please wake up. I need you. I can't lose you." He closed his eyes and leaned down, placing his forehead on his hand. He raised his head slightly, his gaze focusing on the gold band on his left hand. How he missed Lacey's support. His heart beat for only her.

They'd become like strangers since they arrived home a few days ago. She'd come and sat with him at the hospital for a few hours each day and then disappeared to go to the race shop. When they saw each other at the house at night, she'd ask how his father was and then retreat into the guest room to sleep. She wouldn't talk to him and wouldn't even hug him good night.

It was eating him alive. He needed her. He wanted her.

He *loved* her.

No matter how much he'd begged and pleaded for her to listen, she refused to believe he'd never cheated on her. It was as if she'd expected this to happen. Now he stood before his dying father and needed his wife by his side.

Standing up, Reese again touched his father's hand. "Pop, I need to go now. Lacey's angry with me, and I need to try to make things right with her. I'll be back, though. I'll come see you again tomorrow."

He grabbed his keys from his pocket and hurried out the door to his pickup truck. As he drove to his house, Reese flipped on the local country station where the Sports Radio broadcasters were chattering away about the race in Phoenix.

Reese groaned when he heard his archrival, Dylan McCormick, was leading the race. His groan deepened when the announcer reported Reese's and Tommy's cars had suffered engine failures earlier and would finish in the last two spots.

He sighed with disappointment. It had been a banner day all around.

He assumed his crew was already heading back to Carolina in the team plane. He changed to a rock station and tried to concentrate on the music during the ride back to his house.

On a mission, Reese flew into the kitchen at his house. "Lacey? Lacey!" Tossing his keys onto the counter, he stalked into the den. "Lacey?"

"I'm up here!" she called from upstairs.

He loped up the stairs, taking two at a time. He found her standing in the hallway clad in a short, pink satin robe. Her long red hair hung in wet waves, and her gorgeous emerald eyes were wide with concern. She was so beautiful that heat slid through him.

"What's wrong?" Her sweet voice was soft while she put her

hand to her mouth as if expecting the worst.

"He's still alive, but the doctor only gives him only a few days."

She started toward him and then stopped. "I'm so sorry."

"I can't stand this distance between us. It's making me crazy. You've got to talk to me." He stepped forward, and she backed into the master bedroom.

"There's nothing to say." She continued backward until she bumped into the bed.

"There's plenty to say. I can't lose you. I refuse to lose you, especially over something so stupid."

"Stupid?" Her voice rose and her brows knitted together. "I can hardly call cheating on me stupid."

He grimaced, anger ripping through him. "How many times do I have to tell you I didn't cheat on you?"

She wagged a finger at him. "You can say it until you're blue in the face, Reese. But every time I close my eyes, I see you in a lip lock with that-that *slut!*"

His eyes darted to a pile of papers on the bed, and he absently wondered what they were. When he met her gaze again, he shook his head. "Lacey, she came on to me."

She folded her arms, glaring at him with defiance. "I don't believe you."

"It's the truth!" He took a deep breath, trying to curb his anger, but it continued to boil over. "I'd never piss away my marriage like that. You mean too damned much to me."

"Your reputation precedes you. I know about the girls you've dated."

"Oh, really?" He stepped over to her, trapping her between him and bed. "What do you know?"

"I know you dated six girls at once."

Unbelievable. He shook his head, silently cursing the lies that continued to haunt him. "Really? That's news to me. The most girls I've ever dated at once was two." He held up two fingers for emphasis. "It lasted a week before one broke up with me."

"That's not what I heard."

"Do you believe every rumor you hear?" He stared her down. She frowned and blinked with defeat. "No."

"Why on earth would you believe rumors over me?" He jammed a finger in his chest. "I'm your husband."

"No, you're a *business deal*. Remember? You told me to think of this as a way to find out why my father died and not think of it as a marriage."

"That was before I realized how much I love you." He grasped her forearms with his hands and got a glare for his effort.

Crap, he cursed himself. Easing his grip, his hands moved to cup her face.

"Lacey, honey, I love you." His voice grew harsh with anguish. "Doesn't that mean anything to you? I can't lose you like I'm losing my father. It—It'll kill me." His eyes searched hers in desperation. He wished he could read her thoughts. He wanted to get back into her heart and her soul. He loved her so much that his heart ached for her.

Tears filled her eyes. "I'm sorry, but I can't live a lie. I can't stay in a marriage full of lies."

He threw his hands up in frustration. "Damn it!" Shaking his head, he paced. "This is freakin' ridiculous."

He wracked his brain for something, anything, that would make her see he truly loved her. Stopping in front of the bed, he faced her. She sat on the corner, wiping her cheeks.

How could he make her believe the truth? Like lightning, an idea flashed through his mind. He sucked in a breath, hoping it would work.

"Lacey, if you truly think I care about Sandy, then call Rod and ask him who our marketing manager is."

She looked bewildered by the idea. "Why would I do that?"

He gave her a sarcastic smile. "Because he'll tell you Sandy was fired."

"Fired?"

"Yes, fired."

"When?"

"I fired her right after she came on to me Thursday night. If you don't believe me, call Brett and ask him. He and my pit crew saw me fire her."

She blinked, confusion clouding her gorgeous face.

Turning to go, he scanned the bed again. When something caught his eye, he picked up a piece of paper from the bed.

"Oh, that's nothing." She lunged for the paper, and he blocked her by turning his back. "Reese, it's nothing."

He studied the paper and gasped. Resembling a Hollywood movie ransom note, magazine letters were stuck to it and spelled out *Pay up or else*. He snatched another one and read *I know what you did*. Flipping through the stack, he found more with similar messages.

His gaze collided with Lacey's, and biting her bottom lip, her eyes rounded with alarm.

"Where did you get these?" he asked.

"At the shop."

"*Where* at the shop?"

"In your father's office. In the filing cabinet."

He stepped toward her. "When did you find them?"

"Um. . . ." Staring down at the bed, she ran her fingers over the comforter.

"When?"

"Thursday." With her eyes still on the comforter, her answer came in a whisper.

"Why on earth didn't you tell me?" When she didn't respond, his voice rose. "Why'd you keep this from me?"

"I didn't want to upset you."

"Didn't want to upset me?" He shook with rage. "So, you felt it best to keep me in the dark and let me think my dad was stealing from the company when he could possibly have been blackmailed?" He threw the papers down. "Now where's the logic in that?" When she didn't answer, he yelled, *"Will you answer me?"*

When her eyes met his, tears were streaming down her face. "I'm sorry." Her voice trembled.

Good going. Like a bully, I made her cry. "Lacey, I'm sorry."

She got up and ran to the bathroom.

"Lacey!" He started after her, guilt washing over him.

"Go away!" She slammed the door and locked it.

"Crap!" He kicked the bed and then started down the stairs. Frustration gnawed at him. He had to go somewhere. *Anywhere.*

He grabbed his keys from the kitchen counter, stopping when he spotted an unopened envelope addressed to him. He picked it up, studying the preprinted label. Something about it intrigued him.

Tearing it open, he pulled out a piece of paper. He almost dropped it when he read a letter similar to the ones he read upstairs. The letters glued to the page spelled out:

Reese,
If your father doesn't pay up, I will come after your lovely bride.

A digital print-out of a photo showing Lacey and Krista walking out of a restaurant fell to the floor. Picking up the photo, Reese's hands trembled, and his heart pounded in his chest while fear and fury flooded his soul. He had to find out who was threatening him. And he needed to find out fast.

He'd die before he let anyone harm Lacey.

He bolted back up the stairs, snatched up the piles of letters, and headed back down to the garage.

TWENTY-EIGHT

Reese clutched the letters as he entered his father's hospital room. The only sound came from the hum of the florescent lights above the bed.

"Pop, I need your help." He held his father's cool hand. "If you can hear me, you've got to tell me who was threatening you."

He pulled a chair beside the bed and sank into it, hoping somehow his father could hear him and give him a clue, any clue, to this horrible mystery.

Staring down at the letters, Reese trembled with a mixture of fear and anxiety. "I got a letter today, and the person who was threatening you is now threatening my Lacey. I can't let that happen. I love Lacey. She's my life. She's everything to me. Please help me. Please tell me who was threatening you."

Reese bent down, resting his head on the cool metal of the bed guard in defeat. This was pointless. His father couldn't hear him. He was kidding himself. The father Reese knew was gone.

Reese had to figure this out himself. He wracked his brain, trying to guess who could hate his father and why.

After several minutes, he came up with nothing. He couldn't think of one person who disliked his father, and he couldn't imagine anyone who would blackmail or threaten him.

When Reese felt the bed shift, he sat up like a shot. He gasped when his father groaned and moved his head. "Pop?" He leaned forward. "Pop, can you hear me?"

"Reese." His father's voice was a hoarse whisper.

"Hey." His heart fluttered, and he held his father's hand. "You have to get better. I need you."

"I'm sorry," his father whispered.

"What are you talking about?" He stared at his father with confusion.

"I can't live with the guilt anymore. It's killing me."

"What is? I don't understand."

"Greg and Veronica." His dull blue eyes squinted open.

"How?" Reese leaned down to hear his father's faint voice over the humming and clicking of the machines.

"When your mother was dying, I took money from the company. She wanted to come home to die, and I was going to lose the house because of all her doctor bills."

"It's okay. Don't worry about it." Reese brushed some of his father's sweaty hair from his face. Sadness rose in his throat hearing his father's regrets.

"Rod found out and threatened to tell Greg and the police if I didn't pay him."

Reese bit back a gasp. "Rod's been blackmailing you?"

"For over twenty years."

Reese shook his head. "Why didn't you tell me?"

"I didn't want to disappoint you and Greg. I didn't want to lose you."

"It's okay, Pop." Reese's eyes filled with tears at the news. His father had been suffering alone for too long.

"No, it's not. No matter how much I paid Rod, it was never enough. Because of me, the company was losing money. That's why Greg was rushing back. We were going to have an emergency meeting to figure out how to save the company. That's why he died." He paused to cough. "The guilt is eating me alive." His voice was hoarser than before. "I left files out for

Lacey, hoping she'd figure it out and save the company somehow."

Reese bit back tears. "I just want you get better. Lacey and I need you."

"You have to stop Rod. His threats have gotten worse. He said he was going to hurt you if I didn't pay up, but I couldn't do it anymore—especially after Greg died."

"I'll do something. I promise." Reese squeezed his father's hand with hope. "You just rest and get better. I love you, Pop."

"I love you too, son." Closing his tired eyes, his father fell back asleep.

Reese stood, contemplating his words. It was Rod who'd been robbing the company blind and threatening his father. Rod had to be stopped.

Now.

Glancing at his watch, he calculated how long it should've taken the team to get back to Mooresville. If his guess was correct, they could've already made it back to town.

He had to find Rod *now.* He went to the nurse's station and told the nurse that his father had been awake. Trembling with anxiety and blinding urgency, he then hurried out to his truck.

Lacey stepped out of the bathroom. Scanning the room, she saw that the blackmail notes were gone. Why had Reese taken them? She stepped out into the hallway and walked to the balcony.

"Reese?" she called. "Reese, are you here?"

She waited a few moments then went back into the master bedroom. She thought about their argument while lowering herself onto the bed.

Was it true that Sandy came on to him? Had Reese really fired Sandy after she kissed him? He said Brett and some of the pit crew had seen it. She considered calling Brett and sighed with defeat.

Well, there was no better way to find out if he was telling the truth. Crossing the room, she grabbed her phone and dialed.

He answered on the second ring. "This is Brett."

"Brett, it's Lacey." She paced by the bed.

"Lacey. How's Carl?"

"The doctor told Reese he only has a few days."

"I'm so sorry." He lowered his voice. "We've all been thinking of him. How's Reese?"

"He's really upset. He went a little crazy."

"Oh, no." He said something to someone nearby about Carl, and soft voices spoke behind him.

"Where are you?" she asked.

"At the shop. We just got in. I guess you heard how we did at the track."

"Yeah, I did." She stopped pacing and sat on the edge of the bed. "I watched it on TV. I couldn't believe it when both cars blew up within a few laps of each other."

"It was pretty bad. We loaded up and left."

"We'll get through this. Somehow." She folded her arms. "Listen, I need to ask you a question."

"Shoot."

"Did Reese fire Sandy on Thursday?"

Brett snickered. "Did he *ever* fire her! He ripped her apart and then fired her. I believe he told her to stay away from him and you and then he called her a whore. As the icing on the cake, he fired her."

Guilt washed over Lacey. Reese was telling the truth.

Then strange excitement skittered through her at the realization that Reese didn't cheat on her.

Reese loved her!

Lacey stood. She had to find him. She had to apologize. She had to tell him she loved him too.

"Lacey?" Brett asked. "You still there?"

"Yes, I'm here." Crossing the room to the closet, she searched for something to wear. "Look, I gotta go. I'll see you tomorrow at the shop."

"Let us know how Carl is."

"I will. Thanks." She disconnected and threw on a pair of jeans and a sweatshirt. Then she opened her phone and dialed Reese's number. Instead of ringing, it immediately went to voicemail, and disappointment washed over her.

"Reese, it's me," she said after the beep. "Look, I'm sorry. I'm so sorry for not believing you. I love you. Call me." Snapping the phone shut, she grabbed her purse and hurried out of the bedroom.

Reese climbed into his truck and gripped the steering wheel, fury flooding through him. He had to tell Rod he knew everything and was going to call the police. He opened his cellular phone and dialed the team manager.

"Hello?" Rod said.

"This is Reese. We need to talk."

"About what?" Was that defensiveness he heard in Rod's voice, or was he imagining it?

"I want to talk in person." Reese stared down at his speedometer.

"When?"

"Where are you?"

"At the shop."

"I'll be there in twenty minutes." Reese started his truck. "Meet me in the team bay. *Alone.*"

"Fine." Then the line went dead.

Reese stuck the phone in the pocket of his jeans and turned the radio up to drown out his anxiety.

★ ★ ★ ★ ★

Lacey called Tommy and four of the crewmembers, but no one had seen Reese. She tried his cellular phone again, but got voicemail. She needed to tell him she was sorry and wanted to try to work things out. She longed to tell him about the baby.

After stopping by the hospital, she decided to drive around to find him. Merging onto the highway, she motored toward the shop.

Twenty-Nine

Reese's heart pounded with rage as he stepped into the bay. Rod stood on the other side of the shop, his arms folded across his team jacket and a scowl twisting his face.

"I know you've been blackmailing my father, and it's going to stop *now.*" Reese stepped toward him.

"And how do you expect to stop me?"

"I have proof." Reese waved the letters. "I'm going to call the police and tell them everything."

The team manager laughed. "That doesn't prove a thing."

"My father told me everything." He stomped toward him and stood millimeters from the team manager's nose. "You're lucky I don't beat the tar out of you for what you've done to my family."

"Oh, is that so?" Rod smirked, and Reese's blood pressure rose.

"Yes, that's so. Because of you, Greg and Veronica are dead, and my father's hanging on by a thread."

"I'm so sorry." His sarcasm cut Reese to the bone.

"Why, Rod?" He trembled with mounting anguish. "Why would you do this to my family?"

"You know what your problem is?" The older man rammed a finger in Reese's chest. "You've had everything handed to your candy butt your whole life. You never had to earn a place on this team."

"That's not true!" Reese smacked the gnarled finger away. "I earned my ride, and I freakin' earned a championship last year. I've earned plenty." He paused, studying the disappointment in the older man's face. "Is that what this is about? You feel like the team owes you something?"

"You're damn right it owes me!" Rod's voice rose. "I've been with this team practically since the beginning. After Greg took over, he promised me again and again that he'd give me a bigger stake in the company. And year after year, I never got *nothin'*. All I got was a piddly raise."

Reese shook his head. "You selfish old man."

"Selfish? Selfish?" The finger was back in Reese's chest, jamming harder this time. "Greg promised me your father's piece of the company. But he felt sorry for your dad when your mom was dying. Greg gave him *my* piece out of pity. That just ain't fair." A sinister gleam shone in his eyes. "So what if your mom was dying of cancer? People die every day. I was there from the beginning. It was mine!"

With white-hot fury pulsing through him, Reese gritted his teeth and snatched Rod by the front of his shirt. "I oughta beat the living—"

"Not so fast." The team manager moved his arm, and a click sounded.

Reese gulped when something hard and metal slammed into his gut.

"Now who has the upper hand?" An evil grin curled the older man's thin lips.

Lacey spotted Reese's truck near the front of the race shop's lot, and her heart soared. *I found him!*

Bouncing over the asphalt toward the glass doors, she nosed her SUV next to Reese's pickup, grabbed her purse and keys, and hopped from the truck.

Smiling, she trotted toward the front door. She couldn't wait to wrap her arms around Reese and tell him she loved him and that they were going to have a family. She yanked her card key from her purse, unlocked the door, and ran down the hallway.

"Reese? Reese!" she yelled, heading toward the shops.

"Look, you don't need to do this. Let's talk about this." With his hands up, Reese stepped back from the gun. Terror slid up his spine. He had to live through this and work things out with Lacey.

"What's left to talk about? You're going to call the police, and I can't let you do that." Rod gestured wildly with the gun, and Reese's heart hammered against his ribcage.

"Let's work out an agreement." His hands trembling, Reese wracked his brain for something to say. If only he could distract Rod, get the gun, and call nine-one-one . . .

"An agreement?" The team manager snorted. "How about you and your so-called wife sign over your part of the company to me. Or give me your father's piece when he finally croaks."

Reese took a ragged breath, trying to curb the rage and terror surging through him.

"Did I hit a nerve?" Rod smiled, leveling the gun at Reese's chest. "Does it bother you that someone just might steal this empire you and Lacey took over with your marriage of convenience?"

Lacey heard voices coming from the 89 team's bay. Was Reese talking to someone? Who would be at the shop this late at night? She wrenched the door open and spotted Reese standing with his back to her.

"Reese!" she hollered. She stopped short when she saw Rod.

He spun around, gesturing wildly.

Then Lacey saw a gun.

It was pointed at her.

She heard a shot.

A fire bolt hit her shoulder, and she stumbled backward, her body colliding hard with the cement floor.

Someone screamed her name.

Everything went fuzzy, the noise around her sounding like it was filtering through a tunnel.

Something touched her head. Looking up, her eyes met Reese's above her. He was out of focus while yelling something. Was he saying her name?

She wanted to tell him she was sorry and she loved him, but her lips couldn't form the words.

Pain—like fire—surged from her shoulder down her arm. The sensation deepened, and everything went black . . .

"Lacey! Lacey!" Kneeling on the cold cement floor, Reese pulled her limp body to him. His body shook with fear. "Lacey, don't pass out," he whispered while pushing her hair back from her forehead. "Don't leave me."

"What the devil is going on here?" a voice behind Reese yelled. "Did I hear a shot?"

Over his shoulder, he spotted Brett and Tim rushing through the doorway. Rod looked back and forth between the two men. Lowering his head like a battering ram, Rod started to run.

"Get him!" Reese bellowed. "He shot Lacey!"

Turning his attention back to his wife, Reese heard a tussle behind him. Someone grunted and metal banged. Glancing back, Reese found Brett pointing the gun at Rod, while Tim handcuffed him by looping two large white plastic garbage bag ties together.

Looking down, he found Lacey turning paler and paler by the second. He was losing her. His heart plummeted and worry rushed through him.

"Call nine-one-one!" Reese's voice echoed through the bay.

Brett tossed Tim a cellular phone.

"I'm working on it!" Tim dialed and held it to his ear. "I need an ambulance right away . . . A woman's been shot . . . I'm at Southern Racing, the race shop." He rattled off the address. "You have to hurry! Please hurry!"

A warm liquid ran down Reese's arms. He cut his eyes down to where blood pooled on the cool, gray cement floor beneath Lacey. His heart was beating like a drum in his chest. She was losing too much blood too quickly.

Don't die on me!

Please don't die!

He rested her on his lap then shucked off his leather jacket and pulled his t-shirt up and over his head. Wrapping his t-shirt around her shoulder, he held her close.

"Lacey, baby," he whispered in her ear. "Stay with me. Don't leave me. Hang on, baby, hang on." Tears filled his eyes while he rocked her.

Tim rushed to the end of the bay and opened the garage door. Turning back to Brett and Rod, Reese saw the older man gazing at the toes of his boots.

"Rod, you dumb son-of-a—" Reese gritted his teeth. "You're going to pay for this."

Rod continued to stare down at his work boots.

"What were you thinking bringing a gun here?" Reese's voice quavered as he gripped his wife.

He's going to pay for this.

"Hang on, baby," he whispered in her ear. "Please, Lacey. Just a little longer." Brushing her hair back from her face, he kissed her forehead. Her body trembled, and he pulled her closer. His t-shirt was soaked with blood, and her breathing was becoming more and more ragged. "Where's the freakin' ambulance?" His voice rose. "I'm losing her!"

"I don't know!" Tim paced.

Embracing her, he whispered in her ear. When he heard the sirens, his heart leapt in his chest. Within seconds, the ambulance was in the bay and EMTs approached with a gurney. He held his breath while the four men placed his wife on the gurney. He wished her eyes would open. Was she going to make it?

She had to. She just *had* to!

Three police cars roared up behind the ambulance, and four officers stalked into the bay and gathered around Brett and Rod. Reese walked to the end of the bay and bit back tears, watching the EMTs load his precious wife into the ambulance. Within minutes, she was hooked up to an IV and an EMT was checking her blood pressure. The EMTs barked orders to each other, but Reese was so deep in thought and overwhelmed with worry for his beautiful wife that their words seemed like a foreign language.

"She's going to be okay." Brett sidled up to him, looping an arm around Reese's shoulders.

Reese met his crew chief's gaze. He started to speak, but only a stifled sob escaped his throat.

"Here." Brett handed him a team t-shirt. "It's clean. Put it on."

Looking down, Reese realized he was shirtless, and his chest was covered with Lacey's blood. He pulled the shirt over his head. "Thanks," he whispered.

Brett nudged him forward. "Go. Ride with Lacey. I'll talk to the police and meet you there."

He smacked Brett's arm. "Thank you."

Reese started toward the ambulance and then stopped and turned back to Brett. "Call Tommy for me. I want Krista to know."

His crew chief nodded. "Just go."

Sucking in a ragged breath and shivering with anxiety, Reese climbed into the ambulance and prayed his wife would be okay.

THIRTY

Fearing the worst, Reese paced around the emergency room waiting area while wringing his hands. Lacey's blood pressure had dropped during the ride to the hospital, and he'd watched in horror while the EMTs worked to stabilize her.

Upon their arrival, the ER doctors ordered Reese to wait in the lobby and refused to give him any clues on her condition. He'd been silently praying somehow she'd make it through this. She *had* to!

Reese stared out through the large glass windows at the parking lot and wondered where his friends were. He needed their support or he was going to lose his mind. Fishing his phone from the pocket of his jeans, he examined the display and found he had a voicemail message.

Reese dialed the voicemail, gasping when Lacey's sweet voice spoke in his ear. "Reese, it's me. Look, I'm sorry. I'm so sorry for not believing you. I love you. Call me."

After snapping his phone shut, he rested his forehead on the cold window while regret and sorrow tore at his heart.

She'd been coming to apologize to him. She wanted to work things out.

Please, let her make it through this.

"Reese!" a voice bellowed.

Krista and Tommy approached.

Krista crushed Reese into a hug. "Oh, Reese." Her voice trembled.

Closing his eyes, Reese rested his hands on her small waist. He held his breath, trying not to cry while her tears ran down his neck.

"How is she?" Tommy asked, his face clouded with concern.

"I don't know." Reese took a deep breath. "Her blood pressure was falling on the way to the hospital."

Krista wiped her wet cheeks. "I just can't believe it. Why would Rod shoot Lacey? It doesn't make sense!" Her voice broke into sobs.

"Shh." Tommy embraced her. "It's going to be okay. Lacey will pull through this."

"But what about the baby!" Krista sobbed.

Reese's heart stopped and his stomach plummeted. He studied Krista. "What did you say?"

Her eyes widened, meeting his.

"What baby?" When she didn't answer, he grabbed her arm. "Krista, what baby?"

"She's pregnant." Krista's answer came in a whisper.

"Lacey's pregnant? My Lacey?"

She nodded.

Reese's legs gave out on him, and he flopped down into a chair. Pregnant. Lacey's *pregnant.*

And shot.

"Why didn't she tell me?" he whispered. Distraught, he buried his face in his hands.

His body trembling, his eyes filled with tears. Where did he go wrong? Greg told Lacey and him to take care of each other, and Reese had let him down. Now Lacey lay in a hospital bed because of Reese's stupidity. Why didn't he get the gun away from Rod?

Guilt shook him to the core. He couldn't lose her. He just couldn't. Lacey was his life. And the baby—they were a family now. She had to pull through. She just had to.

Swallowing tears, Reese moved over to the window. He stared out over the parking lot, then closed his eyes, pressing his clammy forehead to the glass again.

A hand touched his shoulder. "Reese." Krista's voice quavered. "I told the nurse about the baby. She said she'd alert the doctor right away."

"Thanks." He glanced down at her face, which was full of anxiety. He tried to smile, but it felt like a grimace. "Do you think she's going to be okay?" He hoped to get the answer he needed to hear.

"Of course I do." Her expression betrayed her words. She motioned toward the bank of chairs in the middle of the lobby. "Let's go sit. Tommy went to get us something to drink."

He nodded while she took his arm, leading him to the chairs. Reese flopped down and stared up at the local news on a flat screen television sitting on a shelf in the corner. His mind raced with worry and hope while a weatherman pontificated about the rainstorm heading to the Charlotte area overnight.

Tommy returned with an armload of ice-cold cans of soda. Taking one, Reese opened it and sipped. He couldn't stop worrying about Lacey and their unborn child. Reese would never live with himself if he lost them.

Staring down at the can, he ran his fingers through the cool condensation as questions haunted him. And what about his dad? Was he going to pull through? What if Reese lost the three of them? What would he do then?

Lacey heard the hum of a machine in the distance. She felt as if she were in a fog. Blinking, she opened her eyes. When they focused, she spotted a long fluorescent light above her. The ceiling didn't look familiar.

Where was she?

She tried to move, but pain radiated through her shoulder

down her arm. Then recognition broke through her fog. She'd been in the shop looking for Reese. She'd walked in on him and Rod. Rod had a gun. And he pointed it at her.

Had she been shot?

Was the baby all right?

"Reese?" Her voice croaked. "Reese?"

"Shh, it's okay, honey." A middle-aged nurse in a purple uniform leaned down, patting Lacey's hand. "You're gonna be just fine."

"Where am I?"

"You're in the hospital, honey." The woman's hazel eyes were warm and comforting.

Gazing at her shoulder, Lacey found it bandaged. No wonder she felt like she had a rock on it. "Was I shot?"

The older woman nodded. "You were a lucky young lady. The bullet went clear through your shoulder and didn't do much damage."

"And my baby?" Her voice trembled.

"Your baby's okay, too. Your little one has a good, strong heartbeat."

Lacey let out a sigh of relief. "Is my husband here?"

The woman smiled. "Yes, and he's worried sick about you."

"Can I see him?"

The nurse stood. "I'll be right back. You take it easy now."

Using her good arm, Lacey smoothed the white sheet over her middle while waiting for Reese. She couldn't wait to see him and tell him she was sorry for not believing him.

When he appeared in the doorway, her heart swelled. His handsome face looked stained with tears, and his gorgeous blue eyes were red and puffy.

"Reese." She reached for him with her good arm.

"Oh, Lacey." He rushed over to her and leaned down. "I've been going out of my mind with worry." He gently encircled her shoulder with his arm. "I thought I'd lost you."

Closing her eyes, she breathed in his cologne, resting her cheek on his neck. "Reese, I'm so sorry," she whispered. "Can you forgive me? I never should've doubted you."

"Don't be silly." He moved back and brushed her hair from her face. "I should be sorry. It's my fault you got hurt."

"No, it's mine." She shook her head. "I never should've picked a fight with you. I love you, and I want to be with you, Reese. I don't want a divorce." She took a deep breath. "We're going to have a baby."

He smiled and her pulse raced. "I know." He took her hand in his. "Why didn't you tell me?"

Lacey's throat constricted with guilt for keeping the news from him. "I was coming to tell you when I saw you with Sandy. I thought you were having an affair with her, so I got angry. My stubbornness got the better of me. I was so stupid." She stared into his blue eyes. "I'm so sorry."

He pressed a finger to her lips. "It's okay. It's over now. All that matters is we're together. Don't worry about anything else."

"What happened at the shop? Why did Rod have a gun?"

Reese glowered. "Pop woke up and told me Rod was blackmailing him because he took money from the company back when my mom was dying. My mom wanted to come home to die, and Pop was going to lose the house because of the doctor bills."

"Oh, Reese." Tears filled her eyes and sadness flooded her.

"Pop needed some money just to make it through." He held her hand, running his thumb over her palm. "Rod found out about the money. He was pissed that Pop got a share of the company, so he was blackmailing him. Pop was afraid to admit to Greg or me what happened, so he hid it for all these years."

"My dad would've understood." Lacey bit back tears.

Reese nodded. "I think so, too. But Rod was vicious. He

wanted to take over the company, but we got in the way."

Lacey shook her head. "I can't believe it. Rod was like family to my dad."

"I know." Sighing, he shook his head. "I went to confront him tonight after my dad told me everything, and Rod brought the gun. I told him I was going to tell the police, and he went nuts. You walked in at the worst moment."

"I was trying to find you to apologize."

"I'm just glad you're okay." He squeezed her hand. "I love you."

"I love you too. I always have."

He leaned down and pressed his lips to her, sending liquid heat through her veins. Lacey closed her eyes and rubbed the back of his neck.

As he pulled away, Reese smiled down at her. "I'm the luckiest man on the planet."

Lacey smiled. "And I'm the luckiest woman on the planet."

EPILOGUE

"Can't you drive any faster?" Reese tapped the center console of Brett's SUV while Brett sped toward the hospital. Anticipation and excitement skittered through his veins.

"I'm driving as fast as I can without putting other drivers on the road in danger," his crew chief snapped.

Reese rolled his eyes. "You shoulda let me drive."

"We would've gotten pulled over as soon as we got on the road with you behind the wheel." Brett slowed and merged into the parking lot at the hospital.

"Just calm down," Reese's father barked from the backseat. "The baby will wait until you get there. I'm sure Lacey's not even ready to push yet. You're mother was in labor for close to twenty-four hours with you."

Reese shook his head, and his stomach twisted with anxiety. Why did he think it was smart to drive to Atlanta for a sponsor meeting this week? Lacey had insisted she'd be fine staying with Krista, since the baby wasn't due for another two weeks. Reese told her he wasn't comfortable leaving town, but she promised she'd be fine.

Then he got the call this afternoon. Her water had broken, and she and Krista were heading to the hospital. Last he'd heard they were waiting for something to happen. She'd started to dilate and then stopped.

He bit his lower lip and sucked in a breath. He hoped the baby had waited. He wanted to be there when his child came into the world.

Brett nosed the SUV into spot near the front of the hospital.

"Let's go!" Reese jumped from the truck and trotted toward the main entrance.

"Slow down, son!" his father bellowed. "Grampa is coming, too."

Grinning, Reese waited at the door for his father and crew chief to catch up. It had been a long road with his father's recovery and rehabilitation after his massive heart attack. Reese was so glad his father had made it. At least his child would have one grandparent.

Life had moved so quickly since the day he found out he was going to be a father. Rod pled guilty and was serving twenty-five years for the shooting, blackmailing, and other offenses related to crimes he'd committed against Carl and Lacey. Reese hired a new team manager to replace him. No charges were filed against his father for the embezzlement, since Reese paid back what his father had taken.

Reese and Lacey settled into a comfortable routine of sharing responsibilities of the race team, and the company was rapidly getting back on track.

"Let's go!" Reese rushed through the automatic doors to the bank of elevators at the end of the hall.

"I'm telling you, you have plenty of time. She's only been in labor for a few hours." His father took deep breaths, stepping onto the elevator in front of Brett.

"You okay, Pop?" Reese studied the older man gripping the handrail.

"I'm fine." He waved off the question. "Just get us to the maternity ward so I can see my grandson."

"Or granddaughter." Reese smiled, smacking the button. His heart leaped with the excitement of seeing his child. Lacey had insisted that they be surprised, but Reese had a feeling they'd have a daughter.

"It's a boy," his father said.

"How do you know?" Brett raised his eyebrows.

"I just do." The older man shrugged. "Next one will be a girl."

Reese held up his hands, signaling his father to slow for a caution lap. "Let's get through this one first."

"I can see you and Lacey with six kids." His father's grin widened.

"Six?" Reese's voice squeaked, and the other two men laughed.

When the elevator door opened, Reese flew down the hallway to the nurse's station. He gave the nurse his name, and she led him to the birthing rooms while Brett and his dad waited back in the lobby.

His heart pounding in his chest, he grasped the doorknob of her room. He prayed he wasn't too late. Wrenching the door open, he found Lacey propped up in bed while Krista sat smiling on a chair across the room. His wife cradled a tiny infant wrapped in a blanket and wearing a little blue knitted cap.

His heart swelled. *A boy!*

His wife was radiant. Her creamy white skin glowed as she whispered to the baby. When she met his gaze and smiled, his heart skipped a beat.

"Hi, Daddy." She lifted the baby's head by moving her elbow up. "This is your son."

"I'm sorry I was late." He rushed to the bed and leaned down into his newborn son's face. "Oh, he looks just like you," he whispered. Joy swelled in his heart at the sight of his newborn son with his cute little nose and chin.

She chuckled. "I thought he looked like you."

"I agree. He looks just like you, Reese." Krista came around the bed. "Congratulations. I'll give you guys some alone time." She slipped out the door, closing it behind her.

Lacey looked down at their son. "This is your daddy." She moved the little bundle toward him. "Here."

Tears filled her eyes when Reese took the baby as if he were holding a piece of glass. His expression said it all—his gorgeous blue eyes widened, and his lips trembled. He must've felt all of the emotions roaring within her.

"Hey, buddy," he whispered. "I'm so sorry I missed your entrance into the world. I couldn't get Uncle Brett to drive any faster."

She settled back on the bed, trying to ignore her aches and pains. Even though she was exhausted, watching her husband and son interact gave her renewed strength.

"It's okay, Reese," she said. "It was a surprise for all of us, and the labor went quicker than we all expected. He seemed to be in a hurry to meet us. You made it in plenty of time."

Looking up, Reese smiled. "He's perfect."

"Yes, he is." She fingered the plastic bracelet on her wrist. "I changed my mind about the name."

"Oh?" He settled down in a chair next to the bed, studying the little bundle in his muscular arms.

"I think we should call him Gregory Reese, instead of Gregory William."

"Why after me?" He tilted his head in a questioning glance.

"It'd be after the two most important men in my life."

He smiled. "Okay. But the girl will have to be after you."

"Girl?" She raised her eyebrows.

He snickered. "My dad informed me we're going to have six. Next one will be a girl."

She shook her head. "We'll have to talk about that. I don't know if I want to do this five more times, and we're not going to call our daughter Millicent."

"We'll call her Lacey." He flashed his sexy smile. "I love you."

"I love you, too."

ABOUT THE AUTHOR

Amy Clipston has been writing for as long as she can remember. Her fiction writing "career" began in elementary school when she and a close friend wrote and shared silly stories. More recently, her admiration for fast cars and handsome men in fire suits inspired her to study and write about car racing. After living in New Jersey and Virginia, her love of the South and racing pulled her to North Carolina. Amy lives with her husband, Joe; two sons, Zac and Matt; mother, Lola; and three spoiled rotten cats, Molly, Ashlee, and Jet. No wonder she writes romance. Please visit her website at www.amyclipston.com.

9/09